HIGH PRAISE FOR EVE KENIN!

"Seductive, aggressive, and hot as hell."
—Michelle Buonfiglio

"[Kenin] gives the reader everything they want."
—*RT BOOKreviews*

"Hot romance and truly cool paranormal world-building make Eve [Kenin] a welcome addition to the genre."
—*New York Times* Bestselling Author
Kelley Armstrong on *Demon's Kiss*

"A lush, sensual and compelling read."
—*USA Today* Bestselling Author Cheyenne McCray
on *Demon's Kiss*

"Riveting! A dark, steamy and twisted tale."
—#1 *New York Times* Bestselling Author
Lisa Jackson on *His Dark Kiss*

"Tense, teasing, brooding writing that is lavishly entertaining...a darkly devastating—and darkly divine—romance that will have a shiver or two running up and down your spine."
—Heartstring Reviews on *His Dark Kiss*

ONE LAST CHANCE

Raina circled back, leaning low on the snowscooter, weaving madly as plas-shots rained down on her like deadly hail. She spun an arc around the back of the rig where she'd last seen Wizard. No sign of him.

Her breath came in short gasps, the pain in her side a wretched fire. Her vision shifted, blurred. She hoped she could hold it together long enough to find him. Where the hell was he?

Then she saw it. The charred and twisted remains of his snowscooter sat in the center of a blackened patch of snow. The sight sent a jagged pain slicing through her, an ugly wrenching that hurt way more than her frigging side. She sped toward the still-sparking wreck. Nothing stirred. No sign of life.

"Wizard!" she roared.

He was *not* dead. She would not *let* him be dead.

Driven

EVE KENIN

LOVE SPELL NEW YORK CITY

For Dylan, my light,
Sheridan, my joy,
and Henning, my forever love.

LOVE SPELL®

September 2007

Published by

Dorchester Publishing Co., Inc.
200 Madison Avenue
New York, NY 10016

ISBN-10: 0-505-52709-X
ISBN-13: 978-0-505-52709-7

Printed in the United States of America.

Visit us on the web at www.dorchesterpub.com.

ACKNOWLEDGMENTS

My deepest gratitude to Leah Hultenschmidt for loving this story, to Sha-Shana Crichton for believing in my writing, to Nancy and Brenda for critiques, camaraderie and commiseration, and to the "debs" because you truly understand that "there is always something new to throw up about."

Driven

ONE

The air was stale, rank with the stink of smoke, sweat, and old beer. Bob's Truck Stop. Nice place for a meal.

Raina Bowen sat at a small table, back to the wall, posture deceptively relaxed. Inside, she was coiled tighter than the Merckle shocks that were installed in her rig, but it was better to appear unruffled. Never let 'em see you sweat. That had been one of Sam's many mottos.

She glanced around the crowded room, mentally cataloging the Siberian gun truckers at the counter, the cadaverous pimp in the corner and his ferret-faced companion, the harried waitress who deftly dodged the questing hand that reached out to snag her as she passed. In the center of the room was a small raised platform with a metal pole extending to the grime-darkened ceiling. A scantily clad girl, barely out of puberty, wiggled and twirled around the pole. Raina looked away. But for a single desperate act, one that had earned her freedom, she might have been that girl.

Idly spinning the same half-empty glass of warm beer

that she'd been nursing for the past hour, she looked through the grimy windows at the front of the truck stop. Frozen, colorless, the bleak expanse stretched with endless monotony until the high-powered floodlights tapered off and the landscape was swallowed by the black night sky.

A balmy minus-thirty outside. And it would only get colder the farther north they went. Raina had a keen dislike of the cold, but if she were the first to reach Gladow Station with her load of genetically engineered grain, there'd be a fat bonus of fifty million interdollars. That'd be more than enough to warm her to the cockles of her frozen heart.

More than enough to buy Beth's safety.

Keeping her gaze on the door, Raina willed it to open. She couldn't wait much longer. Where the hell was Wizard? Sitting here—a woman alone in a place like this—drew too much attention. She wanted no one to remember her face. Anonymity was a precious commodity, one she realized had slipped through her fingers as from the corner of her eye she watched one of the Siberians begin to weave drunkenly across the room.

"Well, hello, sweet thing." He stopped directly in front of her, kicked the extra chair out from the table, and shifted it closer before dropping his bulk onto the torn Naugahyde. He was shrouded in layers of tattered cloth that were stained and frayed, the stink of him hitting her nostrils before he finished his greeting.

"Leave. Now." Keeping her voice low and even, Raina snaked one hand along her waist toward the small of her back, resting her fingers on the smooth handle of her knife.

The Siberian smiled at her, revealing the brown

stubs of three rotting teeth. "You can't chase me off so easy. I've been watching you." He gestured at the front of his pants. "You need a man, sweet thing."

Uh-huh. "And you think you're a man?"

The trucker frowned at her question; then his thick brows shot up as he realized he'd been insulted. Undeterred, he leaned forward, catching her ponytail with one scarred and dirty hand. "I'll show you how much man I am. Give us a kiss, sweet thing."

His tongue was already out and reaching as he pulled her face closer to his.

"Last warning," Raina said softly, wishing he would listen.

He gave a hard tug on her ponytail. Raina slid her knife from its sheath, bringing it up with a sharp twist, neatly slicing through the tip of the trucker's tongue. Blood splattered in all directions, thick and hot. With an enraged howl he jerked back, letting loose his hold on her as he clapped both hands over his mouth. Dark blood dripped down his unshaven chin to pool on the tabletop.

Raina sent a quick look at the rest of the Siberians. Their attention was firmly fixed on the girl who was shimmying up and down the pole. Returning her gaze to the moaning trucker, she picked up the stained scrap of cloth that passed for a serviette and slowly wiped her blade clean. She knew that once serviettes had been made of paper, but that was a long time ago, when there had still been enough trees to provide pulp.

"Name's Raina Bowen. Not sweet thing." She sighed. So much for anonymity. "And the last thing I need is a man."

Well, that wasn't exactly true. She needed one man

3

in particular, Wizard and his precious trucking license, but he was nowhere to be seen.

The trucker's eyes widened as he registered her name, and a flicker of recognition flared in their dull depths. Nice to have a reputation, even if she didn't quite deserve it. This lovely little encounter would just add to the mystique. Unfortunately, it would also add to the risk of being found. *Damn.*

He reached for her again, his hands rough, his expression stormy. He was mad, challenged, belittled, and he wanted revenge. What was it with Siberian gun truckers?

Twirling her hair around one finger, Raina shifted her expression, lowering her lashes over her blue eyes in a come-hither invitation, curving her lips in a winsome smile. The trucker blinked, clearly confused by her abrupt change in manner. He leaned in—Lord, some people never learned—and Raina deftly clipped him hard under the chin with the hilt of her knife.

He slumped across the Formica table, unconscious, mouth hanging open, leaving her with a blood-splattered tabletop, a ruined beer, and an end to her patience.

His companions were looking this way now. Raina lowered her head as though enthralled by her tablemate, using her body to shield his inert form from view. Her ruse worked, and the men nudged one another and laughed before turning back to the stripper.

Well, that had bought her about three minutes.

A sudden blast of light sliced through the frost-dusted window, spreading a glowing circle across the floor. Hope flared as Raina wondered if Wizard had finally arrived, but no, there was too much light for just one vehicle.

Trucks. Lots of 'em. They parked in a circle, the beams of their headlights illuminating a circumscribed area.

Like an arena.

She'd seen this setup before. The new arrivals were expecting entertainment, the kind that involved fists, and they were using their rigs to create the venue. She stared through the glass, the muscles of her shoulders and neck knotting with tension. Illegal gladiator games. There was going to be a bloodbath.

Hell. Wizard or not, she'd outstayed her time here. Tossing a handful of interdollars on the table, Raina shrugged into her parka and headed outside, sticking well back in the shadows as she watched the scene unfold. The trucks were huge, as tall as two-story houses, painted slate gray, and on the front in bold silver letters, the name JANSON.

Men were emerging from the cabs. Big, burly guys, dressed in hides and skins, bristling with weapons. Janson company men. How nice. The Janson owned the ICW—Intercontinental Worldwide—the longest highway ever built. Or at least, they acted like they did.

She could feel the tension in the air. Taste it. Someone had pissed these guys off big-time.

At the far end of the lot was a lone truck. Black. Clean. Nameless. Nice transport, she noticed. A noncompany driver, just like her. Poor bastard. He was obviously tonight's planned entertainment.

"Hey, Big Luc," one of the Jansons yelled, moving into place in the circle that had formed. "That's the worthless parasite who jumped line. We gotta teach him some manners."

Jumped line? What moron would jump line on Janson trucks? They went first. It was an unwritten law. Anyone who flouted it was either insane or bent on a quick death. Raina watched as money exchanged hands. Odds were obviously in favor of Big Luc.

"His pressure looks low, don't it? Can't have an unsafe rig on the highway," a second man called, then laughed at his own lame joke. "Wizard's got some balls coming here tonight. He shoulda kept driving. Maybe we'd have let him live another day."

Wizard. Oh, no. Of all the morons in the frozen north, she had to hook up with the one who had picked a fight with a good portion of the Janson army. She narrowed her eyes at the huge black rig, the one at the far end of the lot. Wizard's rig. *Damn, damn, damn.*

He was of no use to her now. Still, she couldn't help but try to figure a way that she could salvage the trucking pass he was supposed to give her.

"Luc. Luc. Luc." The crowd was calling their champion.

In response to the cry, a huge man swaggered into the circle of light, raising his arms as he slowly spun around and around, egging his admirers on. Beneath the flat wool cap that clung to his skull, bushy brows drew down over a nose flattened and skewed to one side, and just below it bristled a thick thatch of mud-colored whiskers. An animal pelt hung over his massive shoulders. The head was still intact, the jagged teeth catching the light.

Raina glanced back at the black rig at the far end of the lot. She'd never met Wizard, had contacted him on Sam's instructions—which in and of itself was a questionable recommendation—but she couldn't imagine he'd be any match for Luc. She had a hard time imagining *anyone* as a match for Luc.

The door of the cab opened, and a man swung down. He was tall, dressed in a black parka, the hood pulled up, obscuring his features. She felt a moment's pity, and then squelched the unwelcome emotion. Not her fight. Not her business. Sam's words of loving fatherly advice rang in her head as clear as if he were standing beside her. *If there's no profit in it for you, stupid girl, then walk away. Just walk away. What do you care for some sucker's lousy luck?*

Not only was there no profit in it for her, but the jackass had cost her. Wizard was supposed to show up an hour ago with a temporary Janson trucking license that would allow her to jump the queue all nice and legal, behind the Janson but ahead of the other indies. Instead, he was an hour late, and he'd dragged a frigging army with him. Too bad the army wasn't on his side.

Wizard strode forward. He made it halfway across the parking lot, halfway to the door of the truck stop before Luc's fist connected with his face. Raina winced. She had a brief impression of long dark hair as the hood fell back and Wizard's head snapped sideways. He went down, rolling head over heels across the inflexible sheet of solid ice.

In three strides Luc was on him, the steel-reinforced toe of his company-issue boots finding a nice home right between Wizard's ribs. Wizard didn't move, didn't moan, and for a second Raina wondered if that first punch had knocked him out cold. With a laugh, Luc kicked him again, and then nudged him with his boot, once, twice. He backed off, waving at the group that surrounded him, shaking hands as he slowly made his way toward the door of the diner, acting as though he'd just rid the world of public enemy number one.

The remaining Jansons closed in, a pack of avid rats, eyes glittering with malevolent intent. There was no doubt in Raina's mind that they were going to beat Wizard within an inch of his life, a warning to anyone who tried to cross them.

Raina glanced at her snowscooter. She'd been smart enough to park her rig in a safe place and use the scooter to get her to the truck stop. No sense inviting trouble. Now she wondered if she could maneuver into the circle of men surrounding Wizard's prone form, nab him, and get them both out of there before someone got killed. She hesitated, the thought going against her every instinct of self-preservation. Why she was even considering this she couldn't say. Hadn't Sam Bowen beaten all compassion out of her? *Stupid girl. Empathy will only get you killed.*

Squelching the voice in her head, she focused on the guy sprawled across the frozen ground. He had the damned trucking license, and she needed it. All she had to do was figure a way to get it.

She cringed as Wizard pushed himself to his feet. Shaking his head as if to clear it, he wiped the back of his hand across his mouth. God, he didn't even have the sense to stay down.

"Hey, Luc," he called softly, the sound of his voice drawing Raina up short. Low, rich, a sensual baritone that sent a shiver up her spine. "While you're in there, you want to fetch me a beer?"

Raina closed her eyes and sighed. Dim. Thick. Brainless. He was a dead man. And all for the sake of what? His machismo? She shifted, trying to get a look at his face, but he'd pulled his hood up again.

Big Luc turned slowly to face him. "You got a death wish, boy?"

"Name's Wizard, and the only thing I'm wishing for is a long, cold beer." Oh, that slow, lazy drawl. It should be illegal for a guy that dumb to have a voice that smooth.

"Well, Wiiiiz-aaard . . ." Luc guffawed, slapping one fleshy palm on his thigh. "You ready to die?"

Run. Run. Run. You might have a chance. Raina willed him to move, because she knew Big Luc would kill him and leave his frozen carcass in the snow. The wild dogs would pick him clean, and no one would care. She'd make herself not care.

Luc lunged at him. Raina expected Wizard to step back, to dodge, to move. Instead, he shot out one fist with lightning speed, dropping Luc in his tracks.

She blinked, certain her brain was processing something other than what her eyes had seen.

For a moment she waited, convinced that Luc would get up, would charge like an enraged bull and cut Wizard down. Without a backward look, Wizard turned and strode in the direction of the diner, as if he hadn't just accomplished the impossible. As if he hadn't just invited his own assassination.

And, oh, the *way* he moved . . . confident, fluid, a man comfortable in his own skin. Raina watched him for a long moment, and then looked away, wondering what the hell was wrong with her. Why should she care about the easy way some useless gun trucker moved his hips?

Whoooo. Get it together, Bowen.

No one spoke. No one moved. It felt like no one dared breathe, and then two guys stepped forward, hauled Big Luc up by his armpits, and dragged him away.

Stupid man. Stupid, stupid man. Wizard had just made a mighty powerful enemy in the Janson Trucking Company. Actually, they'd been his enemy from the second he'd jumped line, but they might have let him live . . . suffer, but live. Maybe. Now she didn't think so. They were likely to gut him and feed his intestines down his own throat.

Her breath hissed from between her teeth. She needed the Gladow winnings. For herself. For Beth.

Frig. She *needed* that temporary license, which meant she was just as stupid as Wizard was, because she was about to step into his fight.

Hugging the shadows, she sprinted to the edge of the wall, climbed onto her snowscooter, and gunned the engine. She spun the scooter in an arc. Heart racing, she stopped sharply near the door of the truck stop, just behind the dumb jackass who had so thoroughly messed up her plans.

"Get on," Raina shouted. Several of the Janson men were closing in, and she was glad that the hood of her anorak hid her features from view. She could only pray that they wouldn't recognize her. *Yeah, right.* "If you have one iota of sense, *get on*."

Wizard whipped around to face her. For a frozen moment he stood silhouetted against the light streaming from the window behind him. She thought he would prove that he lacked even that one iota of sense she'd mentioned, for he just stood there, his head tilted as he watched the line of Janson truckers who were slowly stalking him, closing in behind her. She could sense them, see the hazy reflection of their faces in the windows of the truck stop at Wizard's back.

Then with a shrug, he swung one long leg over the seat of the snowscooter, his arms coming around her waist as he climbed on.

Dragging in a deep breath, Raina gunned the engine and took off into the star-tossed night. Heart racing, she set the speed as fast as she dared, knowing the dangers of hitting a deep rut at high speed. Knowing, too, that there was a strong likelihood they'd be followed. Even over the noise of the engine she could hear the roar of a mob denied.

Heat exploded in a shimmering wave, and for an instant night turned to day as someone fired a round of plas-shot.

Wizard's reaction had to be instinctive. He pushed up tight against her back, protecting her with his body. With a hiss, she jerked her elbow sharply into his gut, sending the message that she didn't need him to act like human armor. *Moron.*

She could feel him behind her, pressed up against her back, his muscled thighs melded to hers, his arms forming a solid vise around her waist. He was bigger than she had expected. When he'd stepped down from his truck, all she'd registered was the size of Big Luc, the danger posed by the Janson drivers.

She'd thought Wizard some harmless prey.

Now, with the feel of his long, hard body pushed up

against her, she wondered how she could have been so wrong.

She shifted forward a couple of inches, putting as much space between them as she could. Her thoughts turned back to the men they'd left behind. She knew for certain that the Janson hadn't expected anyone to play savior to their chosen quarry. And since she'd been fool enough to take on the role . . . well, she could only hope that she'd not been recognized. Making an enemy of Janson Trucking was a fool's work. And that fool was on the back of her snowscooter.

Annoyance curled through her. Now that she'd saved him, just where was she supposed to take him? She stared out into the night, endless star-stippled sky above a frozen waste. *His* rig was parked back at the truck stop, and until the Janson left, she'd be wiser not to return there. *Her* rig was parked to the east, on a little-known access road that actually led to nowhere— a throwback to the days before the Fossil Fuel Edict of 2089. With a shake of her head she turned east, mentally chastising herself for getting involved in something that was none of her affair. But, hell, she needed that license, because she *was* going to win that race to Gladow Station.

The bite of the wind had grown bitter with the advancing night, and Raina tugged her hood closer around her face as she drove. Some thirty minutes passed before the outline of her truck loomed ahead, a bulky, dark silhouette against the midnight sky, chrome trim highlighted by the beam of the snowscooter's headlight.

"Home, sweet home," she muttered as she killed the engine and climbed off the seat, pulling the hood of her parka back. The frigid air slapped her skin as she stalked forward, and she was glad for the discomfort. Maybe it would smack some sense into her. Lord knew she'd left hers in the lot outside the truck stop when she'd offered a ride to Wizard.

Expecting him to be right behind her, she keyed in the code, opened the door of the cab, and climbed inside. She spoke over her shoulder as she flicked on the light. "You can lie low here for the night, get your truck tomorrow. Big Luc and his friends will either be gone by morning, or too drunk to notice when you come back for your rig. Either way, you aren't going anywhere tonight. Too dangerous."

When there was no reply, Raina turned and found to her exasperation that Wizard was leaning against the snowscooter, arms crossed, legs outstretched, face obscured by the hood of his anorak. He was no more than a dark shadow on an equally dark night. His posture was comfortable, relaxed, as though the glacial chill were no more than a temperate breeze.

"Are you planning to sleep out there?" she called.

"Preferably not." He rose and crossed the space that separated them. The light from the cab leaked across the snow, then across him as he stepped into the circle of its scattered rays. "But it is impolite to enter another's domicile without an invitation."

"You want an invitation to my domicile?" She snorted. "Won't you join me for tea?" *Moron.*

Raina had a fleeting impression of dark hair spilling from beneath his hood before he ducked his head and climbed up the side of the cab. She stepped back to let him in, unfastened the catch-seam of her own parka, and hung it on the hook behind the driver's seat.

She led the way into the small living quarters that backed off the driver's cabin. She felt awkward having him here. Gesturing to the plasma screen set into one wall of her rig, she spoke over her shoulder, babbling as she tried to cover her discomfort. "I can track six satellites, and over four thousand channels. Used to be seven satellites, but I think an orbit decayed."

Her companion made no reply. It appeared that he wasn't interested in small talk. Fine by her. She wasn't particularly adept at it herself.

Snatching a pile of microdisks off the plastitech chair, she clutched them against her chest as she looked around for somewhere to put them. The chair was the only place to sit other than the bed, and she wasn't about to offer him *that*. Hazarding a glance over her shoulder, Raina checked just to make certain he was still there, and her breath skidded to a stunned stop.

He was right behind her, his tall frame a hand span away. Up close, with his hood thrown back, the catch-seam of his parka undone, Wizard didn't look helpless at all. A day's growth of beard shaded the chiseled plane of his jaw, and his full lips were drawn into a hard line. He looked dangerous, self-assured, frightening. Not a man who'd needed saving.

Hugging the microdisks like a shield, Raina tipped her head back and met his eyes. Slate gray. Cold. She swallowed. What the hell had she been thinking to bring him here? He wasn't some lost puppy who needed a warm place to sleep.

She blew out a slow breath.

As if sensing her discomfort, Wizard took a step back. Turning, he looked around the interior of her tiny quarters. Barely the size of a large closet, it was actually luxurious for a trucker.

He crossed to the plasma screen, ran one finger lightly across the buttons. Watching him touch her things with those strong, blunt fingers made her feel uneasy.

Annoyed at herself for bringing him here, irritated that he unnerved her, she had an urge to make him as uncomfortable as he made her. "You were late," she said flatly.

"Affirmative." He picked up a microdisk, put it down again.

She'd already surmised that he didn't have much in the way of gray matter, so she spoke deliberately and clearly. "I was counting on you to arrive as agreed with the special license."

Turning his head, he glanced over his shoulder, his silky black hair falling forward to caress the hard line of his jaw. There were marcasite beads woven through a long braid behind his right ear, and they caught the light, glittering as he moved.

"I agreed to meet Bowen with the license. No one mentioned a girl."

A *girl*. She gritted her teeth. Yanking open a cupboard door, she shoved the microdisks inside. "*I'm* Bowen. *Raina* Bowen."

"Yes." He stared at her a moment too long, then slowly paced to the opposite side of the small space.

Yes? What was that supposed to mean?

"I was supposed to meet *Sam* Bowen." He tapped the wall, opened and closed a cupboard. "A well-appointed rig. Hydrogen power? Fuel cell?"

Raina nodded, then realized he wasn't looking at her.

"Yeah. With solar panels on the roof of the cab along with a hydroponics grow-tube." She paused. "Whoever you were expecting to meet, you were still late."

"Acknowledged."

Well, that about summed it up. She bit her tongue against the urge to demand an explanation, deciding that the why of it didn't really matter.

Pushing open the door to the minuscule bathroom, he poked his head inside, and then turned to face her. "Efficient and well designed. Full bathroom. Shower stall. Mind if I use it when we are done?"

"Done?" *With what?*

He shrugged. "I can use the shower before, if you prefer, though I used the one in my rig just this afternoon."

Wizard pulled off his parka, folded it with meticulous care, and placed it neatly on the plastitech chair. He wore a black thermal top that clung to every muscled ridge of his torso. Raina swallowed, looking despite herself. Hell, she could appreciate art as well as the next woman.

He was even taller, broader, more leanly muscled than she'd thought. The realization clanged a warning bell. Slipping her knife from the sheath hanging across the small of her back, she shifted into a defensive stance. Wizard hooked his fingers into the hem of his shirt and began to peel it off, baring a nice strip of golden skin and ridged abdomen.

Oh, man. Somehow this guy had leaped to a conclusion that was just plain wrong.

"Uh, Wizard. Nice show, but I'm not looking for a stripper." *Or a quick lay,* but she couldn't manage those words out loud.

His hands stilled midmovement, and he raised a

questioning brow. Gray eyes glittered beneath dark lashes, scanning her with unhurried interest. She saw him take note of the knife, his gaze sliding over it, unconcerned. "My mistake," he conceded gracefully. "So what *are* we doing here, Raina Bowen?"

"What are we doing here? You thought I wanted . . . with you . . . a worthless gun trucker . . . ?" She tamped down the insidious voice that whispered across her thoughts, telling her that he was one gorgeous specimen of worthless gun trucker, and maybe that was worth something. "Well, I'm not sure about you, Wiii-zaaard," she said softly, drawing out his name in a fair imitation of Big Luc, "but I'm saving your butt."

"My butt?" He blinked, tilting his head a bit to one side. "Saving it for what? Breakfast?"

She couldn't help it. She laughed. His head jerked up, his gaze locked on hers, a flicker of surprise betrayed and then masked.

Hell. He really was dumb as a post. And he clearly had no intention of pushing the issue of coital association between them.

Deciding that while he might not be harmless, he wasn't about to attack, Raina resheathed her knife and reached for the spare pillow.

Wizard lay on his back on the floor. He could hear the deep, even rhythm of Raina Bowen's breathing, knew she'd fallen asleep almost as soon as her head had touched the pillow. For a minute there, he'd thought she was going to tell him to go outside and sleep in the snow. Nice of her to offer her hard, cold floor for his comfort.

17

Staring into the darkness that engulfed the small room, he analyzed the events that had resulted in his current circumstance. At the truck stop, when he'd turned to find a gorgeous girl on a snowscooter, blond hair spilling out her hood and over her shoulder, eyes flashing blue fire, he'd assumed she'd wanted what most women wanted from him: an endless, perfect night. If he hadn't mistaken her intentions, hadn't assumed that she wanted sexual congress, he would never have jumped on the back of her snowscooter. And if she hadn't distracted him, he would have finished with the Janson and he'd be sleeping in his own warm bed right now.

To find out that he'd mistaken Raina Bowen for a girl on the prowl . . .

Mistakes were outside the realm of acceptable conduct. That he'd made one tonight, over something so basic, was intolerable and not in the scope of his normal behavior patterns. Worse, he'd made a joke. Or at least, he'd tried.

People rarely found his attempts at humor funny. But Raina Bowen had been amused. All the years he had worked to understand humor, failing at every attempt, and *this* woman had laughed at his wit.

Until he'd been almost eleven years old, he hadn't even realized that there was such a thing as comedy, and it had taken another decade before he'd begun to understand that he was supposed to laugh, or at least smile, when someone cracked a joke. Guess that made him a late bloomer.

He'd been practicing, though. He tried it now, under the cover of darkness, forcing the corners of his mouth to lift in an awkward parody of a smile. Oh, it might not look awkward to an observer, but it felt inexplicably strange to him.

He heard Raina shift in her sleep. There was a rack of weapons right above her bed. Two knives. A Bolinger plasma gun, modified, from what he could see. *Nice.* She'd made a point of placing a third knife beside her hand as she climbed into bed, made a point of making sure he noticed.

The lady wasn't one to take chances. He didn't need a dictionary to tell him that she didn't know the definition of trust. Of course, there was no reason for her to trust him. An image of Sam Bowen flashed through his mind. Wizard analyzed the probabilities and determined the most likely scenario of exactly how she'd grown up. Bullied. Pushed toward the paranoid. Indoctrinated with the belief that betrayal waited at every turn. Sam Bowen must have taught his daughter the truth as he knew it.

Trust? No reason at all that she would trust *him.* Smart girl. But it would have made his job a little easier.

He knew her by reputation. Raina Bowen. In recent years Sam hadn't mentioned his daughter, never talked about her, but there were plenty of other people who did. The stories made her sound like a crazed Amazon. Hard to believe. He glanced at the bed where she slept. Pitch-black, but he could still see her. Hear her. Smell her subtle fragrance. He couldn't turn off his senses if he wanted to; they were genetic gifts that had been granted him before he was born. And right now he was glad for those gifts, because for some insane reason he liked lying in the darkness of Raina's truck, listening to her breathe.

Frowning, he shifted on the hard floor, his agile

mind sifting through bits of information that had filtered to him over the past few months. While this turn of events explained much, they also complicated his plan, though not significantly. The stories were true. Sam Bowen was dead.

And as he recalled, the rumors said it was his daughter who had killed him.

TWO

With a soft groan, Raina rolled to her side. It was six a.m., and the sun wouldn't creep across the sky for another three and a half hours, with dusk a mere seven hours after that. *Welcome to the frigging frozen North.*

Yawning, she stretched both arms above her head and brushed her fingers over the switch at the head of her bed, sending a small circle of light leaking across the floor. She could barely discern the outline of the man sleeping an arm's length away. At least he didn't snore. Or rustle the blankets. In fact, he'd been so quiet that at one point she'd wondered if he was still alive.

"Good morning." Wizard's velvet voice slid across the space between them.

She nearly jumped out of her skin. "I thought you were still asleep."

"I've been awake for two hours, seventeen minutes, nine seconds."

Okay. A little meticulous with regard to time.

He rose, stretched, his arms reaching high, fingers

21

contacting the ceiling. The hem of his shirt rode up, revealing a peek at a toned abdomen ridged with muscle. And a thick leather belt, studded with glittering throw-stars, razor sharp, deadly.

Wizard followed her gaze.

"Expecting trouble?" Raina asked, annoyed that she hadn't noticed the weapons the previous night. She'd expected he was armed, but she hadn't anticipated a full arsenal. The only thing missing was a fusion missile.

"Always." He turned slowly, as though modeling his apparel, and she saw the sheath that lay across the small of his back. The handle of a knife lay flat against his skin. A man after her own heart.

Raina's right hand strayed to the mattress, where her own blade nestled in the blankets, never far from her side.

"You've been awake for a couple of hours? What were you doing lying there in the dark?" she asked suspiciously.

His eyes met hers, colder than the frigid expanse of Waste outside. "Lying in the dark." He let the words hang, then added with what might have been a hint of sarcasm, "Playing—"

Could he mean . . . ? *Ugh. Well, bully for him.* She resisted the urge to drop her gaze to his crotch.

"—mathematical tabulation games in my mind," he finished.

Yeah, right. She tossed back the quilt and swung her legs over the side of the bed. The move brought the breadth of his chest directly into her line of vision, blocking the cabin from view. "Playing, huh? With yourself? Thanks so much for sharing."

"We could share whatever catches your fancy." His voice was low, husky. He actually sounded serious.

It was the second time in less than twenty-four hours that he'd offered to sleep with her. Did she look desperate?

"No."

Had she asked that out loud? Raina stifled a groan. Tilting her head back, she looked at his face and frowned, distracted from her embarrassment as she studied the carved line of his jaw. It should be swollen, discolored, bruised.

"Didn't Big Luc land one on the side of your jaw last night?"

"I believe the applicable terminology is sucker punch."

"Yeah. Right. If you'd seen it coming he never would have laid a hand on you. Whatever." She squinted in the dim light. "So where's the bruise?"

Wizard lifted one blunt-fingered hand to his stubbled jaw, rubbing it absently. "I heal quickly."

That was an understatement. By rights, his jaw ought to be broken. His ribs, too. But from the way he'd stretched earlier, it seemed that his side wasn't any more painful than his face. She waited for an explanation, but the big galoot just stood there, watching her.

She cleared her throat. "I'm thinking we should be on our way. The sooner the better. You want to use the shower? I have a min-dry."

"A min-dry." He lifted one dark, straight brow. "Impressive."

"I couldn't bear the thought of driving for days on end without a shower or clean clothes." So she'd paid the exorbitant fee to have her rig outfitted with a tiny shower cubicle and a min-dry, allowing her to wash herself and her clothes at the same time, then dry them in an instant. A ridiculous luxury, but one she hadn't been willing to live without. She nodded toward the bathroom. "There's soap in the cupboard over the sink, and a spare hydro-pic for your teeth."

"Thank you." He turned away, pausing in the doorway, his back to her. "What happened to Bowen?" he asked.

Raina winced. Three months and the memory still sliced through her like a dull blade, hacking a jagged edge as it went. Sam Bowen had been a lousy dad. Disinterested on the best of days, downright nasty on the worst. But on his last day he'd died in her place, and the memory still made her feel gut-wrenchingly sick.

"He died. Three months ago. Siberian Ice Reavers."

The broad expanse of Wizard's back filled the narrow doorway of the bathroom. He still didn't turn, and for a moment she thought he wouldn't comment. Better if he didn't.

"The ICW's no place for a girl." He stepped into the bathroom, the door closing behind him with a soft click.

Raina thought that if his throw-stars had been within easy reach, she'd have enjoyed sinking one into his thick, stupid skull. No place for a girl. Well, some might say there was truth in his words, but Raina Bowen hadn't been raised as a girl. She'd been playing by men's rules, by Sam Bowen's rules, all her life. That made her qualified to handle anything the ICW could throw her way. Including one arrogant, worthless trucker with more brawn than brains.

She heard the pounding of the shower and closed

her eyes, imagining Wizard, water sluicing over him, wet clothes clinging to the sculpted muscles of his arms, his back, his buttocks. Then the min-dry sucking the moisture out, leaving him squeaky-clean.

Her breath left her in a soft whoosh. She'd been on the road too long if she was fantasizing about a useless gun trucker, no matter how pretty he was. No way was she ever going to act on any fantasy; no way would she let anyone get that close. If you let someone get close, they took things you didn't want to give. Or they died. Like Mama. Like Sam. Either way, she'd learned to keep the world at arm's length, and a pretty-boy gun trucker was not going to make her bend her rules.

A sound distracted her. Was he *singing*? And did it have to be off-key?

Damn Wizard for being gorgeous, and double damn him for making her notice.

Dragging on her parka, Raina pushed open the door of the cab and braved the darkness and the frigid air. It had snowed during the night. The snowscooter was covered in a layer of crystalline powder, the tracks of the night before vanished beneath the fresh fall. She made short work of stowing the powerful machine in the cradle under her truck, then using a broom to brush away the new tracks she made in the process. No sense taking chances.

Stepping back several paces, she glanced at her rig, glad that to the casual eye the snowscooter was invisible. She didn't want Janson Trucking to recognize her for the Good Samaritan who'd hauled Wizard's ass out of the fight the previous night. With that fifty-million-interdollar prize calling her name, what she needed was the temporary pass and easy passage on the ICW. What she didn't need were complications.

She had plans for that money. Some selfish. Some not so selfish.

As she climbed back into the cab, a subtle throb pulsed beneath her feet. Her head snapped up and she squinted at the horizon, waiting as the sensation changed, coalesced into a hum and, finally, a roar. The lights of three enormous trucks moved into view, illuminating tires as tall as small houses chewing up the snow and spewing it in a wide arc that fanned out behind them. Five minutes, tops, before she found herself entertaining unwanted guests.

This entire run to Gladow Station was skidding over the slippery edge from fairly lousy to just plain miserable.

Raina slapped open the door to her living quarters, sucking in a breath as she caught Wizard in unexpected dishabille, close enough to touch. His shirt was tossed across the back of the chair, the smooth planes of his naked chest shifting subtly as he ran her brush through his thick hair. *Well, help yourself, buddy.*

And why the hell did he have his shirt off?

She froze, drank in the sight of him, golden skin and lean strength. Wide, square shoulders, trim waist, long legs . . . everything about him was beautifully male. Her gaze slid to the band that circled his right biceps, an intricate design of what appeared to be ancient letters and designs ingrained in his skin. A tattoo. *Frig.*

She'd never seen one . . . well, other than in a holopic.

God, what else could go wrong? She was harboring a *criminal.* If he was caught on her rig with that tattoo, they'd both be heading for a life sentence in the stone pits of Africa, where the average life expectancy was three years. Fact was, most people wished for death long before that.

Her gaze shot to his. "You're in breach of the Bloodborne Pathogen Act of 2087."

"Arrest me." He glanced at the tattoo, then turned his head, his attention caught by the trucks that were rapidly eating up the terrain outside the window. With one step he moved to where she stood, trapping her between the back of the driver's seat and the lean, hard length of his half-naked body. "Looks like a party. Is it for me or for you?"

She held up one hand. "Hey, I'm not the one who decked Big Luc."

Wizard's gaze snapped to hers, hard, flat. "But you could have."

Raina swallowed, strangely pleased by his observation, acutely aware of the length of him pressed up against her. Solid male muscle, tense and ready. She wondered what was wrong with her that she didn't simply knee him in a strategic spot and firmly move him outside of her personal space. She usually had very definite rules about personal space.

His hand closed around her upper arm, and he pulled her behind him, using himself as a shield. *Frigging Sir Lancelot.* Like he could stop three Janson and their arsenal of plasguns with his bare chest.

"If they find you here, we're both no better than a meal for the wild dogs. So cut the chivalry act and hide. Or better yet, *leave.*" Placing both her palms flat on the smooth skin of his back, Raina shoved him toward the rear of the truck.

Wizard hesitated for a fraction of a second, as though he were going to give in to some macho need to stand his ground. Raina gave another shove, hard, against his back. His skin was warm, and she could feel the play of muscle beneath her touch. She huffed out a breath and dropped her hands.

He reached for his shirt, tugged it over his head, then grabbed his parka and slid his arms through the sleeves. "Tsk, tsk, Raina Bowen. You invite a man to spend the night, then throw him out before first light. Cold. Very cold."

Two steps and he was right in front of her, so close she could see the thin lines of blue that fanned through the gray of his irises, smell the scent of him, soap and skin. A wave of confusion washed over her, but before she could fathom its cause, Wizard leaned in and brushed his lips across hers. Warm. Firm. Raina sucked in a startled breath.

He turned away and crossed to the far end of the cab. Opening the door, he leaped down, knees bent as he landed with the grace of a gymnast. He pulled one glove from his pocket and used it to sweep back and forth, dusting away any evidence of his footsteps in the snow.

"Wait!" She let out a soft hiss of frustration, angry at herself that she hadn't taken a swipe at him for daring to touch her, angry at him for the unexpected heat that his kiss had ignited. "I need that frigging temporary license."

"My apologies, Raina Bowen." He actually sounded sincere.

Raising his hand in a farewell salutation, Wizard

stepped back to blend with the shadows and the darkness.

Big Luc himself pushed his way into Raina's truck. She swallowed against the surge of revulsion that clawed at her throat as his eyes skimmed her body hungrily. It was all she could do to resist the opposing urges to cross her arms over her breasts, or to pull out her blade and slice Luc's soft white belly, gutting him like a fish.

"Pretty girl. Pretty rig." Luc caught a strand of Raina's hair between his fingers, rubbing it lightly before bringing it to his nose and inhaling loudly. His nails were chewed to stubs.

Raina swallowed her disgust and looked away, choosing her time, choosing her battle. The sun was coming up now. Luc and the two men with him had spent the past couple of hours taking her truck apart while she skimmed the satellite link, feigning disinterest in their activities. Now she rose, facing Luc with a carefully arranged expression of vacuous stupidity. The move brought him too close for her comfort, but she preferred to face him on her feet rather than at the disadvantage of being seated.

They'd found the snowscooter, but no tracks. Lots of truckers carried a spare vehicle. It was a fact that had saved her life so far. They had no proof that she was connected to Wizard in any way.

"You were at Bob's last night. Alone. Who were you waiting for, pretty girl?"

She shrugged lightly. "I was there for a drink."

"You cut a Siberian gun trucker. Embarrassed him in

front of his comrades." Luc circled around behind her, then leaned in and spoke close to her ear. "He would be very interested to know where you are right now."

So that was how they had known she was there. She had stupidly told the Siberian her name. Raina bit back a curse, careful to let her expression betray nothing. This was Wizard's fault. If he'd been on time . . . if he hadn't jumped the line on the ICW, drawing the Janson's attention . . .

"This man, this Wizard, he's trouble. He jumped line last night on the ICW."

Tell me something I don't know.

"And before that, he stole two temporary passes—"

There you go. Something I didn't know.

"Stole? From the Janson?" she asked incredulously, turning to face Big Luc. There was no need to feign surprise. Wizard was certifiably, irrevocably insane. He was supposed to buy the passes on the black market, not steal them directly from the company. "Who in their right mind would steal from you? The Janson own the ICW."

That wasn't strictly true. According to the New Government Order, the ICW belonged to the people. But anyone who drove the highway knew it belonged to the man who owned the Janson: Duncan Bane.

The thought of him made her skin crawl.

"You're a smart girl." Big Luc smiled at her, baring crooked yellow teeth in an expression of genuine approval. She'd said the right thing, and for the moment he looked positively benign. Then he shook his head balefully. "I doubt that boy is in his right mind," Luc said with exaggerated concern. "Don't you know his story?"

Raina frowned. She didn't know Wizard's story. Didn't think she wanted to. One thing she did know—her dad had hooked up with Wizard and made a bargain. With his dying breath Sam had made her promise to look the guy up. Only, from what she'd seen so far, that meant her dad hadn't known squat.

"He's a mercenary." He grinned, an ugly stretching of lips and skin. "Used to work for the New Government Order before he decided to sell himself to the highest bidder."

Not just a no-account gun trucker. A mercenary. My, my, isn't Wizard just full of surprises? Raina shrugged. Being a mercenary wasn't any worse than working for the Order. Either way, you ended up employed by slime.

Luc's gaze strayed to his companions. "Doug, Glenn, go meet the others at the Line Sixty-four fill station." His gaze raked Raina, lingering on her breasts. "I'll be along in a bit."

As the two men left, Raina suppressed a satisfied smile. She'd be alone with Luc. She could have taken out all three if she had to, but it would be easier, quicker, to deal with only one.

Luc stood by her side, watching as his two companions drove away.

"Come play hide the salami, pretty girl." He grabbed her hair, roughly yanking her head back as he tried to kiss her on the mouth. Twisting her head aside, she diverted his lips to her cheek. She could smell beer and garlic, and the metallic stink of rotting teeth. Big Luc could use a visit to the dentist. What was it with Janson truckers and personal hygiene?

Jerking away, Raina dragged the back of her hand

across her face. "Go away, Luc. Tell your boys that we did the wild thing, and I won't deny it."

"We'll do it. And I'll tell them." He puffed out his chest, leering at her. "You won't deny it, pretty girl. You'll dream about getting it again."

Uh-huh. Raina shook her head. "Last warning," she said softly, twisting away as Luc's thick fingers grasped at thin air, hating the fact that she knew he wouldn't listen.

He growled, lunging for her. With a sugary smile she stepped into his rough embrace, dropping her hand to the front of his filthy jeans. He hesitated, disoriented by her apparent acquiescence. She closed her fingers tight around Luc's testicles and gave a sharp, hard twist. He howled, doubling over. Raina glanced up, over his shoulder, momentarily distracted by a shadow of movement.

"I have this thing about personal space," she said, shifting to the side and tightening her grip around his family jewels. "I don't like people getting close. Ever."

With her free hand she lifted a metal pot from the counter, for once infinitely glad that her home was so cramped. And without a moment's hesitation, she rapped Luc hard on the head, watching in satisfaction as he slumped to the ground.

"ICW's no place for a girl," she mimicked irritably, raising her gaze as the shadow she had noticed shifted and became a man. "You could have at least lent a hand."

Wizard leaned against the door of the cab, watching her, his gray eyes glittering. He smiled, a controlled movement of his lips, a little stiff, as though he wasn't exactly sure whether he was doing it right.

For a second she forgot all about the rancid trucker sprawled unconscious on the floor. All she could think about was the fact that when he smiled, white teeth flashing, one cheek creasing in a sexy dimple, Wizard was too perfect to be real. Her breath left her in a sharp hiss.

God, why this man? It was the last, the absolute last thing she needed right now—a mindless attraction to a worthless gun trucker who couldn't even deliver the pass he'd promised her.

"You didn't look like you needed my help," he said, smoke and velvet.

She blinked, dragging her mind back to reality. "Well, I wouldn't mind it now. Drag him out to his truck—"

"Yes, ma'am," he interrupted. "You do not want me to leave him outside in the snow?"

"I don't like killing." She thought of Sam, the darkness, the bitter wind, the cold, and the blood. "What do you think would happen to him in this temperature?"

Wizard narrowed his eyes, and for a second she regretted revealing so much. What would he do with the knowledge that she hated to take a life? But, no, she reminded herself. He'd been dumb enough to steal trucking passes from the Janson. No way was he going to see inside her mind, understand its workings. The comment had probably gone right over his head.

"The temperature outside is minus-thirty-six degrees." His voice was devoid of expression. "Primary accidental hypothermia resulting from environmental exposure results in decreased heat production. At rest, humans produce forty to sixty kilocalories of heat per square meter of body surface."

Ohhh-kay. With a start, she realized that his contemplative expression had nothing to do with what she'd divulged. He was actually answering her rhetorical question. "I need to know this because . . . ?"

"Exposure at these temperatures would result in frostbite. Tissue cells would be subject to ice-crystal formation, cellular dehydration, protein denaturation, inhibition of DNA synthesis, and abnormal cell wall permeability—"

"Uh, Wizard," she cut him off as he paused to draw breath. "I just don't want the Janson any more pissed at me than they already are. A dead carcass definitely won't sway them in my favor." She smiled thinly. "But, um, thanks for the lesson about the dangers of cold weather. I'll keep it in mind."

"You asked what would happen to him in this temperature. I provided the requested information."

"Umm, yeah. But I didn't mean it literally."

He tilted his head to one side. "Then why ask?"

"It was a rhetorical question."

"Understood." He gave a sharp nod. "In the future please clarify." He hooked his hands under Luc's arms and dragged him outside.

Raina stood staring at the empty space Wizard had just vacated. He'd been like some kind of frigging human computer, standing there spouting facts as if he were reading them from a book. *Weird.*

Crossing to her tiny bathroom, Raina carefully scrubbed her hands, disgusted by the fact that she'd touched Luc. She splashed water on her face, then brushed her teeth, desperate to take away the feel, the smell of Luc on her body. She could hardly spare the time, but the shower stall beckoned. Three minutes later she was out and dry, her physical comfort sorted out, her emotional well-being in turmoil.

Here she was, in the middle of the frozen frigging Northern Waste, persona non grata with the Janson army. No pass. No apparent way to get to Gladow Station. And no idea what to do with Wizard, a man who wasn't anything he appeared to be.

She wanted—*needed*—that frigging interdollar prize. For herself. And for Beth.

Hell. Trust Sam Bowen to get himself killed and leave her with the responsibility of a sister she'd never known she had.

THREE

Port Uranium, Janson Transport Head Office

"She's with him. At least, we think she is." The words skulked across the cavernous space on a whisper, echoing hollowly. The man who had spoken hovered hesitantly near the door.

Duncan Bane, owner of Janson Transport and special Adviser to the president of the New Government Order, did not immediately acknowledge the news, did not turn from the vast window that formed the east wall of his office. He liked the view, the sight of the enormous plasma screen set atop the city's highest tower, warning the citizens of Port Uranium about the size of the ozone hole that day, the level of deadly solar radiation. He derived immeasurable pleasure from manipulating their minds with the false data he posted, and from the pungent aura of their fear. It was almost . . . sensual.

"You *think* she is with him?" he questioned softly. "I pay you to know for certain."

In the window he could see the reflection of the huge man who stood a respectful distance away, lingering near the door of the beautifully appointed office, nervously shifting his weight from foot to foot. Duncan felt a primal surge of satisfaction, a glow of power as his tongue darted out and he tasted the unseen molecules that embodied the man's fear. The flavor was sweetest nectar.

His gaze shifted, and instead of the unwieldy bulk of his minion, he saw his own reflection before him. Tall. Lean. Groomed to perfection. Except for that one flaw.

Of its own volition, his hand moved to the black patch that covered the gaping hole that had once held his right eye. His index finger traced the raised, puckered skin that sliced a jagged path along his cheek and dragged the corner of his mouth into a perpetual sneer. He had been perfect once, his face an even compilation of chiseled features and boyish charm. Gone in an instant with the single slash of a sharp blade. And all because he had tried to take what he wanted, what he considered his due. The only time in his life that he had been forced to take no for an answer.

Raina Bowen. Just the thought of her brought the familiar cold, hard knot of rage to the fore, made his hands itch to wrap around her neck and squeeze, watch her gasp and struggle for breath. . . . But, no. Dead, she would be released from her suffering, freed from paying the price that she owed him. Better to keep her alive for endless days and pain-racked nights. Her pain. His pleasure.

Reining in his thoughts, Duncan turned and walked

around his impressive desk, one hand trailing over the polished mahogany. A luxury, to be sure. So few trees remained in this part of the northern hemisphere.

"She was not supposed to find him. Your men were to deal with him before he ever reached her." He paused, then continued, more to himself than to his companion: "Mother dead. Father dead. Never in one place long enough to build any relationships. I have planned and worked toward this end for years. I wanted her to be totally, irrevocably alone. Nervous, frightened, cowed by years of watching for me over her shoulder . . ." He stalked his underling until mere feet separated him from the sweating, stammering fool who hovered near the door. "Mistakes are so very costly." He could smell the man's terror now, rich and sharp. Lovely. "Do you remember John Brooker? Your predecessor?" He let the question hang in the heavy silence. "Well, Earl? Do you remember?"

"Yes, sir," Earl muttered, keeping his eyes downcast, long, greasy hair falling forward.

"Unfortunate accident. Caught in the blades of a grain harvester while on routine inspection . . . terrible. Terrible. It took him so many days to die, the physicians cutting away parts of him as they became infected until there was really nothing left to cut. Tragedies strike so unexpectedly." Duncan waited, let the implication sink deep into the man's brain before continuing. "The mercenary Wizard is an inconvenience, a splinter I cannot seem to ignore. I should have killed him years ago, but I found his pathetic predicament entertaining. He amuses me no longer. Alive. Or dead. Whatever. I care little about his life. I simply want him removed."

Earl cleared his throat. "Consider it done, Mr. Bane."

"Excellent. Now as to Miss Bowen . . . ahhh, but she is an altogether different matter. I want her alive and unsullied. No one is to put a mark on her." He smiled, imagining the feel of her soft skin, the sound of her terrified cries. "Putting marks on her is a pleasure I reserve only for myself. You have three days."

"Yes, sir." Recognizing his dismissal, Earl backed away, a bowing, scraping subordinate taking leave of royalty.

"Earl." Duncan stopped him as he pulled open the heavy door. "Our allies in the Northern Waste would be put out if anyone other than a Janson man made that first delivery."

His fingers twitched with the urge to stray to the edge of the black leather patch. Ruthlessly, he wrested the desire under control. "Appearances are everything, you understand. It must be a Janson trucker who wins the Gladow race."

"Yes, sir." Earl swallowed and scuttled out, closing the door softly behind him.

"Such a limited vocabulary." Duncan shook his head, striding across the antique hand-knotted Persian carpet that covered the floor, a priceless artifact from a bygone era.

Sinking into the body-molded chair behind his desk, he punched a button, bringing up a hologram of a globe, the borders of the Northern Waste outlined in red, the ribbon of the ICW shown in green. The New Government Order had rules about the ICW. All truckers had equal rights. There was no special treatment for any specific company. Bribes were dealt with in a harsh and immediate manner.

Duncan smiled, well pleased with his own work. After all, he'd helped draft those rules as head of the Committee for Fair Traffic on the Intercontinental Worldwide. So easy to fool those who saw only what they *wished* to see. He stared at the thin green line that wended its way through the Alberta Corridor, north to Dorje Station, then along the Nunavut passover. The longest highway ever built. The safest highway in the world, according to the New Government Order.

Imperceptive and thickheaded wretches. The politicians could drone and posture all they wanted. The Northern Waste was *his*, an untapped treasure. Not because of any natural resource, but because of the lack of resources. The vast and ever-growing population of Northern Waste settlers needed food, materials, supplies, and via the ICW, Janson Transport was the source.

Supply and demand. A concept of inexplicable simplicity and beauty. He supplied, and he demanded whatever price he chose. Money. Loyalty. A man's nubile daughter, or his wife. Leaning back, he relaxed into the soft embrace of the obscenely expensive chair. His own little throne. And he, Duncan Bane, ruler of his own frozen kingdom.

FOUR

Sunlight streamed through the windows of the cab, refracted off the glittering crystals of snow, nearly blinding Raina as she shifted the truck into gear and headed toward Bob's Truck Stop. A few short hours and the light would be gone. She snagged her antiglare lenses from the overhead visor, slipping them on as she listened to the hum of the powerful engine, felt the throb roll through her body. To her left the raised platform of the ICW ran parallel to her route, extending in an endless line to disappear over the horizon. The ICW ran right through Gladow Station. It wasn't just the easiest and fastest route. It was the *only* route. And it was off-limits to her, thanks to Wizard, his stolen passes, and the momentary lapse in sanity that had led her to offer him a ride on her snowscooter.

"So what brilliant plan do you have, Wizard? You think you can just walk casually up to your truck and drive away happy?" He'd asked her to drive him back to the truck stop so he could retrieve his vehicle. The guy was nuts. If the Janson weren't there waiting for him, it would be a miracle.

"That is my brilliant plan." He stretched his long legs out in front of him, leaning back in the seat and looking way too relaxed for her rising temper. And way too warm. He'd doffed his parka and hung it over the back of the chair. With a burst of perverse pleasure, she opened her window nice and wide, letting the frigid air fill the cabin. After all, *she* was wearing her coat.

He pushed up the sleeves of his thermal shirt, baring his forearms, apparently impervious to the cold.

"Listen, you worthless screwup. You were supposed to meet me with a pass. One that was bought and paid for, not stolen." Gritting her teeth, she silently acknowledged that she was annoyed as much with herself as she was with him. First because she should have had a backup plan—she always had a backup plan—and second because she was supremely irritated that her gaze kept straying from the road to Wizard's strong forearm where it rested casually on the arm of the passenger seat. Corded muscle. Lightly dusted with dark hair.

She narrowed her eyes and focused on the road. "Thanks to you, I'm not only out one temporary license, but I can't even drive the ICW until things settle down. You're about as reliable as a busted comlink."

Wizard shifted on his seat, turning his head to look out the side window. "It was your choice to render Big Luc unconscious and leave him sleeping in his rig. That choice is the reason you cannot drive the ICW. There is no correlation to my activities."

Rolling her eyes at him, she jammed her temper back to a slow simmer. "If it weren't for you, Big Luc wouldn't have been in my rig in the first place. *Your* actions were foolhardy."

"Foolhardy. Showing boldness or courage but not wisdom or good sense." He continued to stare out the window.

Raina blinked. "What the hell was my dad thinking when he hooked up with you? Your word to supply that damned pass was as good as mud."

She felt rather than saw the change in him, a subtle shift of current, and suddenly he wasn't relaxed anymore. There was a sharp edge to him.

"My word is my only law." His tone was clipped. "I gave my word to Sam Bowen that I would provide a temporary trucking pass—"

"No. You gave your word to me, Raina Bowen. Sam was never part of the picture."

"Clarification noted. At the time, I knew my contact only as Bowen and made the logical extrapolation that Sam required my services."

"Uh-huh."

"When the Janson refused to sell the pass, I stole it," he continued. "The time it took me to carry out the theft made me late for the meeting. Had you not called attention to yourself by inviting me to join you on your scooter, then I would have let things die down, contacted you, and delivered the pass as agreed."

Raina let out a snort of irritation. The guy really was dumber than dirt. "A stolen pass isn't worth the techslab it's laser-imprinted on."

"I am aware of that. My word was given to provide

the pass. There was no stipulation as to its value after delivery. Besides, Sam Bowen was not there to receive delivery. His absence nullifies my commitment."

Her insides twisted at his words. Sam wasn't there to receive delivery because he was dead, his belly cut open, his guts lying in a steaming heap on the snow. The one time in his life that he'd actually thought about her rather than himself, and then he'd gone and died before she could thank him, before she could say any of the things that she'd really wanted—no, *needed*—to say. She glanced at Wizard, forcing the words past the unwelcome tightness in her throat.

Yeah, that was Sam. Tell her about a sister she never knew she had. Get himself gutted. And then go and die on her.

"Why would anyone want a pass they couldn't use?"

"My word was given to provide the pass," he repeated.

"Yeah. I get it. Your word was given to provide the pass." She gestured impatiently at the icy tundra beyond her window. "Which is about as useful to me as a bikini right now."

Wizard was silent for a moment, long enough to draw her gaze. "A bikini would be a poor choice of apparel, given the current subzero temperature," he pointed out, serious.

She sighed. Dumber than dirt.

Leaning a bit forward, Wizard shoved his hand into the back pocket of his pants and withdrew a small rectangular piece of techslab with a hologram insignia laser-imprinted on the front. The useless temporary license. Astounded, Raina stared at him, looking for some indication that he was kidding, but finding none. She slapped his hand away and shook her head in exasperation, then turned her attention back to the rimed tundra that served as a road. "What is it with you anyway? Some of the things you say, the way you think . . . it's like you've got a computer chip in your head. Or like you're one of the New Government Order breed dogs, latched on to one thing, hanging on to it and shaking it back and forth like a trophy."

"An unflattering comparison," he said without rancor.

"You think?" Gearing down, she slowed the truck, simultaneously closing her window. Wizard didn't seem to care about the cold, but she'd had quite enough of it herself. "That's Bob's up ahead. Looks pretty dead."

The truck stop seemed deserted, and beyond it, the shabby buildings that housed the waitresses, the strippers, the bartenders looked equally dead. Likely everyone was still asleep.

Wizard's eyes moved slowly across the frozen rectangle of ground that served as a parking lot. At least he had the sense to watch for trouble. There were no Janson trucks here, and Raina couldn't help wondering why they hadn't left anyone to guard Wizard's rig. Unless they were all on the ICW, barreling toward Gladow Station and the fifty-million-interdollar reward. Of course, the ICW was exactly where *she* wanted to be. That prize was slipping through her fingers, and she didn't like the rope burn it was leaving as it went.

"Is your rig loaded?" she asked, wondering if he wasn't after the prize dollars for himself.

"No. Yours?"

So his rig wasn't loaded for a run to Gladow. Interesting. Then what was he doing here?

"Yeah. I stopped at the Arctic Line Station. Got a full load of grain in government-sealed containers. I'm all dressed up with nowhere to go," she muttered.

He slanted her a quizzical glance.

What was it with this guy? "It means I've got a full load and no way to get to Gladow Station. The Janson will likely be waiting for you at any fill station you pull into. . . . They'll kill you before you can get your rig loaded, so I guess that puts you out of the race. Too bad. Aren't you just a little anxious to get your hands on those interdollars?"

"No." He met her gaze, and she could read no guile there. He meant it. He didn't care about the prize. *There you go. Certifiable.*

Better for her. One less truck to compete with.

After setting the brake, Raina yanked on her gloves and pulled the hood of her parka up with one hand as she swung down from the cab. Bob's looked worse in the pallid daylight than it did in the more forgiving darkness of the long northern night. One of the front windows was broken, boarded up with layers of plasti-glass. The sign hung crookedly, flapping noisily with each gust of wind, an eerie creaking sound that made Raina's back teeth ache. Barren. Bleak. Grim. Like her prospects. At least fate was consistent.

Shrugging into his parka, Wizard climbed down from the cab and closed the door behind him with deliberate care. She couldn't help noticing the way he moved, the easy grace, the masculine perfection of his form. He was tall and hard and muscled, and she wondered what it would feel like to touch—

No. No. No. She was *not* going there.

She had heard stories of people who went insane in

the Northern Waste, who lost their grasp of reality. Yes. That must be it. She definitely preferred that explanation to the possibility that she was wildly attracted to a worthless gun trucker.

Shifting her focus, she scanned the vicinity. No sign of anything amiss. The Janson were long gone, which Raina figured was the first bit of good luck that had come her way in a long while. If one believed in luck. Sometimes she thought she did, but mostly she just believed in herself.

"Hey, man, that your truck?" A teenager's tenor, laced with arrogance.

Raina turned to find a cadre of scruffy youths slinking from the side of the truck stop, their grimy faces gaunt with hunger. They focused on Wizard, kept their eyes on him. Likely they didn't see her as a threat.

These kids would as soon knife you as talk to you. With good reason. Killing was often their sole means of survival. The New Government Order promised food on every table, a warm home for all. Except orphaned kids of the Northern Waste settlers didn't seem to qualify as "all," and they ended up on their own, scrabbling out an existence, just waiting for their turn to die.

She felt a little sick at the thought, knew exactly how desperate they were. She'd grown up little different from them, one step away from freezing, or starving, or being knifed for a crust of bread. Home. Family. What the hell did she know about those things? Only the hazy memories of a mother whose face she had forgotten—and worse, what Sam had taught her, when he was sober enough to remember she was there.

The boy at the front of the pack pushed back a hank of brown hair, and though his filthy hands were wrapped in rags, Raina noticed that the baby finger of his left hand was missing. He glanced at her then. She met his whiskey-colored eyes, read the flat desperation there, and knew that he'd hacked the finger off himself.

"Frostbite. It was either cut it off or let the black rot eat the whole hand," he said with a shrug, then turned his shrewd gaze back on Wizard. "So is that your truck or not?"

"No. It is her truck." Wizard tipped his head in Raina's direction. "The black one over there is mine."

The boy's gaze slid slowly to Wizard's truck, then back, and his face took on a sly expression. "Nice rig. You left it here alone? Lucky for you nothing happened to it."

The kid knew something, and Raina had a feeling that whatever it was, it didn't bode well for Wizard's vehicle. Shame. It was a fine rig.

"What'll you pay us to give you a bit of information?" the boy asked, jutting his chin out mulishly as he subtly passed an indecipherable hand signal to his companions. They moved to form a loose ring around her and Wizard.

Raina tensed. Defending herself against a grown man was one thing, but she hated the idea of hurting a kid, even a dirty, devious kid who was just as tall as she was, probably outweighed her, and who'd knife her in the back the second she turned away if he thought there was any profit in it. She had this thing about kids. Orphan kids. Kids who had to fight for everything.

One more reason to win that race to Gladow, to make certain Beth never became one of them.

Before she could say anything, Wizard had his hand jammed in his pocket and was dragging out a fistful of whisper-thin plastitech interdollars. She wanted to hit him. If he gave over the money, these kids would think they were tough—tough enough to take on the Siberian gun truckers or the ice pirates. Maybe even the Janson. Better to let them think they could *win* the money. At least that way they wouldn't get an inflated sense of whom they could go up against. Reaching over, she snatched the interdollars from Wizard's hand.

"We don't pay for information, especially when there's no guarantee you can tell us anything we don't already know. Like the fact that the Janson hung around last night waiting, maybe even left us a surprise in that rig."

The kid's eyes shifted to Wizard's truck and back.

"Tell you what." Raina leaned in, as though offering a secret. "We won't pay, but we'll *play* you for whatever information you have. Three-dice Jacey."

The boy narrowed his eyes thoughtfully at her suggestion. She could feel Wizard close beside her, and she just hoped he understood her motivation. At least he hadn't gainsaid her, which was a start.

"What is your name?" he asked the boy. "I cannot play against a man if I do not know his name."

"Name's Ben." The kid puffed out his chest. "Yours?"

"Wizard. What have you got to bet, Ben, besides information that is questionable at best?" he asked, his insolent drawl mimicking the boy's.

"How about *her* life?" The kid was all macho posturing and bravado.

Wizard shook his head. "Not good," he said impassively. "She is not mine. And she is not yours, so no bet." His eyes roamed the motley group, stopping on a little boy near the front and the puppy by his side. "I will take the dog."

Well, Wizard caught on fast. That dog was the only thing of value these kids had. The fact that they hadn't eaten the animal counted for something, though the actual value of the lop-eared mutt to anyone other than them was debatable. But they needed to feel they had something to lose, or the whole deal was a worthless venture.

The little boy stepped in front of the puppy, as though to shield him, his small face tense, his dark eyes wide. Ben glanced at the boy, then the dog, and Raina saw a flicker of emotion cross his face. He again communicated silently with the younger child, his hand signal sending some sort of message.

"Fine." Ben grunted. "You win, I'll give you information and the dog." He nodded in the direction of the wad of interdollars. "I win, you give me all of that."

The money was enough to feed these kids for a month.

"Three thousand interdollars is my stake. Information and the dog are yours," Wizard agreed. He hunkered down in the snow, shoving the interdollars into the rusted tin can one of the vagabond children thrust in front of him.

Ben grabbed the little boy by the hand, dragging him forward. The puppy followed.

Wizard pulled three dice from the pocket of his parka. Three-dice Jacey. Make the call. Roll the dice.

You had to be dead-on to win. The game had been invented here in the frozen north, where men had nothing but time, endless time, on their hands. Raina rolled her eyes. They could be here all day.

"How do I know your dice ain't fixed?" Ben demanded with a scowl as he squatted opposite Wizard. Raina looked around and saw only smug certainty on the faces of Ben's crew. That he would cheat was a given, as far as she was concerned, but that was fine by her. It was Wizard's money.

"You have dice?" Wizard laid his own dice on the ground.

The boy fished out a set from a small skin bag that hung on a leather strip from the rag at his waist. He tossed them on the ground. They landed up seven. Wizard gathered the dice, hefted them in one hand, then rolled. Again they landed up seven. Raina hid a smile.

"Okay. We'll use mine." Wizard scooped up Ben's dice and tucked them away.

Ben tilted his head, his expression betraying his concern, but when he looked up to see Raina watching him, he quickly masked it.

They played, roll after roll, the bitter wind swirling around them, biting deep, but not as deep as Raina's impatience. She was eager to end this and get moving. Then Wizard called seven and won. The little boy sank his fingers nervously into the puppy's fur. Raina felt a pang of regret. However bad she'd had it with Sam Bowen as her father, these poor kids had it much, much worse.

The next roll came up in favor of Ben, who promptly sent a telling glance at the boy beside him.

Suddenly the puppy was loose, gamboling across the small area they squatted beside. From the corner of her eye she caught Ben's movement as he scooped up the dice and tossed down a second pair. She'd almost missed it, and either Wizard did miss it or he had a strong urge to divest himself of some money, because he said nothing about the switch.

So now everyone in the game was cheating.

Ben won the next roll. And the next. The dice were definitely fixed. It was near impossible to win consecutively at Three-dice Jacey. With the fifth roll, Wizard lost the tin can full of interdollars, and heaving a sigh, he got to his feet.

"Nice try," Ben said, snatching up the money and tying it into his pouch. In a flash he had a homemade knife in his hand, whittled bone tied to a hand-hammered blade. He eyed Wizard warily as he shifted the knife from hand to hand. The blade was nicely balanced, Raina noted, and the kid's grip was confident. He'd obviously been taking care of himself for a very long time, and she suspected that more than once he'd had to fight for his winnings. Maybe even for his life. "You lost. No information. No dog."

Rising slowly to his feet, Wizard reached into his pocket, withdrawing a handful of plastitech disks. "Vid-credits for Bob's," he said. "I'll trade them for that information."

A dozen sets of eyes were fixed on the disks in his hand. Raina wondered if they'd ever had vid-credits to spend. Not often, if ever.

She sighed. *For frig's sake.* They were back to where they started, only Wizard was about three thousand interdollars poorer, and he was about to hand vid-credits to a bunch of kids who were already full of overblown bravado. Maybe it would be a kindness if she scared them a little, just enough to remind them that they weren't as tough as they thought.

A Siberian trucker would eat them for breakfast. An ice pirate would do the same, but he wouldn't be kind enough to kill them first.

Ben skewed his lips to the side, making a show of considering Wizard's offer. Finally he nodded, and the little kid reached out to snatch the vid-credits, dropping them in the metal can.

Raina shook her head and slid her hand to the small of her back. She hated to do this, but it would be worse for these desperate kids if they tried to take on the next ice pirate that came through. She was about to unsheath her blade, intending to wave it around a little and put a healthy dose of fear into Ben and his raggedy pack, when she felt Wizard's fingers close around her wrist. Not enough to hurt her, but enough to send a warning. Annoyed, she turned to glare at him.

"Next time you're through here, I won't be in such a generous mood." Ben tossed his head defiantly.

"I will remember that," Wizard said. "And I'll take that information now in payment for the vid-credits."

"Two Janson truckers stayed all night. Right there beside your rig. Three other trucks drove out after you. East. Following the scooter tracks. The two that stayed were really, really interested in your rig. Didn't leave it even for a second." As Ben spoke, Raina realized that he must have been there last night, watching what happened, must have seen her and Wizard take off for the access road. For a moment she wondered if he'd sold that information to the Janson. Probably.

"That's all I've got." Ben puffed out his chest. "Me and the crew are going to make good use of these vid-credits. I'll give you a couple of hours to clear out. Don't be here when I get back." Warning issued, Ben turned and sauntered away, the pack of sunken-eyed children following behind.

"Ben," Wizard called softly. The boy stopped but didn't turn.

A soft hiss disturbed the cold air, and a metallic glitter shone for a millisecond beside Ben's right ear. A lock of ragged brown hair fluttered to the ground just before one of Wizard's throw-stars lodged in the ice several feet away.

Okay. As far as warnings went, that was fairly effective. Raina unclenched her fingers from her knife hilt.

"The soldier who is attacked from behind is the one who dies," Wizard said softly as he casually strode over to retrieve his throw-star.

Something in his tone sent a chill chasing along Raina's spine. She could almost hear Sam saying those exact words to her, knew they were part of the training of the New Government Order forces.

The boy gave a sharp nod and kept walking, but his shoulders were tight and the swagger was gone. That was a warning he'd remember, she thought.

"Glad you caught on, smart boy," Raina murmured as she watched them go. "Can't just hand over money to kids like that. They have to fight and scrabble for everything they get. They'd never trust easy pickings, and if they did, it could mean their death."

"I am cognizant of that fact." Wizard turned and strode toward his truck.

"Cognizant?" Raina called after him. "Can't you just say, 'I know'?"

FIVE

Halfway to his rig, Wizard froze, then veered sideways and made for Raina's truck instead. He circled it slowly, as though searching for some flaw. After a moment he popped open the hood, climbed up, and looked into the engine.

Annoyed, Raina followed, filing away her questions for now. "What?" she demanded, watching him lean in to get a closer look at the motor.

Wizard glanced at her. "Not combustion. That is good. Fuel cell is better. And graphite storage for your hydrogen. What do you get? Eight thousand yuales? Better than cylinder storage. Less bulky. Solar panels up top."

"Yeah, I get about eight thousand yuales. And yes, I have solar panels, for what they're worth at this time of year, when we're getting about four hours of sunlight."

"Eight thousand isn't enough." Wizard poked at one of the tubes leading into the fuel cell. "I will modify it."

"Not enough for what?" She narrowed her eyes at him.

Jumping down from the bumper, Wizard turned and studied the horizon. "There are no hydrogen fill stations on the I-pole. Eight thousand yuales will not get you to Gladow Station."

Raina shook her head, certain she'd heard him wrong. "The I-pole? You can't mean what I think you mean. . . ."

He just stood there, focusing on the horizon, saying nothing. And that made her so very nervous.

"No one would be crazy enough to drive the I-pole. Not even you." The Polar Interlink—or I-pole, as it was commonly referred to—was a prewar throwback, a highway built before the Fossil Fuel Edict, before the Second Noble War.

She always found it strange, that name: Noble War. As if there were anything noble about a nuclear holocaust. The Second Noble War had ended about a third of the lives on the planet along with civilization as it was known at the time. It had also ended travel on the I-pole. There were deserted petroleum stations along the way, but no hydrogen fills. No rig could go twenty thousand yuales without hydrogen. If that wasn't deterrent enough, the ancient highway ran smack-dab through the center of ice pirate territory. Then it went over the pole directly under the biggest, nastiest hole in the ozone layer. Though, she had to admit, if they *could* drive it, they were pretty much guaranteed to be the first ones at Gladow Station. The I-pole could be a straight line to riches or, more likely, an early death.

Suddenly the second half of Wizard's statement

registered in her mind. "What do you mean, you'll modify it? You are *not* going to modify my engine. If there's any work to be done on my rig, I'll do it."

He turned, his gaze moving to his own truck and then back to her face. "My rig runs off water."

"Uh-huh. And mine runs off strawberries."

He stared at her blankly, then smiled, that gorgeous turning of his lips, there, then gone so quickly she thought she might have imagined it. She wanted to see him smile fully, openly, white teeth flashing in the sun.

Oh, man. She'd been bitten bad.

"Off strawberries . . . A joke," he said, his face lighting with wonder.

Weird. "Uh, yeah, my rig doesn't actually run off strawberries."

He nodded slowly. "But mine runs off water."

Raina puffed out a short blast of air. "That's impossible. To split hydrogen from water, you'd need to input energy. The point is to remove energy from hydrogen, use it to run your rig, and end up with water as your exhaust." She patted him gently on the arm. "You're confused. Nice dream, though. If you could run off water, you'd never need a hydrogen fill. The I-pole might even start to look like a possibility. And if you sold that technology, you'd be rich, rich, rich."

"I have no need for money."

"Uh, yeah, you do. You just gave all your interdollars to those kids." *Gave.* That was the key word. He'd *wanted* those ragged children to have the money.

"My rig runs off water," he reiterated. "Input H_2O. Utilize energy from solar source to split hydrogen. Pump it through the fuel cell. Easy."

The guy was odd with a capital O, and his story

about running off water was about as wacky as could be. If he *was* actually able to do what he claimed, he'd be the richest man on the entire stinking planet, wealthier even than Duncan Bane.

She shivered. Duncan Bane. Would she ever hear his name—think his name—without feeling the cold talons of dread curl about her insides? Maybe. On the day she celebrated his death.

Deliberately turning her attention elsewhere, Raina circled Wizard's truck. "Yeah. So show me your amazing miracle fuel, smart boy."

"Not good." He spoke from just behind her as his hands closed around her arms and he yanked her back against the solid wall of his chest. Raina's breath left her in a whoosh. She could feel his heat even through the thermal gear they both wore, feel the firm grasp of his fingers around her arms, holding her close against him. And she wanted to lean in, to revel in the feel of his solid warmth.

"What . . ." Her voice came out as a hoarse croak. Closing her eyes, she steadied her thoughts, focusing on the reason for his actions rather than the inexplicable frisson of electricity that shimmered between them. This was so out of character for her as to be almost laughable. "What do you mean by 'not good'?" she finally managed as she took a very deliberate step away from him.

He dropped his hands back to his sides. "Our friend Ben gave us a warning about the Janson's keen interest in my rig. Look." He pointed to the fine layer of fresh snow that surrounded his truck.

Frowning, Raina squinted in the direction he indicated. "What exactly am I looking for . . . ?" Her voice trailed away as she saw them—the faintest indentation of footprints, covered now by the fresh layer of snow. She narrowed her eyes, focusing on the details. The warning—it was always there in the littlest details. She saw it then, a thin wire that ran up the side of the truck. Her gaze followed it to the door handle. Trip wire. *Nice*. The Janson had left Wizard a present. Most likely a tiny, deadly blob of cytoplast stuck to the underside of the rig, wired to the door handle.

"I was expecting it, and I still almost missed it," she said. "On the way over here I was wondering how the Janson could just leave your truck without a guard. I would have sworn they wanted you dead." She jerked her head in the direction of the trip wire and spun to face him. "Guess they want you better than dead. They want you in tiny little pieces."

As she turned, she realized that he was still too close. His scent, warm and male and clean, mingled with the hard, cold edge of the winter air, and she had the strangest urge to lean in and sniff him. His gaze shifted, dropping to her mouth, and his pupils dilated, leaving his eyes dark and mysterious.

"Today is not my day to die." His voice was low, the sound reaching deep inside her and tying her in knots.

"Maybe. But your truck's a goner. There's no way to defuse a cytoplast bomb." Unnerved by his proximity, by the subtle invitation in his tone, she used her forearm against his chest to push him out of the way. "Come on. I think we can use my rig to tow yours out a ways so the debris doesn't wreck this place. But first I want to check out the size of the cytoplast and figure the blast radius."

She strode across the frozen lot. When she reached

his rig she glanced over her shoulder. He stood exactly where she'd left him, watching her, his gaze hot and hungry.

Squatting down, she used her actions to shield herself from him and to cover her confusion. She was so not herself. Raina Bowen did *not* turn into a quivering mass of lust just because some guy with a gorgeous face and a body she itched to touch gave her a look that could melt the polar ice cap.

She leaned in, squinting at the underside of the rig. Yes. There. Enough cytoplast to blow an entire town.

Crossing his arms over his chest, Wizard watched as Raina crouched on the ground to examine the underbelly of his rig. The hood of her anorak was pulled close about her face, hiding her features from view, but the long golden tail of her hair sneaked out one side and trailed over her shoulder.

He knew what that hair smelled like. He'd lain in the dark, wrapped in her scent. He'd sat in the seat beside her, attuned to each beat of her heart, the soft sound of each breath she took. Tough, smart, sexy. There was something about her that was more than that, though there was definite appeal in a woman who was tough and smart and sexy. There was a vulnerability, subtle, nearly hidden. He wanted to protect her, and the thought was absurd, because she was a woman who would spurn any attempt he made.

Besides, the thing she needed protection from most right now was *him*. He had planned to meet Sam, and use Sam to find his daughter.

Instead, Sam's daughter had found him.

She leaned forward, lending him a better view of her legs, long and lean, encased in weatherproof black thermal leggings, poking out from beneath the hem of her oversize parka. His fingers flexed. He could almost feel her softness beneath the touch of his hand, taste her beneath the brush of his tongue.

Wizard blinked. He was not prone to unguarded moments of fantasy. In fact, he had long doubted that he possessed any imagination at all. Yet here he was, imagining the woman in front of him with her golden hair falling over her naked shoulders, her body arching into his touch—

He blew out a short huff of air, his warm breath sending a cloud of steam up in front of him. Dragging his thoughts back to the reality of the moment, he watched Raina examine the underside of his rig. He already knew what she would find there: a small, innocuous ball of cytoplast, a completely stable, completely lethal explosive that could be neither disarmed nor removed once set for detonation. The Janson were nothing if not predictable.

Raina's anorak rode up as she moved, revealing the rounded shape of her bottom. Wizard mentally traced the enticing curves, then frowned in annoyance at the baffling turn of his normally ordered thoughts.

Bait. Raina Bowen was *bait*, he reminded himself. Nothing less, and absolutely nothing more.

"Your rig's a goner," she said, throwing a glance at him over her shoulder as she pushed herself to her feet.

"Agreed. There is no way to defuse the cytoplast." Wizard felt a momentary pang at the imminent loss of his truck. "The wire cannot be cut or disconnected without achieving detonation. The truck must be sacrificed." A small price, and, in fact, it was an unexpected development that fell perfectly in line with his plans. If he had no transportation of his own, then he could request passage in Raina's truck. Easier to keep track of her.

"Sacrificed? Nice word choice." And just what else would be sacrificed? she wondered. If he blew his rig, did that mean he expected to hitch a ride with her? *No. Oh, man, no, no, no.* She liked her own company. Preferred it, really. Her privacy was not something she particularly wanted to sacrifice. Best to clarify the outcome right now. "And once your truck's history, you'll do what? Stay on at Bob's for a while?"

He kept his gaze fixed on his rig. "No."

"You'll contact an associate to come fetch you?"

"No." Dismissing the topic, Wizard began to walk toward the truck.

"Wait." Raina stopped him, intent on clearly and concisely putting an end to any thoughts he might have of tagging along with her.

He turned at the sound of her voice, his gray eyes meeting hers, and for just a second she thought she saw pain. Sadness. Regret. Her heart clenched as she realized how depressing it would be to lose *her* vehicle the way he was about to lose his. She turned to his rig, taking in the sleek, dark lines, the polished chrome, and with a sigh she acknowledged the fact that she wouldn't be able to do it. To watch his rig blow and then leave him stranded here, halfway beyond hell's frozen cousin.

"Let's tow it out a ways," she said. "So long as we leave the trip wire untouched, the cytoplast should remain stable. I'd feel really lousy if we detonated here and damaged this lovely facility." Not really, but she couldn't help thinking about those vagabond kids, worrying that they might be harmed by the blast. Besides, if the truck blew here at Bob's, damaged any property, there would be an investigation. That would mean her departure would be delayed, and she really disliked that possibility.

A part of her, albeit a really unrealistic part, was still hoping she could win that damn race. She needed that money, needed to pay for her sister's care, needed to make sure the kid had a chance at a real life. A safe life.

She wasn't sure why she cared. She had never met her sister. Never seen her except for one hazy holopic that she hadn't dared to keep. But somehow, it seemed so important that someone in this world care about an orphaned girl. That someone keep her safe. And safety required money.

Beth. Her sister had a name. *Beth*.

Blowing out a breath, she turned to Wizard, who was looking around the truck stop, his gaze lingering on the dilapidated shacks that served as living quarters and the pile of garbage to one side of the bar. The only thing that kept the air from being completely polluted by the stink of rotting trash was the frigid temperature.

"Man, I pity anyone who's here for the spring thaw," Raina muttered. "Still, I can't stomach blowing the place up."

"Agreed. Destruction of this facility is unnecessary, although statistical probability suggests that some structures will soon fall on their own." Wizard inclined his head in the direction of one of the outbuildings. "I will attach the towline."

The operation went reasonably smoothly. Wizard

shimmied under the front of his rig and hooked up the towline. Raina fought the feeling of nausea that churned in her gut as she imagined the cytoplast detonating and Wizard raining down on her in pieces. Of course, she knew that was ridiculous. Cytoplast was stable unless the specific trigger was applied. In this case, someone would need to tug on that trip wire.

"The cytoplast is approximately the size of a tangerine," he reported when he returned to her rig.

A tangerine? She stared at him, then spread her hands wide and gave him a look that she was sure conveyed her every thought. *What the hell is a tangerine?*

"The cytoplast is approximately the size of my closed fist," he amended. "Estimated blast radius, five yuales."

"Lovely." If the bomb discharged before the rig was moved, innocent people would be blown to mangled shreds just so they could kill one man. What value human life? "They didn't care if they took out the whole truck stop right along with you."

"Apparently not." No inflection. No concern. A statement of fact.

She stared at him, at the black, straight fall of his hair, silky and thick, the kind of hair that was perfect when he woke up. And his eyes. Open, clear, rimmed in dark, dark lashes that made the cool gray irises all the more startling.

She imagined those eyes gone dim, the life snuffed from their glowing depths, and she felt faintly ill.

"Let's go," she said, angry at herself for her inexplicable fascination with this strange, beautiful man.

Slowly, moving at a steady and unremarkable pace, they towed Wizard's rig a distance away, skirting the truck stop and heading out into the Waste. They stopped when Bob's was a mere speck on the horizon.

"Sacrifice it," Raina insisted when Wizard told her he was going to retrieve the towline.

"There is no need. The cytoplast is stable. I will untether the vehicle."

She shook her head, her heart pounding as she watched him from a distance. They were already pushing their luck. The guy had nerves of titanium.

His task complete, he jogged back to her rig and climbed into the cabin, the coiled line looped over his shoulder. She put the truck in gear and drove a significant distance away.

"Uh, Wizard. Great plan, but you forgot one small thing. How are you going to detonate the cytoplast from way back here?"

Rising, he pushed back the side of his parka, revealing the belt he wore and the glittering razor-sharp edges of his throw-stars.

A bark of laughter escaped her at his silent reply. "Right. Even if you could actually throw a star that far, you'd need to hit a trip wire as thin as an optic fiber."

He didn't laugh with her. His expression was ruthlessly neutral. "Affirmative."

"Affirmative?" She cocked her head to one side, studying him. He didn't *look* as if he were joking. . . .

Doffing his parka, he hung it over the back of the seat and stepped from the rig wearing only his thermal shirt. Raina wrapped her arms around herself, feeling cold just watching him. Nerves of titanium and molten lava instead of blood.

The bitter wind whipped his hair about his shoulders, and he reached up to gather the thick strands, tying them off with a cord at his nape. Tipping his head back, he stood, legs braced slightly apart. Then he angled his shoulder toward his rig and removed a throwstar from his belt, barely pausing before he drew his arm across his body and let the star fly free with a clean, sharp jerk. Power. Precision.

For an instant nothing happened, and Raina almost laughed at his arrogance. As though anyone could possibly hit a trip wire from this distance. Then the air rippled and curved, expanding with the force of the wall of fire that ascended from the spot where Wizard's truck had been. She felt her rig rock to and fro, buffeted by the tremendous power of the blast, and her teeth snapped together with a loud clack as her head was thrown back and then forward. From the corner of her eye she saw Wizard's body lift, caught by a giant unseen hand and thrown back against the frozen ground like a child's toy.

The breath left her in a rush, chased by a wave of nausea, and her eyes slammed shut against the sight she was certain awaited her. *Frig.* He'd be strewn about in gruesome little pieces. The strength of that explosion had nearly unhinged the metal plates of her truck. Wizard's body, regardless of how hard and rugged it was, stood no chance against the force of that blast.

It was a shame to see a beautiful thing torn to pieces. That was all. There was nothing personal in the knot of dread that tightened her throat, no emotional attachment to the man who'd just gone and gotten himself blown into fragments. It was just that she hated the sight of blood. Red, red blood on white, white snow.

Frig. Frig. Frig.

The reality couldn't be any worse than her imagination. Grimacing, she opened one eye, then the other.

For a moment she sat, stunned by the fact that the snow was still pristine white and not stained deep red by Wizard's blood. Then she clambered out of the rig and ran, her feet slipping and sliding on a patch of ice as she made her way to his side.

Blood or no blood, the guy was dead. She was certain of it. The blast had thrown him against the ground with such force that she expected every bone in his body to be broken. Just what she needed: a corpse to deal with.

She dashed the back of one hand against her cheek. She was *not* crying over some worthless dead gun trucker. It was the harsh wind making her eyes tear.

Skidding across the ice, she lost her balance and slid the last of the way on her rear end, coming to a stop when her bent knee banged Wizard's side. She winced. That had to hurt.

Or not. The guy was dead.

Taking shallow breaths of cold air that cut at her lungs like shards of glass, Raina leaned in close and peered at Wizard's face. His eyes were closed, the length of his dark lashes fanning along the curve of his cheek. There was an angry scrape on his jaw. She reached out and grazed the tips of her fingers along his still body, not even sure why, knowing only that she wanted to touch him, one final human touch to send him on his way.

And then he lifted his head, his gray eyes clear as they locked on hers.

With an involuntary squeak, she jerked her hand back, watching in amazement as he sat up and shook his head slowly from side to side as though clearing his thoughts.

"You're not dead." Her brilliant observation brought his attention back to her. "Are you hurt?"

He raised one hand to his cheek, drew his fingers away, and looked at the blood.

"I am unhurt," he replied, pushing up the sleeves of his thermal shirt.

"You're bleeding," she pointed out. *And you should be dead.* She stared at his bare forearms, at the dusting of dark hair and the shift of muscle beneath supple skin, and she huddled deeper in her parka as the bitter chill seeped all the way into her bones and joints. "At the very least, you should be hypothermic, standing around in nothing but a thin shirt."

His shoulders lifted and fell in a careless shrug. "I do not feel the cold. I was designed to withstand extreme temperatures."

"Designed?" A shiver coursed through her, and it had nothing to do with the cold.

Wizard laid his hand along his side where she'd accidentally hit him with her knee when she'd gone careening across the ice. The same side that Luc had nailed with his metal-reinforced boots. "What did you hit me with?"

"It was an accident. I slid on the ice—" Snapping her mouth shut, she refused to explain further. A gale-force blast threw him like a kid's doll, and he was asking what *she'd* hit him with?

Narrowing her eyes, she glared at him. Was that a smile?

Apparently unconcerned with her lack of explanation, Wizard pushed himself to his feet and offered her his hand. She stared at his fingers, marveling that the limb was still attached to him. The blast had been enough to rock her rig, almost knock it off its tires, but it had barely put a bruise on Wizard. The man was either unnaturally lucky, or just plain unnatural.

Ignoring his proffered hand, she got to her feet, struggling to ignore the irrational tide of anger that swamped her. He'd frightened her, and she was as much angry at herself for feeling concern as she was at him for causing it.

"Come along, Raina Bowen," he said as he headed for her truck.

Okay. She'd had just about enough. *Come along? What the hell?*

"Hey, Wizard," she called. He paused, slowly spun to face her.

In three steps she was by his side, and with each step her temper flared higher. He'd gotten her into this frigging mess, effectively blocking her access to the ICW, hurting her chances for the interdollar prize, and each moment she spent with him seemed only to dig her deeper in the mire.

And he'd made her care, though the admission stuck in her gut like a six-inch spike. She did not want to have any feeling for this man, for any man. She wanted to get in her rig, drive the ICW, and win the frigging race to Gladow. Use the prize to buy her freedom, her safety.

Use it to buy her little sister a life.

Maybe buy a miracle that would let them be together. A family. The family she'd never been lucky enough to have.

"Do not tell me what to do," she said softly. Reasonably.

"I thought your intention was to reach Gladow Station with all haste. You are wasting time."

She thought about it for a millisecond. Maybe less. And then she hauled back and decked him. One minute he was standing there looking down at her from his superior height, and the next, he was on his butt on the cold, hard ground, staring up at her as he ran his fingers over his lower jaw.

"Sucker punch," she said, striding past him, shaking her hand loosely to work out the sting on her knuckles. "Amazing. I actually learned something from Big Luc." She glanced back over her shoulder, feeling inexcusably smug at the confusion on his face. "Come along, Wizard. You're wasting time."

SIX

As they drove back through Bob's Truck Stop, Raina
noticed that the massive explosion that had shredded
Wizard's rig hadn't been loud enough to drag a single
person from his bed to investigate the noise. *Welcome
to the Northern Waste, where death and destruction don't
warrant a second thought.*

Except she'd had second thoughts about Ben and
his crew, and she'd stopped long enough to unload a
crate of supplies and leave it where she was certain
they would find it. She couldn't explain why. She'd
never thought generosity to be one of her strong suits.
Hell, she had enough trouble keeping *herself* alive.

But she had this soft spot for orphan kids.

As she set the crate on the ground, she caught Ben
watching her from the shadows. For a long moment
their gazes locked and held, and she felt warm despite
the frigid wind.

To her utter amazement, Wizard modified her truck
just as he said, and they were soon barreling along
toward the I-pole, powered by hydrogen supplied as

water. Raina slanted a glance at him, still marveling that he'd actually been able to do it.

Long legs stretched in front of him, he lounged in the passenger seat, calm, relaxed. Asleep. Maybe. She had a feeling that with Wizard, she'd be wise not to trust first impressions.

Thinking back on their encounter with Ben, Raina tried to figure the angle. Wizard had lost a huge chunk of interdollars and shown no emotion at all. Then he'd been impassive as his truck blew sky-high, his gorgeous, expensive, perfectly maintained truck. She wondered what the deal was. *Why don't you seem to care that you've just lost an unbelievably expensive rig, not to mention three thousand interdollars to those vagabond children?*

She doubted he would provide an answer to that question, so instead she asked, "So what's your plan, Wizard? You got someone you can contact to come retrieve your sorry butt? I don't want to cart you around forever." She didn't dare cart him around at all. There was something inexplicably seductive about him, and she didn't want him around any longer than necessary. He was not good for her peace of mind.

His eyes were closed, his breathing even. Asleep. Except she knew he wasn't. An almost imperceptible tension tugged at the corners of his mouth, an edgy readiness that suffused him. Definitely awake, but choosing to let her think otherwise.

"You're awake," she said flatly. She almost reached over and prodded his forearm, but the thought of touching him unsettled her. Mostly because she *wanted* to touch him, to feel firm muscle and hot skin under her fingertips. She closed her hands tighter on the wheel.

Wizard opened his eyes, sent her a hard, indecipherable look, and closed them again. The muscles of his arm flexed as he pushed his thick, long hair back from his face. The marcasite beads were still there, catching the light, drawing her gaze to follow the dark strands that kissed the hard line of his jaw, the strong column of his throat. Barbed little stabs of awareness shot into the pit of her belly.

Raina looked away. *Great.* She'd been driving the ICW for years, the tiny cabin in back her only home, and never once had she felt confined or crowded. But now, with Wizard sprawled in the seat beside her, the truck had shrunk to the size of a pinhead.

Not because Wizard was over six feet of hard, broad, muscled male who might put the moves on her. She could always decline any amorous offer. He'd made that pretty clear last night. Besides, she was confident in her own ability to defend herself. A strategically placed knee could do wonders for cooling a guy's passionate intent.

No. What made the rig so small was the fact that he'd stood behind her that morning while the Janson trucks pulled up, his solid, half-naked body pressed tight against hers, and she hadn't decked him in protest. Hadn't wanted to. What the hell was wrong with her that she was letting this worthless gun trucker under her skin?

Blowing out a breath, Raina spoke sharply. "An answer would be nice. What do you intend to do now?"

"I have business in the Waste." His tone was even. "But I prefer not to contact anyone. Better if I do not broadcast my presence here."

She couldn't help the snort of laughter that escaped. The guy really was odd. "Better if you don't broadcast your presence here? Last night you took on the frigging Janson, and this morning you blew your truck to kingdom come. I wouldn't call that subtle."

"There are those who will assume I was incinerated along with my belongings. Right now I prefer the anonymity."

His impassive statement reminded her that he had cost her her own anonymity. The thought was less than welcome.

What business did he have in the Waste? Raina was silent for a moment, pondering the possibilities. Whatever it was, he wanted to carry out his task without drawing attention. He had as much chance of that as she had of being mistaken for a man.

And he still hadn't given her any indication of what he intended to do now.

"You're planning to hitch a ride all the way to Gladow, aren't you?" she asked with a definite sinking feeling in her gut. He was going to be sitting right there, sprawled in the seat next to her, long legs stretched in front of him, arms folded across his broad chest.

"Affirmative."

Great. Just frigging great.

"Mind if I use your satellite link?" he asked after a brief silence.

"Help yourself." She focused her attention on the road, kept her gaze fixed on the glittering snow as Wizard rose and headed into the back cabin.

She hadn't asked what he wanted to use the link for, but curiosity gnawed at her. Research? Entertainment? He'd said that he wanted anonymity, so it

wasn't likely he'd use her satellite link to contact anyone. Even if he did, no one would be able to nail her
signal. She'd paid top interdollar for her encryption
program.

A lifetime spent hiding in plain sight had made
caution as natural to her as breathing. After all, Duncan Bane had wide-reaching power. All he had to do
was find her, and her freedom was forfeit. Her freedom? *Hell.* Her body, broken bit by bit, then her sanity, and ultimately her life. She knew that with
certainty, had spent most of her life looking over her
shoulder, wondering when he'd decide to collect on an
old debt.

Which made it all the more out of character for her
to have let Wizard into her rig. She never let anyone
get that close. She must be losing her damn mind.

Wizard closed the link, satisfied that payment had
been made, that Beth Bowen would remain at the
Sheppard School in Port Uranium, hidden in plain
sight, cared for, safe. He owed Sam that much—the
safety of his younger daughter—because he could not
guarantee the well-being of the older. In fact, his mission put her in jeopardy.

Were there another path, he would choose it.
Something close to regret tugged at his thoughts, and
he ruthlessly contained it. There was no place on a
mission for conscience or remorse.

Do the job. Speed and efficiency are the only criteria.

He closed his eyes as the memories rose, sharp, precise. Ugly.

Wizard . . . save her. Please. She has a chance.

A whisper from the past. Tatiana.

The memory was fresh, clear.

Wizard recalled how he had looked back and forth between his sisters, their faces marked by Duncan Bane's fists. There would be more. He had known that without question.

To make you stronger. To make you invincible. Bane's justification. And the simple truth. But Tatiana was not like Wizard. She was not like Yuriko. She did not recover as quickly. She bruised easier. Her bones broke where Wizard's and Yuriko's bent to absorb the force.

Bane had been particularly brutal that session.

"Because you are soon to go on your first mission," he had explained in that soft, soft, cultured voice. "This will ensure that you are ready, that you survive. You, Wizard, will be the commander, and a commander must be able to make rapid decisions." Bane had smiled and run his finger along Yuriko's cheek. She had met his gaze coldly, refusing to jerk away, refusing to show any weakness. "So decide now, Wizard. Who will be subjected to ten more minutes?"

In the time it took to draw a single breath, Wizard had already calculated the statistical probabilities. He could easily handle the beating, would come back stronger, faster. Yuriko as well. But Tatiana would not likely survive.

"Me. I will take the ten minutes." The logic was clean. He was the most physically resilient.

Bane had laughed. "You are the commander. The fastest. The strongest. You have the best chance of finishing your mission. I may send you out tonight, before you have time to heal, though. Choose the weakest, Wizard. A good commander knows when to calculate the odds, when to sacrifice for the good of the mission."

Logical. "Understood."

"Wizard . . . save her. Please. She has a chance." Yuriko had pleaded for their sister's life.

Wizard knew, then and now, what emotion was, had read about it, studied the phenomenon. It was essential that he be able to present a passable imitation of humanity. But he did not *feel* the way Yuriko and Tatiana did. He could not teach himself to feel.

"Calculate the odds," Bane had ordered, ignoring Yuriko.

The odds. The odds: 99.966 percent probability he would survive another ten-minute beating and recover in time for the mission; 99.872 percent probability for Yuriko. But Tatiana . . . Tatiana's chance for survival and rapid recovery had been less than 11 percent.

Her eyes had locked on his. Hit by a strange sensation in the pit of his belly, he had hesitated.

"Choose." Bane had whispered the word against Wizard's ear.

Choose. Choose. Choose.

Wizard's memory was of the face of his sister, but here in the dim light of the living quarters her features shifted and changed until it was Raina Bowen looking back at him.

Sucking in a breath, Wizard stared straight ahead. His pulse was steady and slow, his breathing calm. But there, in the pit of his belly, that . . . sensation.

A memory. His sister.

Tatiana.

Raina let her mind wander as she drove, dreaming of palm trees and a white-sand beach, the kind she had seen only on holopics and satellite links. The kind she'd never experienced in person. That fifty-million-interdollar prize made for some pretty vivid imaginings, and when she was the first to reach Gladow, it would make for a very warm reality.

Maybe she wouldn't just pay for Beth's school. Maybe she'd go get her, take her with her to paradise. They could be a family; they could find a home; they could—

She tensed as the door to the living quarters opened and Wizard came forward from the back cabin. He stood behind her seat, staring out at the clear dark sky. Again she noticed that his broad-shouldered form felt too large for the cramped space of the cab. The smell of him, fresh and clean and male, told her that he'd made use of her shower and min-dry.

"Nice night." He took a small step back, as though he sensed her unease. The small talk sounded awkward coming from him. "Pleasing scenery."

Pleasing? "Uh-huh." Raina glanced to the left, where the enormous, smooth face of a giant glacier thrust its sharp summit skyward to slice the dark expanse of endless night. The full moon cast an eerie glow over the glittering surface. She turned her attention back to the uncertain expanse of the I-pole. There was no section of the Transport Ministry responsible for the upkeep of this road, and that meant it was little more than a shallow groove in the endless terrain of rimed tundra.

Up ahead was an archway formed of snow and ice. Of massive proportion, it curved over the path of the ancient highway, towering above them as they drew near. The lights of the rig bounced off its monolithic walls, accenting every icy angle and frozen crevice.

"We're on the ice field. With any luck we'll be at Gladow Station in about forty-six hours," she said, raising one hand to stifle a yawn.

"Forty-seven hours, twenty-eight minutes."

She gritted her teeth. "What? You can't tell me the exact second?"

"Taking into account speed variation, ratio of acceleration versus deceleration, wind resistance, friction created by tire tread on snow, unforeseen—"

"Forget it," Raina muttered. Again she raised one hand to stifle a yawn.

"It would be logical for me to drive while you sleep," Wizard observed.

Over my rotting carcass. She didn't need his help, didn't want his help, did just fine on her own, thank you very much. "I'm used to driving." Then she added in a high-pitched sim-sweetener voice, "But thanks so much for the offer."

"You are going to drive the entire way without rest?" He didn't sound skeptical, just curious.

"No. I'll do what I always do: pull over, sleep, and then I'll drive some more. Rules for the Gladow race say one driver. *One.* That's me. You drive, I get disqualified." She could feel him standing close at her back, and she was acutely aware of his presence. Did he not understand the concept of overcrowding? "Look, Wizard, I'm used to doing for myself. I don't need any help. You're just along for the ride. Got it? And I'm not even sure why you're here, why you didn't just catch a ride at Bob's and head back to wherever you came from."

"You want that interdollar prize," he pointed out, ignoring her monologue.

"Yeah. So what's your point?"

"If you are sleeping instead of driving, you lose precious time."

"If I fall asleep and crash my rig, I'll be dead instead of driving. If I let you drive, I get disqualified." Besides, she didn't want anyone else driving her rig. It was hers. *Hers.* Hard earned with sweat and blood and tears. "I'll just nap for a short while. Besides, the I-pole is way faster than the ICW. I'm already ahead of the game." And she wasn't about to accept his help. Anyone's help. She'd learned to count only on herself. No disappointments that way.

"The ICW—"

Whatever he'd been about to say was lost as he tensed and glanced at the side mirror. She waited a heartbeat and then she saw it too—a glint of light. Reaching overhead, Raina doused the internal cabin lights and turned off her forward illumination as well. Someone was following them, and as she caught a second glinting reflection, she realized that whoever it was, they were coming in fast and they didn't care if she knew it.

Sliding into the passenger seat, Wizard unrolled the window and leaned out. As if he'd be able to see anything at this distance in the dead of night. Raina shook her head.

After a moment, he straightened and closed the window. "Three rigs. Janson trucks. Speed, seventy-five yuales. Acceleration, five-point-three ckuales per second squared. Estimated time of contact—"

"And you know this how?" Raina asked, then thought better of it. "Never mind."

She geared down, slowing the truck, allowing her

pursuers to draw ever nearer. Wizard met her gaze. "You do not wish to outrun them?"

"There are times to run and times to fight." She glanced at the side mirror and saw the headlights of the Janson trucks drawing closer. Her heartbeat accelerated as she watched them split apart. They intended to flank her, to make a kind of Raina sandwich. Effective. Not creative, but effective. She could hear the powerful roar of their engines as they began to draw abreast of her.

"A little closer, boys," she murmured, thrusting one hand beneath her seat and pulling out a Setti86. Nice plasgun. No recoil. Good for shooting tires. Or men, if the need arose. She'd prefer to go for the tires.

With her elbow, she pushed the button and unrolled her window, watching the progress of her unwanted guests.

"You could outrun them," Wizard pointed out. "You have no need of fuel, but their supply is limited."

"True." She forced herself to take slow, even breaths. "But what would be the fun in that?"

"Fun?"

"It's an expression." Raina balanced the barrel of the Setti86 on the padded rim of the door where it met the open window. She let the muzzle poke through, ready. The cold air rolled through the cabin, making her cheeks sting, and she welcomed the feel of it. In her state of exhaustion, she could use the stimulation. Although come to think of it, the adrenaline surge was doing a fairly efficient job. "Sam always said there's a time to run and a time to fight. If you know you'll win, fight. Because you don't want a rat gnawing on your tail. You get it?"

"Affirmative."

Actually, she didn't care if he got it or not. She did things her way, end of discussion.

"I'm making the assumption that if you wish my assistance, you will request it," Wizard said, leaning back in his chair and folding his arms across his chest.

Raina glanced at him, then back at the side mirror, a little surprised that he was so willing to leave his fate in her hands. She frowned, confused. He was a man. Didn't he want to take over?

"Thought you said the ICW's no place for a girl."

He slanted her an unreadable glance. "You do hold a grudge, Raina Bowen."

Yeah. Maybe she did.

"I won't ask for help." She didn't need help.

The truck on the right drew level with her tailgate. The two trucks on her left were coming in fast. Her heart pounded in rhythm with the throb of the engine, but her palms were dry, her aim steady.

Shifting in her seat, she steered with her right knee, the Setti held at the ready in her left hand. With her right hand she flicked the com-link, setting it to the Janson feed.

"Hello, boys. I do thank you for dropping by, but I'm afraid I'm not in the mood for company. So I'm going to ask you to leave. Now." She settled her right hand back on the steering wheel, felt the plastitech smooth and cold beneath her grasp. They wouldn't listen. She knew that.

With a sigh, Raina ran her thumb over a small switch on the side of the plasgun, unlocking the trigger.

Time to take out the trash.

Static crackled through the cab, and then the sound

of raucous laughter carried through the com-link. She shrugged. "You know, the Janson just never take a woman seriously."

The truck on her right was abreast of her now, as were the two on the left. With a sharp jerk, she veered her rig to the side. The horrible crunch of metal on metal sliced the night. Raina braked, making sure she had caught the rig on hers. Then she hit the accelerator, turning her wheel sharply left then right, shaking the Janson truck like a wild dog with a baby squirrel in its jaws. She spun the wheel hard in the opposite direction, sending her rig slamming into one of the trucks on her left as she peeled off a plas-shot at the third truck. The squeal of tires and the lurid curse that came over the com-link told her she'd hit the tire. *Good.* That meant she might not have to shoot any men today.

She fired off a second round for good measure. The two trucks on her left careened into each other, and the sound of rending metal and shattering glass bruised her ears. She glanced at Wizard. The guy looked cool as metal in the snow.

"Crazy bitch!" a voice came through the com-link. She recognized that voice: Big Luc. "What the hell's the matter with her? What the hell's the matter with you, you crazy Waste-trash bitch?"

Well, what did he expect? That she'd slow down and let him catch up, maybe invite him in for a nice cup of tea? Raina blew out a breath as she thrust the truck in gear and peeled away from the wreckage in her wake. "What's the matter with *me*? Didn't I ask them politely to leave? Wasn't I just driving the I-pole, minding my own business? Frig."

"That was Luc," Wizard commented unnecessarily.

"Thanks ever so much for pointing that out." With a last glance behind her, she reassured herself that the Janson were in no condition to continue their pursuit. "You know, Wizard, you're a magnet for trouble."

"I could say the same about you."

Raina sighed. She supposed he could. Trouble had a way of trailing close in her wake, no matter how hard she tried to outrun it. Truth was, she wasn't certain exactly who the Janson had been after. Maybe him. Maybe her. Maybe both.

"They after you? Or me?" she asked after a few moments, feeling drained. That adrenaline had crashed her just as fast as it had pumped her up. She kept her focus on the ground ahead of her, knowing how very dangerous it was for her to drive when she was so done-in.

Wizard didn't say anything. He stared at her intently for a moment, and then he leaned across her and took the Setti86 from her limp fingers, pressing his bent elbow against the button to close the window. He was so close, the clean scent of his skin teasing her senses. A blast of cold air rushed in through the closing window, lifting the dark strands of his hair so they fanned across her cheek.

If she shifted just a bit, she would be able to press her lips to his. The thought came out of nowhere, hitting her hard. He was in her space. But she didn't shove him away.

She did not want to feel an attraction to this man, did not want to acknowledge the urge to lean in and burrow against the heat of his skin, to trace the hard line of his lips with her tongue, to tear the clothes from his gorgeous body and touch him until she finally felt warm. God, she was so cold.

And he was so hot.

Raina blew out a harsh breath, watched it form a white cloud just beyond her lips. Her hands were shaking. She ground her teeth together to keep them from chattering.

Squatting beside her with the plasgun in his hand, Wizard locked the trigger and reached between her ankles, thrusting the Setti back under her seat. She tensed, every cell in her body aware of how close he was. As though sensing her conflict, he rose and without a single word returned to the back cabin.

So much for Mr. Personality.

She turned her headlights to full, squinting for a moment as the sudden glare hurt her eyes. She dared not slow. Though she was fairly certain she'd stopped the Janson, she figured it was better to put just a bit more distance between them before she stopped to rest. And she *did* need to stop. Her eyes felt as though they were weighted down, and her limbs were rubbery.

For as long as she could remember, she'd had an uncanny ability to go for lengthy periods of time without sleep, but in the past three days she'd clocked only about six hours of rest, total. That was pushing it, even for her.

"Here." Wizard came up beside her and thrust a portamug into her hand. The smell wafting from the spill-proof seal tantalized her, making her stomach rumble.

"Uh, thanks." She glanced at him in surprise, feeling awkward, not used to having anyone do anything nice for her. "I just wanted to put a bit more distance between us and Big Luc before I stopped to make myself something to eat." Frowning at the mug, she sniffed it suspiciously, hiding her annoyance with herself for offering an explanation. She didn't owe him one. "What's in here?"

"Soup." Wizard sank into the passenger seat. "I ate it and it didn't kill me."

She took an exploratory sip. Not bad. Veggi-sim, protein supplement, spices. Edible. Heck, she'd even go so far as to call it tasty. She couldn't find it in her to get pissed off that he'd helped himself to her supplies, not when he'd made enough for her as well.

"So you think they were after me? Or you?" Wizard asked casually, and that was exactly what made Raina wary of answering. He didn't do casual very well. Besides, he hadn't answered when she'd asked the same question of him.

"I think that Big Luc didn't like getting decked by a girl. I think he wanted to even the score a bit." Not the complete truth, but not a lie either. She took another sip of her soup, already feeling refreshed.

Wizard was silent for a moment. "Good answer. Truthful, but less than forthcoming. Why else would the Janson follow you?"

Well, she'd slashed their fearless leader's face as if she were gutting a fish. That was a pretty good reason, she figured. But it wasn't *the* reason. Duncan Bane had had years to come after her if he'd wanted to. So why go into action right now? She was starting to suspect that just maybe the frigging Janson were following them because of Wizard. "No reason for them to come after me. What about you?"

He didn't reply. Not that she'd actually expected

him to. After a moment he leaned forward to turn on the broadband. "You mind?" he asked after the fact.

"Just make yourself at home." She made an overly grand sweeping gesture with her hand. He settled back in the seat, and she figured her sarcasm was lost on him.

"Welcome to *Talk About It* with Lissy Abbott." A feminine voice, firm and professional, wafted from the speakers set into the walls. "For several months, escalating incidents of piracy and murder on the ICW have caused growing concern among settlers of the Northern Realm. Numerous new safety measures have been introduced at the Nunavut pass-over, accompanied by growing vocal opposition to the methods that the New Government Order is using in order to maintain security."

"The Order maintain security. How's that for irony?" Raina gave an incredulous hoot of laughter.

"Piracy is escalating," Lissy Abbott continued. "Reports of attacks on independent trucks are growing exponentially, and there is speculation that illegal gunrunning is on the rise in the region. The devastation is enormous. Refugees are moving en masse to the relative safety of Gladow and Dorje stations."

"So much for the promise of peace and safety," Raina murmured, shooting a glance at Wizard. He was staring straight ahead at the endless plane of frozen Waste, his expression as hard and set as the rigid ice outside.

"Our guest today is Duncan Bane, chief executive officer of Janson Transport and special adviser to the president of the New Government Order." The woman's voice took on an inviting tone. "Our com-lines are open. Our topic is ice pirates in the Alberta Corridor and Nunavut pass-over. Let's *Talk About It*. Welcome, Duncan Bane. Can you comment on the reports of piracy?"

Raina forced her hands to remain steady on the wheel as a cultured masculine voice responded to the interviewer's greeting. She hated the sound of that voice. Hated *him*. Duncan Bane. Owner of the largest trucking company in the world. Businessman. Respected politician. Wealthy philanthropist.

Sadistic bastard.

"Got something against Mr. Bane?" Wizard's voice was soft and even.

She took a slow breath. The man saw too much. Sensed too much. She'd have to try harder to hide her inner demons.

"Not a thing." And she turned to meet his gaze, certain that she betrayed none of the hate, the memories, the decade-old revulsion that simmered deep inside of her every time she thought about Duncan Bane. She'd practiced long and hard to keep the seething hatred in check.

Wizard's gray eyes were flat, cold as polished steel. No compassion, no understanding flickered in their depths. Here was a guy who definitely lacked the sympathy gene, and she was enormously glad of it. She didn't want his pity.

She turned her attention back to the road, wondering if Wizard knew that she preferred his lack of sympathy to any overt show of emotion, or if he was simply a man who really felt absolutely nothing.

Duncan Bane's voice droned through the speakers,

making the hairs rise on the back of her neck, and hatred boil, turbulent and bitter, inside of her. She blinked, thought about the odd look in Wizard's eyes. Maybe the lack of emotion had nothing to do with her. . . . Maybe . . . "What about you?" she asked. "You have something against Mr. Bane?"

There was a brief silence, and then he said, "Yes. I have something against him."

Okay. She imagined her jaw hitting the floor with a great big bang. That was one question she definitely hadn't expected him to answer, at least not with honesty.

"You going to tell me what that something might be?"

"No."

Well, he was nothing if not consistent.

Wizard turned up the volume on the broadband, and Duncan Bane's voice swelled to fill the small space.

A soft hiss of air escaped her, and with an impatient flick of her finger Raina turned off the volume altogether. She concentrated on the stillness, the silence, refusing to let the sound of Bane's voice drag her memories free of the cage she had put them in. They would not tear her down from the place she had finally reached. She was independent. She was in control. She was not a scared little twelve-year-old girl betrayed by those she trusted. Not anymore.

Clearing her mind of everything but the long ribbon of ancient highway that snaked out ahead of her, she drove, fixing her thoughts firmly on the interdollar prize, ignoring her exhaustion, allowing herself to focus on the positive, like the fact that she'd gotten rid of the frigging Janson.

Then the com-screen let out a metallic ping, and another.

"Looks like our night for company," Wizard said softly.

So much for focusing on the positive.

SEVEN

"Perfect." Raina shook her head as the com-screen sounded again and a light blipped on and off.

"They are at seventy yuales, coming in fast." Wizard leaned forward, his attention focused on the screen. Raina glanced at it and counted five yellow blips shifting closer on the radar tracking device.

"Possibly Janson reinforcements. Too many trucks for just Big Luc and his pals. Besides, I don't think their vehicles were in any shape to come after us." She glanced in her side mirror but saw nothing.

He paused before replying. "Possibly Janson, but I think not."

She didn't like the way he said that. The Janson were bad, but the alternative was worse. Ice pirates. Reavers. Whatever you called 'em, they were the dregs at the bottom of the barrel.

"What have you got in the way of artillery, besides the impressive array of knives on the wall above your bed and the Setti under your seat?" Wizard asked.

"Bollinger plasma gun on the wall."

"I saw that. AT100?"

"Yeah. Modified to cut the delay. And an AT850 in the kitchenette, under the sink. In front of the mixing bowls."

"In front of the mixing bowls . . ." He met her gaze, blinked. "A joke?"

"Space is at a premium, in case you didn't notice. I use the mixing bowls more often than the AT850, so I was tempted to put them in front." She shrugged. "But I guess Sam's training is so ingrained that I couldn't help but put the plasgun up front. Easier access."

"Point taken. The AT850 could take out a city block. Good choice. What else do you have?"

The screen pinged again. "Echoes at fifty yuales," Raina said. "We definitely have company, and I think they're interested in getting here sooner rather than later."

"Any other long-range weapons?" Wizard prodded.

"Nope." She paused, thinking, forcing her sleep-deprived brain to focus. "And I guess whatever you had went up with your rig."

"There were two plasguns in my rig."

"Two? That's it?" She tipped her head to one side. "I saw the miniarsenal you carry on your body. Two knives, stars. Garrote. And whatever else I didn't catch a glimpse of. I'd have expected you to pack an 850 . . ."

"In my line of work, short-range weapons are key."

"Your line of work?" She shot him an assessing glance and found him watching her. *Short-range weapons are key.* What the hell was he, an assassin for the New Government Order?

Lean. Hard. Cold as liquid nitrogen.

Perfect assassin material. *Oh, frig.* She had Wizard's number, and it wasn't exactly lucky seven.

Maybe Luc and his boys really were after him and not her.

She knew the exact second he realized the conclusion she'd reached, the exact second he knew that she knew what he was. The refuse of the earth. Worse even than the Reavers. A mercenary assassin for the New Government Order, with *assassin* being the key word. Mercenary was bad. Assassin was worse.

Wizard was a frigging death machine for hire.

My word is my only law, he'd said earlier. Suddenly she believed him, and she was surprised that he obeyed any law at all. She had a nasty certainty that Wizard was a member of a very select group, an elite killing machine rumored to have no conscience and no remorse. Nice traveling companion she'd picked up.

No wonder he'd said that he preferred to maintain his anonymity. After his altercation with the Janson the previous night, word was bound to travel quickly that Wizard had arrived in the Waste. Which might provide a warning to Wizard's intended victim. What better disguise for an assassin than the rumor that he'd been blown straight to purgatory?

"You never needed my help with the Janson. At the truck stop . . . you could have taken them out, one by one, without even breaking a sweat," she whispered.

"Affirmative."

"So why the hell did you climb on the back of my scooter?"

He glanced at her, held her gaze, looked away. "I liked your hair."

Raina opened her mouth, snapped it shut, and finally settled for a snort of disbelief.

The radar scope pinged again.

"Echoes at twenty-five yuales," Wizard said, tapping his index finger lightly on the screen. "Kill your lights."

"There's a full moon. Either way we'll stand out like a stain against the snow."

Wizard shrugged, tapped his finger a little harder. "Agreed. But why give them any help? Kill your lights."

She didn't appreciate being told what to do, but he was right, and now was not the time to argue. Raina switched off her lights. "I use those mixing bowls to make cookies. You know how to make cookies, Wizard? 'Cause we've definitely got someone coming to tea."

He rose, and within seconds Raina heard him rummaging through her kitchen cabinet. Then he was back, with the AT850 slung over one shoulder. His expression was cool, smooth. Like polished steel. "Do not stop," he said. "If you continue along this route for about twenty minutes, you will see—"

"No," she snapped. "Do *not* give me orders." Raina pointed her index finger at him, then at the seat beside her. "You. Sit. Do not think that you're going to play hero and take over *my* run to Gladow, in *my* rig."

He didn't immediately move back into the passenger seat, and Raina felt her temper boot up a notch from simmer to boil. With her right knee she knocked the panel out from under the steering wheel and flipped the tiny Setti9 she stored there into her hand. She aimed the lethal little shooter directly at Wizard's head, and snarled a one-word command: "Sit."

He stared at her with those cold, cold eyes. And then he sat.

"Thank you." She suddenly felt a little foolish. Right now he wasn't the enemy.

"You are welcome." There was no trace of emotion in his tone. She would have preferred a little sarcasm. The man was unflappable. It was a bit eerie. She wondered what it would take to get a reaction from him. A plas-shot to the head?

"What were you planning to do, leap out of a moving truck and go gun down the bad guys all by your lonesome?"

He stared straight ahead. "I am the bad guy."

"Oh, for frig's sake." She rolled her eyes. "Look, I appreciate the tough-guy thing. 'I am the bad guy.' Really. Let me tell you something, Wizard. I've met the bad guy, and he wasn't you." He was evil personified. He was Duncan Bane. A short huff of air escaped her. "I've got phosphorous mines."

Wizard pursed his lips, nodded slowly. "Phosphorous mines and a Setti9. Any other long-range weapons you forgot to mention?"

"The Setti9 is short-range." Raina geared down and began to slow the rig, turning a wide circle so she was facing her pursuers rather than running from them. The five blips on the radar screen began to disperse, moving away from one another until they formed a horizontal line. Frontal attack mode. These bastards were cocky.

Reaching up, she snatched her antiglare lenses from the visor and pushed them up the bridge of her nose. Just in time. The lights of their pursuers sent a bright blaze spilling across the ice field. If she'd been any slower with her glasses, the glare would have temporarily blinded her. From the corner of her eye, she noticed that even without glasses Wizard appeared unaffected. He didn't even blink.

Mechanically she flipped open the control box for the phosphorous mines and jammed her hand inside, closing her fingers around the stick. Letting her breath escape slowly from between her teeth, she aimed.

Her eyes were accustomed to the light now, and she saw the hulking outlines of five ugly piles of twisted metal that passed for vehicles. She could just make out the silhouettes of their gun turrets and, projecting from the grilles, ramming horns.

Not the Janson. Much, much worse than the Janson.

"Reavers," Wizard observed.

Icy fingers dug deep into the dark morass of her memories, making her shiver. "I do see that. Any other bits of enlightenment you'd like to share?"

There was a high-pitched whine, followed by an explosion that tore up the ground in front of her rig. Shards of frozen earth pebbled the windshield.

"They have guns," he commented.

"What gave it away?" Was he joking? She shook her head. "That was meant as a warning shot."

"They want something."

Raina shook her head. "What could they want from me? A load of grain? They don't exactly qualify for the interdollar prize." And what the hell were they doing here, so close on the heels of her altercation with Big Luc and his posse?

A second shot landed in front of them, the force of the explosion rocking the rig from side to side.

Okay. Maybe she needed to rethink her plan. They wouldn't settle for warning shots in the long term. At some point her guests would get tired of the game and get serious. Perhaps waiting around to gauge their intent was not the way to go.

"So what could they possibly want?" Raina mused. "Definitely not my load of grain . . . My rig . . . ? What?"

"Guns," Wizard said.

"Yeah. You noticed. And you've already mentioned it. They have guns."

Only that wasn't what he meant. She knew it with a dark, ugly foreboding, and suddenly Lissy Abbott's cool, professional reporter's voice rang in her head. *Piracy is escalating. Reports of attacks on independent trucks are growing exponentially, and there is speculation that illegal gunrunning is on the rise in the region.*

"I'm a dupe." The words escaped her in a whisper. She felt the cold edge of fury pour through her as certainty coalesced in her gut. It explained so much. The Janson and the Reavers . . . an unholy partnership. "I'm not carrying a load of grain for desperate settlers. Those sealed crates have *guns*, and that prize is just a way to make sure they get where they're going." She turned on him, her anger finding a convenient target. "You knew. You bastard, you knew."

"Perhaps now is not the moment to muse over your concerns." Wizard cocked his head toward the window, and Raina saw that the ice pirates were edging their vehicles ever closer. "In this case, retreat may be the better part of valor."

"If you mean we ought to hit them and run, I'm going to have to agree. Hang on." Slamming the truck in gear, Raina closed one hand around the steering wheel and simultaneously fired off a round of phosphorous mines. They streaked through the air and found their marks with a loud report and an eerie green glow that sliced the night.

"Clean hit." Wizard sounded impressed.

"Good, because that's all I've got. Enough to temporarily distract them, but definitely not enough for a war." Pressing her foot to the floor, she peeled off the highway, willing her rig to move like it never had before as they raced across the tundra. From experience she knew the best-case scenario—they'd kill her if they caught her, just as they'd killed Sam. Of course, unlike Sam, her death wouldn't be quick. Ice pirates had a reputation for having their way with the ladies, whether the lady was interested or not.

Driving blind without lights posed something of a challenge, but Raina dared not do anything that might give away their position. She aimed for the monolithic range of ice mountains that she had seen earlier, hoping against hope that there would be a crevice or cave that she could slide the rig into and disappear. As they drove between the craggy peaks, the moon's light was diminished and they were wrapped in darkness.

"There." Wizard pointed to the right.

Leaning forward, Raina whipped off her antiglare lenses and squinted at the window. *Hell.* She couldn't see a thing.

"Where?" She could feel the sweat trickling down her back. Her palm was slick against the wheel.

"Right. Two o'clock. Steady." Wizard's voice guided her, calm, unfazed. Did anything bother this guy?

"Hard right. Four o'clock."

"I can't see a damn thing." Still, she turned as he indicated, sensing that though the night hid their destination from her eyes, Wizard was subject to no such limitation. It galled her to depend on anyone else, even for directions. Actually, it more than galled her. She wanted, *needed*, to be completely independent. Trusting anyone else for anything went against her grain.

And hadn't Wizard already proven himself to be untrustworthy? He'd brought her a frigging *stolen* trucking pass. And he'd known about those frigging guns.

"There," he said again, and this time she did see it: a narrow fissure in the sheer face of the wall of ice.

Edging the truck through the constricted opening, she eased to a stop, hoping they were far enough in to be invisible. Her heart was still pounding wildly, exhilaration tinged with an ugly dose of fear. She turned off the engine and shivered, feeling the cold and the dark close around her.

Raina reached back blindly, snagged her parka, and shoved her arms through the sleeves. This was going to be one long, cold night, a night of wasted opportunities. While she was stuck hiding from the ice pirates like a mouse in a hole, every minute that ticked past was costing her. The other truckers would be barreling toward Gladow Station, toward that interdollar prize, while she—

"Oh, hell." She smacked her open palm against the steering wheel as realization nailed her right between the eyes. "Frigging hell."

"What?" Wizard's voice reached across the space between them.

"No grain. No settlers. No frigging prize." She

fought off the wave of disappointment that threatened to swamp her. Par for the course. She was no novice to setbacks; only she'd really, really been counting on that prize. Her vision of her own place, somewhere warm, wilted before her eyes. It wasn't just the warmth that seeped away; it was the hope that at last she'd stay in one place long enough to sink some roots, maybe even cultivate some friendships—a luxury she had never been allowed. It was too dangerous to let anyone matter, too unfair to let people close enough to care about her. One of them might end up dead.

But if she could get away from the Waste, buy her way into the Equatorial Band, away from Bane and his minions, then she might have a chance to live, a chance to collect Beth and build a home, a family. Anguish clogged her throat. That dream was dead.

Struggling to contain her emotions, Raina forced herself to slow the rapid puffs of air that were huffing in and out of her like a piston.

"Why no prize?" Wizard. Always calm. Always cold as the frigging ice they were hiding in.

What was he? Dense? "No prize because there is *no frigging grain*. There's just a load of guns that aren't meant for those settlers at all. I'd bet my rig that they're destined to be handed over to the Reavers, and the Reavers just decided to collect their spoils a little early."

"The prize is offered to the first driver to arrive at Gladow Station with their load. You could still be that driver," he pointed out reasonably. "Regardless of what the load is."

She wanted to punch him. He just didn't get it. It

was like he was missing the emotion chip or something.

"I don't deliver guns to murderers," she ground out.

He was silent for so long that she thought he wouldn't reply, and then he said quietly, "Understood."

An automaton. He was a frigging automaton. He *didn't* understand. She was certain that he just didn't get it, and suddenly she had a target for the maelstrom of her emotions—fear, adrenaline, anger, disappointment, he was the target for all of it.

"What the hell? Don't you feel *anything*? I deliver those damn guns and they'll be used to kill kids. Or shoot the parents and leave the kids to wander the Waste and get frostbite and hack off their own damn fingers. I don't deliver guns to murderers, no matter how badly I want that damn reward."

Her voice rose with each word, and she was appalled by her loss of control. Sam would beat her senseless if he were here to see it. With Herculean effort, she restrained herself, balling her hands into fists, wishing that it weren't so damn dark and that she could see Wizard. That she could let him see her, let him read exactly what she thought of him in her eyes. Take him down a notch, shake his unflappable control. The truth was, she really wanted a good argument, an outlet for her disappointment. But he just wasn't rising to the bait.

Damn him.

She turned in the dark, raised her clenched fist. Extending her finger, she made the crudest gesture she could think off. Not very mature, but it did make her feel marginally better.

A strangled cough reached her through the dark, or maybe it was a grunt of laughter. If it was laughter, it sounded rusty, unexpected.

"I, um, I can see in the dark," Wizard said.

Okay. Definitely laughter. Raina shrugged and gave in to her instincts. Raising her other hand, she repeated the gesture, two-fisted.

And this time when he let out a short bark of laughter, she laughed right along with him, letting the tension of the past minutes drain out of her. She was barely aware that he sat in silence while she laughed, arms crossed over her belly until finally her odd euphoria passed.

"Better?" he asked, his voice tight, strained.

"Yeah." She let the sound of silence settle around them, wrapping them in its barren cocoon. If she concentrated really hard, she thought she could hear him breathing, but even then she wasn't certain.

She had been terrified. That was the ugly truth of it. Memories of Sam's murder fresh in her mind, she had been afraid of those damn Reavers, afraid that they would catch her. Kill her. Even more afraid of what they would do to her before they finally slit her throat. Her fingers curled tight around the armrests of her seat, she wondered if Wizard had heard her ragged gasps for air, the pounding of her heart as she had confronted those damn pirates.

"Hey, Wizard," she said. "You ever . . ." She cleared her throat. "You ever get scared?" Why did she ask that? She wished she could call it back.

"No." Wizard's calm voice slid through the darkness.

"Never?"

"Never."

She'd opened the can of worms, so she figured that she might as well follow the trail to the end. "So you've never felt panic, terror, dread?"

"No."

"For real?"

"Emotions such as you describe are . . . unfamiliar to me."

"What are you? An automaton?"

He hesitated for a moment, and she almost expected him to admit that yes, he *was* a robot. "I am a mercenary. There is no place for fear on a mission. I have a job to do. I do it." His tone was flat.

"I figured you were an assassin for the New Government Order."

Again he hesitated, then said, "I was. And now I am not."

"Who do you work for now?"

"The highest bidder."

Well, that didn't put too fine a point on it. "No apologies, no regrets, huh? So who's the highest bidder right now?" Raina was glad for the chance to question him, to fill her thoughts with something other than her own fear.

"My current contract is with the Northern Waste Settlers Committee. I have been hired to scout and to train their troops."

The breath left her in a rush. The Northern Waste Settlers Committee was a polite name for the rebels who had taken up arms against the New Government Order. They were a loose collaboration of scattered settlements that had banded together to fight against the Order. A swarm of gnats against a grizzly. If she had delivered her cargo to Gladow, they were the ones the weapons would have been used against. And right now, Wizard worked for *them*.

"So what would you have done if I'd said that I was going to deliver those guns to Gladow Station? They would have been used against the settlers. Against the rebels who hired you." Would his job description have included killing her before she ever reached her destination?

He didn't answer, and in his silence she figured she had her reply. Wizard would have done his job. He would have stopped her. And perverse woman that she was, she couldn't help admiring his offbeat integrity.

A mercenary with a code of honor. Didn't that just beat all?

"I need to sleep." Raina paused and then continued in a grudging tone, "I trust that you'll wake me if there's trouble."

Wizard gave a sharp nod, then realized that though he could see her clearly, she could not see him. "Yes." He rose and reached for his parka. "I will backtrack and ascertain whether we are being followed. You should—"

Holding up one hand palm forward, Raina shook her head. "I thought we already agreed that you wouldn't tell me what I *should* do."

He glanced at her and ran his hand along his jaw. "You do pack a punch, Raina Bowen."

"I'll take that as a compliment." She adjusted her seat to a more comfortable angle. "I'm leaving in two hours. Don't expect me to wait if you're late."

"Understood." He had no doubt that she would not wait if he was late. She would fire her engine and leave him alone and without shelter in the frozen Waste. Though she clearly had a conscience, Raina also had a strong instinct for self-preservation. Waiting around for a missing guest, especially one she clearly didn't want, was something that was not in her best interest.

He left the cab and strode around the side of the truck, intent on assessing the damage done by their encounters with the Janson and the Reavers. Not bothering with a light—having no need for one, as his eyes adjusted to the dark in milliseconds—he rapidly evaluated the situation. The front of Raina's vehicle had fared surprisingly well, with only cosmetic damage, scrapes and scratches. There was also a deep scratch that ran the length of the trailer, a gift from Big Luc. The back fender was twisted into an odd angle, but it would hold. Maybe.

Not one to take chances, Wizard moved to the tool kit mounted on the side of the rig near the back. Laser-locked, with voice-recognition release. Raina invested in the best.

It took him thirty-seven seconds to crack the code and disable the voice lock. With Raina's fusion welder in hand, he set to work on the fender, and he couldn't stop the smile that tugged at the corner of his mouth as he imagined the look on her face when she realized he'd gotten past her impenetrable security.

Suddenly he sobered. He was doing it again—using an imagination he hadn't known he possessed, enjoying sparring with a woman who was a blond tsunami with a backbone of pure steel. Maybe that was the attraction. He knew she'd been afraid earlier, yet she refused to succumb to it, choosing instead to follow her course to the end. It made her all the more attractive, more likable.

Confusion skittered through his thoughts, making him uneasy. He was analytical. He was decisive. He was never confused or uncertain.

He wasn't supposed to like her. But he did.

He was supposed to use Raina Bowen as bait in a trap. But suddenly he had no wish to.

For a moment he longed to vent the frustration that mounted inside of him, an unfamiliar and displeasing sentiment.

"Frig." He tried the word aloud, attempting to copy Raina's tone. The level of his irritation did not alter. "Frigging hell," he tried again, louder, but with no more effective result. The echo of his words bounced back at him from the frozen walls of the crevice.

Emotions were foreign to him, even nearly two decades after he first discovered their existence. This frustration was something he barely recognized, a foreign virus that invaded his thought processes and made them jittery and unclear.

But one thing was definitely clear: he couldn't get the image of Raina out of his mind, and that *hadn't* been in the plan. Get her to the Waste. Use her to draw Bane out. Pay back an ancient debt. For Tatiana. For Yuriko. And, yes, for himself.

Simple. Straightforward. Nowhere in the design was an annotation that told him to think about kissing Raina Bowen hard, deep in her mouth, wet and hot. Of pinning her beneath him, touching her, skin to naked skin. He'd already lost it and kissed her once, a quick brush of his lips on hers, and for all the logical angles he explored, he couldn't explain why he'd done it.

He'd tried reason, telling himself that any woman would do, that his basic needs had gone untended far too long.

But it was a lie.

He wanted *her*. Only her. Raina.

And that wanting just might get them both killed.

EIGHT

Raina jerked awake with a start, choking on the scream that clogged her throat. Her chest felt heavy, crushed by some unseen weight. Her back ached where he'd kicked her, the pointed toe of his boot bruising her again and again. She dragged in a breath and brought her closed fist up, ready to fight for her life.

Except he wasn't there.

Duncan Bane wasn't there. No one was there.

Her chest felt heavy because she'd forgotten to release her safety harness before she'd fallen asleep, and it had pulled tight with her thrashing. Her back ached not from a bruising beating, but from the awkward position she'd been sleeping in. Exhaling a sharp huff of air, she willed her pulse to slow, her taut muscles to relax.

There was no light and little sound, just the hum of the night generator that was keeping the rig warm. Twisting in her seat, she looked out the passenger window. Darkness pressed against the glass.

Fumbling with the harness, Raina released it and

pushed herself out of the seat. She glanced at the lumi-clock. She'd slept for just under two hours. Not bothering with a light, she stumbled back to her living quarters and fell into the shower, turning her face into the pounding stream of water. The ache in her back eased, and the knots of tension in her shoulders melted away. She had never been so glad that she'd spent a fortune in interdollars on the shower and min-dry.

When she came out, scrubbed clean and immensely refreshed, the nightmare fading from memory, she found that Wizard had returned. He gave her a long, searching look, one she met with quiet confidence. Her nap had done her a world of good, and that shower had been a true blessing. She felt almost human.

"Find anything while you were out sightseeing?"

"No."

Chatty, wasn't he? Well, she wasn't a particularly diligent conversationalist herself, so no problem there.

From the small utility box on the back of the passenger seat, she retrieved a lumi-light. After snapping the light to activate the phosphorous beam, she shrugged into her parka, pushed open the door of the rig, and nimbly jumped down to land on the frozen ground. The impact jolted through her legs.

"Where do you go, Raina Bowen?"

Glancing up, she found Wizard framed in the open door of the driver's cab, the interior light surrounding him, accentuating the breadth of his shoulders. He was an incredibly beautiful man. With a sigh she turned away.

"I'm going to check the damage before we get moving again." She spoke over her shoulder, fanning the beam along the side of her rig.

"There is a scratch from one of the Janson trucks. Aesthetic in nature." Wizard's voice trailed after her, pointing out the damage even as her light revealed it.

"Could be worse." She shrugged, not bothering to hide the hint of irritation in her tone. She'd check her own truck, thank you very much.

A dull thud sounded behind her, and she assumed that Wizard was now on the ground, following after her.

She rounded the back of the trailer, the lumi-light glinting from the polished metal of the back fender, and she was surprised to find it still intact. Lightly touching her finger to the luminosity trigger, she increased the brightness of the beam. Frowning, she leaned closer. There were signs of fresh welding.

He was there, right at her back. She could feel him. Sense him. Whirling, she found Wizard not a foot behind her.

"You fixed my fender." Her tone was low, trembling with barely leashed anger. "How did you get at my tools?"

"Your precautions are effective and sensible. They would stop all thieves."

She stared at him incredulously. "All thieves except you. Laser lock and voice recognition. I spent a month's earnings on that system, and you broke through in how long . . . ten minutes?"

Wizard said nothing. He just stood with his hands resting on his hips, head tilted to one side. "You are angry."

Raina sucked in a breath, battling with her temper. She *was* angry. And a little afraid, which made her even angrier. She didn't want his help, didn't want to accept anything from anyone. That path led to weakness, and she refused to travel it, refused to let herself rely on anyone. For anything.

"Do not touch my rig again. If it's falling down around your frigging ears, do not touch it. Got it?"

Wizard stared at her, his face cast in a harsh contrast of light and shadow by the glow of the lumilight. "Got it," he said.

For a second she thought he sounded hurt. And for an equally brief second she actually cared.

"We need to get moving." She stalked back to the rig, not caring if he followed. Knowing he would. A prickly unease skittered through her. Wizard was insinuating himself in her life, and it was making her nervous.

"Where do we go now, Raina Bowen?"

She had no answer, and for the first time in many long years, she hesitated, uncertain. She had trained herself to react, to make instantaneous decisions and follow them through, to ignore all ambiguity. Sitting here in the frigid cab, faced with the load of illegal weapons in her trailer and the very limited prospects in her future, she was uncertain how to proceed.

Her gut clenched, and Sam's voice echoed in her mind. *Faster, girl! Too slow and you're dead. Right or left? Choose. Now!* She'd turned left that day and earned a beating for making the wrong decision. Best make the right choices today, or she might earn an early death for herself and for Wizard. She didn't want his blood on her conscience.

She swallowed. "Gladow Station is no longer my

destination. I'll try to find a band of rebels and sell the weapons to them."

"You think the rebels have money?" Wizard shucked his parka, even though it had to be minus-ten in the cab despite the blowing heat from the vents. The man was hotter than a stone sauna.

Narrowing her eyes, Raina mentally cataloged Wizard's oddities. The cold didn't seem to bother him at all. Last night, the glare of the ice pirates' lights hadn't blinded him. He could see in pitch dark. And that first night, when Big Luc's beating should have left him black and blue, if not half-dead, he'd shown no sign of discomfort or damage. *Weird.*

She shook her head. Not her business.

"The rebels must have *some* money. They hired *you,*" she said.

Watching him from beneath her lashes, Raina couldn't help noticing the way his muscles rippled under his thermal shirt as he stretched. No fatigue showed in his face, no shadows gave testament to tension or nerves. She didn't need a mirror to know the same was definitely not true for herself. How could anyone look that good after a sleepless night?

Suddenly the nature of her thoughts registered, and she wanted to kick herself. What was she doing noticing how good Wizard looked? His pretty face wouldn't get her the money she wanted.

"Anyway, whatever money the rebels have, I won't get nearly the fifty-million-interdollar prize I would have gotten at Gladow, but right now I'll take any reasonable payback. They're my only choice. It isn't as though anyone else will buy weapons I've basically pilfered from the Order."

Wizard ran one hand over his stubbled jaw and turned to face her, catching her watching him. The intensity of his gaze pinned her in place. When he spoke, his tone was bland, as if he asked from mere curiosity, though she suspected there was more to it than that. "And if you find the rebels, would you later sell them out to the Janson or the New Government Order? They would pay a significant finder's fee for the location of a large rebel camp. That would definitely increase your payback."

She wanted to punch him, nice and hard. He didn't have much of an opinion of her. "Who the hell are you to question my integrity?" she asked, her voice tight. "An assassin. A mercenary who sells himself to the highest bidder. Is there anything *you* won't do for money?"

He tilted his head to one side, as though seriously considering her question. "Yes, Raina Bowen," he said at last. "There are things I will not do for money."

"How comforting." Resisting the urge to ask what those things might be, she laced the words with sarcasm, but oddly, his reply *was* comforting. There *were* things he would not do for money. Somehow, it mattered to her that he had some kind of ethics. *Pathetic.* She was falling for a pretty face. A perfect body. A really warped code of honor. *Frig.*

No. Not falling for him. She was smarter than that. Wasn't she? Sighing, she put the truck in gear and backed slowly out of the narrow crevice. With the Janson and the Reavers looking for her, she wouldn't be able to drive the ICW or the I-pole. The rebels were her best choice. Her only choice.

As she cleared the ice mountains, she looked slowly

about her, scanning the horizon in the thin light. She sensed that Wizard was scouting the terrain as well. Flat, frozen ground shone dully in the predawn gray. There was no cover for the ice pirates. In the distance she could see the jagged peak of the monstrous glacier they had passed the previous night. Most of the body lay below the surface of the ice, hidden from view, with only a hint of its magnificent proportions touching the heavens. Glancing at Wizard, she couldn't help wondering what depths were hidden beneath the surface of this mercenary who had the audacity to challenge *her* ethics and ask if she would sell the rebels out.

"Anyway, to answer your earlier question," she said. "No. I would not sell the rebels out. If I had a mind to do that, why not just deliver the guns to Gladow in the first place and claim the prize?"

"A rational question. A logical train of thought." He stared at her, his expression intent.

Against her better judgment, she let her gaze drop to his mouth, a little hard, a little grim, a lot sexy. Her breath escaped her in a rush. What the hell was wrong with her?

"Now, if I can only find a rebel camp," she murmured, dragging her gaze away. "I'll head back to the I-pole. Try to raise some other independent truckers on the com-link. Someone might have a lead." Pondering her dilemma, she sank her teeth into her lower lip, turning the huge rig in the direction of the ancient highway that sliced the Northern Waste. "I definitely need to watch my wording, keep it light, just in case there's anyone listening, looking for us."

Wizard rose and took a step toward the door that

separated the cab from her tiny living quarters. "I will get breakfast," he said, pausing in the open doorway. She glanced at him. He rested one hand against the doorjamb, his arm extended in front of him, his head bent forward. He looked as though he pondered some weighty question, and it felt out of character for what she knew of him.

"You okay?" she asked.

"Affirmative." He stepped through the door, and then asked over his shoulder, "You mean what you say? If you found them, the rebels. You would not sell them out?"

"No." She didn't even have to think about it. Closing her eyes for a second, she had no trouble imagining the massacre that would result if she informed on the rebels. She'd seen it more than once as Sam dragged her from town to town throughout the Waste. No way would she ever be able to live with that kind of destruction on her conscience, no matter what reward was offered. "I told you I don't deliver guns to murderers. I don't deliver rebels for execution, either. I drive my truck. I mind my business."

He was silent for a moment, and she could sense him watching her. Then he said tersely, "Head due north, then turn north-northwest at the Maori Talisman. If we maintain our current velocity, we will be there in six hours, forty-two minutes."

Raina gritted her teeth. She didn't need to ask *where* they would be. Of course Wizard would know where she could find a rebel camp. Of course she'd have to pass some test that only he could define before he'd give her directions. "You could have said so."

"I just did."

She thought she heard him laugh softly, but maybe it was just a whisper of the northern wind.

Following Wizard's directions, she drove into the camp from the southeast, to a barren terrain of low, rounded snow huts scattered between blown-out buildings that reached jagged gray concrete and twisted metal frames into the clear canopy of darkening blue sky. These were the remnants of a civilization that had once built skyscrapers. The sun sank low on the horizon, the day having exhausted its precious hours of light.

The dogs penned to one side threw themselves against the walls of their cage, snarling and barking, and the rebels made no attempt to hide the guards that patrolled the perimeter in pairs.

"They're well armed," Raina commented as they drove closer, aware that all eyes watched, assessing the new arrivals, and that all weapons were trained directly on them. There were more people here than she had expected, and the camp had a strange aura of permanence that surprised her. "Let's hope they talk first, shoot later."

"There." Wizard pointed at the bombed-out shell of a building straight ahead.

Raina drove toward it and parked her rig to one side. Warily she climbed down and followed Wizard as he strode confidently into a dark hole that appeared to serve as the doorway into the building. No one stopped them. No one challenged them. The guards seemed to have melted into the landscape, and the very lack of greeting made her a little nervous. Her right hand snaked instinctively toward the small of her back, and her fingers closed around the handle of her knife.

They were barely inside before a harsh voice cut from the shadows. "You're late."

Spinning toward the sound, Raina pulled her knife from its sheath and shoved her left hand into the pocket of her parka, reaching for the Setti9 that she had grabbed before leaving the rig. The air shimmered with tension, and she sensed that at least one rebel had her in his plasgun sights. Wizard stepped in front of her, and, using the pads of his fingers, he pushed the barrel of her gun down. Realizing that she was outnumbered, she allowed Wizard to redirect her weapon, but made no move to put it or the knife away just yet.

"Late. That I am," he said calmly. "My apologies."

Raina noticed that he gave no defense, made no excuse.

Several men glided from the shadows, wraiths draped in thick swaths of clothing, ragged and worn, their appearance reminding Raina of the vagabond children at Bob's Truck Stop. Only these men were cleaner, bigger, and definitely more dangerous. They were well trained. Though logic had warned her they were there, she had neither seen nor heard them.

A huge man stepped into the light, his dark face weathered from long years in the harsh northern clime. "You've brought a . . . guest." From the sound of his voice, Raina realized that he was the one who had spoken earlier, and from his tone she surmised he was the leader of this ragtag group.

Wizard gave a casual shrug. "She is Raina Bowen."

Tension passed through the group in a palpable wave. Or was it surprise?

The leader of the rebels took a step closer and peered into her eyes. "Sam's girl?"

Sam's girl. She hated that label. She was a person in her own right.

"Sam Bowen was my father."

"I knew him many years ago. He was a good man. A good commander."

Raina kept her expression neutral, but it was an effort. A good commander? This was the first she'd heard of it. A good man? She hadn't known him as one. Could a man be good to strangers but harsh and cold to his own blood? From the reaction of this man, she supposed he could.

"I am Juan. Accept my condolences on your loss, Raina Bowen."

Her loss. Years of cold treatment, being berated and bullied by her father; then the first mission they'd done where he'd treated her—as what? an equal?—he'd gone and gotten himself butchered. She swallowed. "Thank you for your condolences."

He inclined his head, and turned to Wizard. "Come. We will talk."

As they strode along a narrow, dark hallway that seemed to descend into the ground, Raina realized that they had let her keep the Setti9. Either Sam's reputation gave her some level of trustworthiness, or Wizard's did. Both possibilities felt absurd. She re-sheathed her knife and tucked the plasgun back into her pocket, fairly confident that she wasn't about to be shot where she stood. Still, she left the sheath unfastened, just in case.

At the far end of the hall the group passed through a large metal door into a windowless chamber with a handful of chairs set about a worn and scarred round table. A huge nucleoplast screen dominated one wall. Strange that a destitute group of rebels should have a state-of-the-art visual device. Perhaps the rebels *could* afford her load of weapons. The thought was cheering.

Beneath the screen sat a narrow table. Raina paused, surprised, her gaze drawn to the corner of the table, where a large plant with full green leaves and delicate flowers on narrow stalks glowed beneath a suspended lumi-light. The subtle fragrance of the flowers wove through the air, tickling her senses.

"Sit." Half invitation, half command. Juan gestured with one hand.

Wizard moved to a seat near the door, angling his chair so his back was to the wall. Thinking that he'd taken the exact seat she'd have chosen if she'd gotten there first, Raina slid into the chair to his left. There was an energy about him, a subtle tension that made her uneasy. He seemed to be waiting for something.

Keeping her posture purposefully relaxed, she studied each new arrival as several other people made their way silently to their seats. The leader, Juan, sat across from them. Two men soon joined him, each taking a seat on one side of him. Both were tall and lean, one with long white hair tied back in a leather thong so it hung in a thick mass nearly to his waist. His eyes were brown and sharp, his face wreathed in lines of age and wisdom. The second man was a younger, broader replica of the first. Handsome. Forbidding. His face was marked by a jagged scar that ran across his jaw.

Her gaze shifted to watch as three women assumed their places at the round table. Raina felt a flicker of surprise. The New Government Order didn't allow women in positions of power. Clearly the rebels had different ideas.

"Commander Yuriko," Juan said, his booming voice echoing off the walls of the chamber as he inclined his head to the woman on Raina's left. She was tall and sleekly muscled, dressed in swaths of cloth similar to her contemporaries, her dark hair cropped in a ragged mop that fell carelessly to her shoulders. Yet despite her tousled appearance, the woman held herself like royalty. The others watched her with obvious respect.

Well, hell, Raina thought. She'd been wrong about Juan's position here. These rebels didn't just allow women in positions of power. A woman was their *leader*.

The commander swept those around the table with her cool, assessing gaze. Her gray eyes lingered for a moment on Raina, and then moved on to Wizard. She leaned forward, tapping her index finger on the table-top, the movement at odds with the impression of still confidence she portrayed. Raina felt a strange sense of déjà vu as she watched the simple action, but she couldn't place its source.

"Have you brought us an extra mouth to feed, an extra body to protect? I can only hope that whatever information you can provide will compensate for our inconvenience." The commander aimed her comments at Wizard, her chin tilted to a haughty angle, her tone glacial, yet there was a subtle undercurrent, as though she were secretly pleased by some turn of events.

Raina opened her mouth, intent on clarifying the

fact that this group of ragged rebels did not need to feed her or protect her or offer her shelter, despite what their leader might think. She was self-sufficient, and whatever paltry supplies they had, she could easily match them in her well-provisioned rig.

Wizard's hand settled lightly on her thigh, then was gone. A warning. Or perhaps a request for her to hold her tongue. The contact surprised her as much as the fact that he had sensed her desire to contradict the other woman. Frowning, she turned her attention to his response, deciding to hold her silence for the moment and proceed cautiously. After all, there was no profit in alienating the very people who would soon be bargaining for her goods.

"There is a race to Gladow Station, with a fifty-million-interdollar prize for the first to arrive with their load of sealed containers." Wizard leaned back in his chair, crossing his arms over his broad chest.

"And in the containers?" Yuriko asked.

"The government seal states they carry genetically engineered grain."

The commander raised one dark brow derisively. "For this information we paid you?"

To Raina's surprise, Wizard accepted her scathing tone without comment, without any outward reaction. He seemed impervious to insult and derision.

"You have yet to pay me, *Commander* Yuriko, but I look forward to the transaction," he said. Raina wondered at the odd emphasis he placed on the title of commander. "The sealed containers do not hold grain. They hold plasguns, phosphorous mines, hydrogen cannons."

Crossing her arms, the commander sat back in her

seat, mirroring Wizard's actions and looking decidedly unimpressed.

Raina glanced at him, uncertain how he knew exactly what the crates contained. She clenched her jaw as she realized that he'd probably climbed back and looked while she'd slept during the night, and that he'd done it without mentioning it to her. Even worse, he'd gotten through the security blocks that had cost her even more than the ones that guarded her side-mounted tool kit. Did any lock or barrier deter this guy?

She'd assumed there were plasguns in the crates, but mines? Cannons? She was loaded with a frigging arsenal. A valuable arsenal, and she wasn't about to let someone else negotiate her price, especially someone who, according to his own admission, hadn't bothered to get paid himself.

"The rig that carries those precious weapons is mine," she interrupted before Wizard could continue. "I'm Raina Bowen, by the way. I believe that some of you knew my father?"

"Sam's daughter." Something flickered in the commander's eyes. She glanced at Wizard, and then returned her attention to Raina. "I am truly sorry for your loss. I knew him many years ago."

Frowning, Raina wondered if they were talking about the same Sam Bowen. These people seemed to hold Sam in high regard, seemed to think he was a man whom his daughter would miss.

"Uh, thanks." Suddenly she realized that Commander Yuriko was about her own age. If she had known Sam many years ago, she would have been little more than a small child. "How old were you when you knew my dad?"

The commander iced over, her expression going from remote to positively arctic. "I was younger than I am now."

"Yeah. I figured." *Okay.* Talkative. Kind of reminded her of Wizard that way. Still, Raina could understand the desire for privacy. "So if we're done with the stroll down memory lane, let's focus on the race to Gladow." Time to turn the conversation back to opportunities for profit. *Her* profit. "Everything Wizard says is true. In fact, I've brought a whole truckload of toys for your little army. All we need to do is negotiate a fair price."

That got her. The commander half rose, her gaze intent as she leaned across the table. "Here? You've brought those weapons here?"

Raina frowned. "I said so before. The rig that carries the weapons is mine."

Yuriko's gaze shifted to Wizard as her mouth curved in a smile. "You have pleasantly surprised me."

"An unimaginable compliment." Wizard inclined his head in acknowledgment, his tone flat. "I wasn't aware that you had added surprise to your repertoire of emotions."

He spoke to her as though there were no one else in the room, as though the rebels weren't armed to the teeth and likely to take offense at such insult to their commander. Raina wanted to kick him.

There was something here that she didn't understand, some relationship, some history between these two. Was Wizard's barb about emotions aimed at Yuriko because she was an old lover? Did he harbor some regret for a failed relationship? Raina swallowed, aware that the thought of Wizard and Yuriko together didn't sit well with her, and equally aware that she *disliked* the fact that it didn't sit well. *Damn.*

Her gaze returned to Commander Yuriko. The woman reigned in remote flawlessness over the gathering, a confident and regal presence, her perfect features schooled in a look of competent authority.

Wizard with Commander Yuriko. Raina felt her admiration for the other woman wane, replaced by a cold knot of jealousy that coiled in the pit of her belly, an unfamiliar and most unwelcome sensation.

"We will not pay you fifty million interdollars for the weapons," Yuriko said softly.

Raina shoved aside her disconcerting thoughts, glad for something else to focus her attention on. "Yeah? So make me an offer."

The piddling amount the commander named made Raina think she heard the door of an imaginary cell clang shut with an abrupt finality. All her dreams of warmth and home—a place that was her own—evaporated in an ugly little puff of smoke. No one would pay top dollar for weapons stolen from the New Government Order, which meant that the rebels were her sole customers. And whatever the rebels could afford to pay was clearly something that was far from enough. She needed a fortune to keep Beth safe, a fortune to take her far away from the Waste.

She glanced around the room, then returned her gaze to Yuriko. They haggled back and forth, and finally Raina knew she'd hit the maximum. "You have a satellite link?" she asked.

The commander inclined her head. "We do."

"Encryption to the eleventh degree?"

"Affirmative."

"And a place where we can have some privacy?"

Yuriko lightly touched the side of her finger to her forehead in a gesture of salute. "Indeed."

"Then we can do business." Forcing her body to relax, Raina sat back in her seat, giving the impression that she had all the time in the world, when in fact she was nearly jumping out of her skin. As far as she was concerned, the sooner they completed this transaction, the better.

"A job well-done," the woman said softly, her gaze shifting from Raina to Wizard. Again, Raina had a sense that there was some weird current between the two of them, some unspoken bond.

A job well-done. The commander's words echoed through her thoughts. What job did she mean? Bringing the weapons? What did that have to do with Wizard? Those weapons were in Raina's rig.

Glancing at Wizard, Raina narrowed her eyes. Could he have been manipulating her from the first second they met, twisting her actions in such a way that she had no choice but to end up here with her load of plasguns and mines? Had he intended this as their destination all along?

She met his gaze, measuring him. Was he truly capable of shaping events to that degree? The thought was in equal measures far-fetched and objectionable, but even worse was the realization that she did not want him to have brought her here in order to please this woman, this cold rebel commander.

Raina slowly unclenched her fists in her lap, aware that even as she was watching him, he was watching her, studying her. Acting while in the heat of a jealous snit was the worst thing she could do.

A jealous snit . . . She was losing her frigging mind. Wizard was nothing but a worthless mercenary, an assassin who sold his deadly skills to the highest bidder. What the hell was she doing worrying about the women in his life?

Unsettled by the dispassionate depths of his gray eyes as much as by her own musings, she looked away. She'd been skirting the edges of danger for over a decade, falling into the acid mire more than once, and always coming out stronger, if not unscathed. Yet this man Wizard, this mercenary killer, threatened her stability as nothing—and no one—ever had. A faint nausea rolled within her as she wondered if it was possible to fall in love in the heartbeat span of two nights and a day.

No. No. No. That was just plain nuts.

Besides, what the hell did she know about love?

He was gorgeous.

She was horny.

End of discussion.

With a murmured command Yuriko cleared the room, and to Raina's surprise Wizard rose to leave along with the others. She felt an odd pang as he moved around the table and leaned low to speak softly against the commander's ear, and an even stronger pang when the dark-haired woman lifted her face and gifted him with a subtle smile.

Turning, he crossed the room, passing close beside Raina to reach the door. She watched him, determined to give no hint of the emotions he generated. He stopped in front of her, a breath away, his cool, assessing gaze locked on hers.

"Until later." That mouth, that gorgeous, carnal

mouth, curved at the corner, just a little, just enough to make her skin tingle and her breath catch.

Yeah. Later. Her heart gave a sharp kick against her ribs.

His gaze shifted, drifting down, and without thought she licked her lips. She had an insane urge to grab him, rip the clothes from his body, and do him right here on the table. Forget later. Now was looking better and better.

As though he could read her thoughts, he smiled fully, a hard, masculine smile that flipped her insides upside down. And then he turned and walked away, closing the door behind him with a firm click.

NINE

Annoyed with Wizard, with herself, with her traitor-ous libido, Raina turned to find that Commander Yuriko had unveiled a linkboard and keypad built into the table at the far end of the room.

"Nice growth," Raina gestured to the plant she had noticed earlier. The large dark green leaves spilled over the sides of the pot, and the soft pink flowers bal-anced atop thin, delicate stalks. Clearly the plant flourished, yet Raina found it strangely out of place in this harsh, barren environment. Plants were a pre-cious commodity here in the Waste.

"This is a hosta. A hardy plant, sturdy, strong. It can be uprooted many times, split, replanted in soil that is poor, and still it will find a way to grow." Yuriko glanced up, her expression unreadable. "You enjoy plants?"

With a shrug, Raina looked away. "They remind me that somewhere in this world the ground isn't frozen solid. I have a small vegetable garden in a hydroponics greenhouse rigged with solar panels. I don't do anything. It takes care of itself."

"What do you grow?"

Looking back at Yuriko, Raina found the other woman regarding her with interest. "Carrots. Tomatoes. Lettuce. Cucumber."

"I treasure plants. Without them, this world has no future."

The poetic sentiment was at odds with Yuriko's cool exterior, and Raina frowned as she stared at the commander, feeling an inexplicable liking for her. Hell, the woman grew plants . . . How bad could she be?

"Where do you wish the funds deposited?" Yuriko asked, her tone changing from warm to brisk.

So much for friendly conversation. Raina moved closer and waited until Yuriko stepped away. She keyed in the necessary information, knowing that she had a perfect fail-safe mechanism that would forward her funds, then close the account, moving the interdollars to a series of accounts that would hide her trail. It was one of the many precautions she had learned to take over the years because she had never stopped looking over her shoulder, knowing that one day Duncan Bane would want his revenge, and she'd best have a way to burrow in and hide when that happened.

She had access to money in twenty-seven different accounts, each with a unique name and code. And just in case all else failed, she had the equivalent of buried treasure in five relatively accessible sites. When Bane decided to come after her, being on the run for her life would be bad enough; doing it without funds would be even worse, and she had no intention of letting that happen.

"Because of all the encryption, it will take seventy-two hours and fifty-six minutes to finalize the transaction," Yuriko observed. "We will wait until the finances are secure before unloading the weapons. You may remain in our compound until that time, if that is your wish."

Raina blinked at the other woman's tone. For a second she'd sounded exactly like Wizard: cool, analytical, emotionless. Yet another perfect bit of proof that the two had some history, that they'd shared enough hours for Yuriko to take on some of Wizard's characteristic speech patterns.

Again, an ugly little twist of jealousy speared Raina's gut. She blew out a breath and turned from the keypad. "Yeah, I'll stay. Once I get transfer confirmation, you can unload the weapons and our transaction will be complete."

Yuriko studied her for a long, uncomfortable moment. "Where will you go then?"

"Here and there," Raina muttered, unnerved by the question, thinking of her defunct dreams of home and knowing that whatever money she gleaned from this transaction, it wouldn't fill her bank account for long.

An image of the ragtag kids back at Bob's Truck Stop formed in her thoughts. Their desperation hit too close to her conscience, reminded her of a girl she'd once been forced to leave behind. Ana. She tried to push the memory aside, but it sank sharp talons into her soul and refused to let go.

Maybe that was why she was so obsessed with getting her sister, Beth, making a home for her, making sure she wasn't alone. Restitution of sorts, because she hadn't been able to take Ana with her that long-ago night, because she'd had to leave her to her fate.

Raina had known misery, hopelessness, fear. Lived it, breathed it, tasted its bitter tonic for more years than she wanted to count. Which made her determined to lessen the misery of any kids she could help.

Man, she was such a sucker. First those orphans near the Nunavut pass-over last year. Then those half-starved kids at Dorje a few months later. The kids at Bob's. And Beth. Hell, at the rate she was going it was a wonder she had enough funds left over to power up her rig.

With a sigh, she pictured the boy from the truck stop, Ben, with his mangled hand and tough-guy air, and she wondered how far Yuriko's interdollars would go toward some warm clothes, food, and shelter. *Hell.*

Someone ought to get a home out of this deal.

The wait brought only edginess. Raina thrashed about on her narrow bed, restless, anxious, her bottled tension threatening to burst free of her body. The hour was late and she wanted to sleep, to lose herself in a dreamless nothingness and awake refreshed. She hated this—the waiting. It was making her crazy. Staying in one place for too long always did that to her, yet her heart's desire was a little place of her own that she could stay in for a good long while. The irony of it wasn't lost on her.

Turning on her side, she stared into the dim interior of her quarters, the darkness cut by the lumi-light she'd left burning near the door. Thoughts of Wizard crept up on her, uninvited. She hadn't seen him since he'd left Yuriko's conference room with the others, and though she tried, she couldn't quite convince herself that she didn't care if she never saw him again. When he'd shared the rig with her during their wild ride across the Waste, she'd thought he crowded her, felt like the place was too small for the two of them. But now that she was alone, she kind of missed him.

No. She did *not* miss him. She refused to miss him.

She rolled over on her narrow bed, trying to sweep Wizard from her thoughts, to focus instead on the hours she had spent that afternoon with Yuriko, scouting the terrain. Raina had found herself enjoying the other woman's company. It was a strange feeling to ride side by side with another person, to stop and talk about a recipe for sim-steak stew or an adjustment to her hydroponics growth equipment that would allow for a better yield; strange to think she had begun to develop a friendship.

Just as it had felt strange to have Wizard beside her as she drove the I-pole. And then it had felt even more peculiar to have him gone.

Gone. Leaving her alone. When in hell had she decided that she liked company, that she didn't like being alone?

Damn Wizard.

With a sigh Raina snuggled deep under her covers, fighting what she knew was a losing battle. No matter how much she wished it weren't so, Wizard was on her mind.

And then he was there, just as she had imagined him, his hair hanging straight and thick about his muscled shoulders, his eyes glittering in the glow of the lumi-light as he stared at her. Eyes like molten silver, bright against the dark fringe of lashes, intent, hungry, heavy lidded with primal need.

He leaned close, resting one palm flat against the bed, his lips a breath from hers. The heat of him came over her like a mist. The corners of his mouth kicked up in a hard, masculine smile. Knowing. Hungry. Raina shivered as he pulled the sheets aside, baring the curve of her shoulder, the arc of her collarbone. Her breath came in short gasps, leaving her dizzy.

And still he did not touch her.

She licked her lips, waiting, every inch of her skin yearning for his caress. Running her palm along his forearm, she felt corded muscle under smooth, hot skin. She closed her eyes, thinking that she'd like to wrap her hands around other smooth, hard parts of him, to touch him and claim him and make him her own. Everything inside her melted at the thought, pooling into a dull ache that throbbed between her legs.

"Touch me," she whispered, nearly desperate to kiss him, to taste him, to tunnel her fingers through the thick length of his hair, to run her hands over his warm skin.

Surging upward, she reached for him.

Her arms closed around emptiness, and the chill air of her cabin embraced her.

"Frig." Raina fumbled for the lumi-light.

The phosphorescent glow filled the cabin, and the face of her clock revealed what she'd already figured out: the night had passed.

Dreaming. She'd been dreaming.

Wizard wasn't there. She was alone, shivering, her covers a twisted tangle around her hips, her body aching for a Waste-trash assassin who'd walked away from her without a backward glance.

* * *

Wizard clambered silently up the side of the icy ridge that offered a windbreak to the Reavers who had set up camp on the plain below. He surveyed the vicinity, gauging distance, movement, threat. Apart from Trey, who climbed nimbly behind him up the glacial face of the ridge, nothing moved.

"Three guards on each of two plascannons. Five on the munitions cache," Trey said by way of greeting as he hauled himself up the last bit. "No dogs."

Trey's report matched what Wizard had seen. "An additional seventeen Reavers asleep in their thermarolls," he added.

"Two of us. Twenty-eight of them." Trey shook his head.

"The probability of success is within acceptable limits," Wizard pointed out.

Trey was silent for moment, digesting that, and then he laughed, a short, harsh sound. "Commander Yuriko would call us stupid. Or suicidal."

"Yuriko is not here."

"Right. Commander's back at camp, snug as a bug. But if she were here, she'd tell us to move out and report back. This assignment was recon only." There was a hint of bitterness in Trey's tone, and Wizard knew that he was thinking of another day, another reconnaissance mission. A life lost.

One more sin for Duncan Bane. One more reason to seek justice.

"When she assigned this run, Yuriko did not know that a line of refugees moves toward Dorje Station," Wizard pointed out. "They are in the direct path of the Reavers, and they have no warning. Intersection estimated at seven hours."

"They'll be annihilated." Trey blew out a breath, then muttered, "And if we try to take out twenty-eight Reavers, *we'll* be annihilated."

"The probability of our success is—"

"I don't want to know." Trey cut him off. "Let's just do it." Surging to his feet, he pulled the pack from his back and set it to one side.

Wizard followed his actions. They would travel weapons-only into the ice pirate camp. Time enough to retrieve their sleeping rolls and food supplies when their task was complete.

"Live to see peace, because Yuriko will be displeased if you do not."

Trey sent him a sharp look. "I think the only thing the commander will be displeased about if we don't come back intact is the loss of a couple of fighting machines." He grunted. "But your Raina Bowen might be a tad put out if I have to haul your corpse back on my scooter."

Your Raina Bowen. Wizard blinked, recalling the words he had spoken to Ben at Bob's Truck Stop when he had told the boy that Raina was not his. Raina. Brave, resilient, bold. Fighting even in the face of her fear. He thought of the way she handled herself in a fight, the clear blue of her eyes, the soft scent of her hair.

There was no logic in it, but for just a second he let himself wonder what it would be like if she *were* his.

Raina looked at the clock. Three hours before the sun would rise on another long day of waiting for her funds. She was edgy. Again. Because she'd dreamed of Wizard. Again. Shoving her quilt aside, she swung her legs over the side of her bed, determinedly pushing thoughts of him aside, only to have them bounce back at her.

Frig. She was half-infatuated with him, holding her breath at each creak of the rig, each gust of wind, wishing that it were him coming to her. She needed to get a firm grasp on her reality.

No emotional attachment. No frigging emotional attachment.

That would only put him in harm's way. She knew that with certainty. Every time she'd started to put down roots, every time she'd started to build a life, build relationships, Duncan Bane had come.

And no matter how strong, how careful, how well trained, Wizard wouldn't stand a chance. Bane had an entire army at his disposal. Not just the Janson, but the whole corrupt New Government Order. What chance would Wizard stand, one man against the world?

After a quick shower, she dressed for the weather and headed out, wanting—no, needing—the blast of cold air, hoping it would blow a certain mercenary assassin right out of her mind. Her breath formed vapor clouds as she walked the perimeter of the compound. She identified herself to the guards she passed, but at this point she didn't need to bother. They greeted her by name. Joked with her about the temperature. It was weird; she'd been here long enough for them to know that she hated the cold, long enough for her to know that the taller one, Jake, was addicted to early twenty-first-century romance novels, and the shorter one, Sawyer, was a wisecracking joker.

It was a little frightening to realize that she had gotten to know them well enough to like them.

Head bent low against the wind, she walked at a brisk pace. Her thoughts wandered, and each time they circled back to Wizard. She needed to concentrate on something—anything—else.

Money. That was a safe subject. But even that betrayed her, and she found herself recollecting the cadence of Yuriko's voice as she discussed the money transfer. Which made her think of Wizard again, because hadn't Yuriko sounded just like him? *It will take seventy-two hours and fifty-six minutes to finalize the transaction.* The commander's comment had been eerily reminiscent of something Wizard would say.

To Raina's thinking, that, along with the subtle glances and the undercurrent to their exchanges, was proof that the two had a shared history, a bond from the past. For some reason the thought depressed her.

No. It more than depressed her. In spite of the companionable rides they'd shared, the conversations they'd enjoyed, it made her want to yank Yuriko around by the hair and smack her silly. Get in a catfight over a guy. And that definitely depressed her. She had to be losing her mind.

As she rounded the bombed-out shell of a building at the edge of the compound, Raina drew up short.

"Speak of the devils," she muttered, drawing back into the shadows as she saw Wizard and Yuriko standing beside a gleaming black snowscooter. Her heart slammed against her ribs. He was back. Wizard was back.

He leaned close to Yuriko, and Raina swallowed the lump in her throat, trying to ignore the fact that it was jealousy that curdled there as she watched the two, heads bent close together, engaged in private conversation.

Yuriko reached out and laid her hand on Wizard's arm, speaking earnestly as she gazed into his eyes. There was true emotion there, affection; Raina was sure of it. Wizard took a step closer and enfolded the commander in a stiff one-armed embrace that suggested that offering comfort was an unfamiliar experience for him. Or maybe it was a certain level of awkwardness with an old lover.

Her jealousy was a living entity now, writhing inside her, and Raina sucked in a breath, stunned that she was feeling this way, at a loss to explain why this man engendered such an uncharacteristic response. She began to turn away when he ended the embrace and stepped back from Yuriko. Turning, he faced in Raina's direction, his gaze trained on her despite the shadow of the wall that should have hidden her from view.

She recalled his assertion that he could see in the dark, recalled the way he had seen the Janson trucks even at an enormous distance. There was no doubt in her mind that Wizard knew she was there, could see every nuance of her expression. Caught, Raina swaggered forward, determined to brazen it out.

Her gaze lingered for a moment on the snowscooter. It was loaded for travel. Which meant he was leaving. Again. Obviously he'd had no intention of checking in with her during his brief time in camp. And why should she think he would?

"You going somewhere?" She kept her tone neutral.

"Yes."

She almost asked where, but figured that it would

be a waste of breath. If he'd wanted to tell her, he would have. They'd had conversations like this before, like the one they had had in her truck when she'd asked if he had something against Duncan Bane. *Yes. I have something against him,* he'd replied. *You going to tell me what that something might be?* she'd asked. *No.*

With a shrug, she turned away. He didn't owe her an explanation, and she didn't want one. The less she knew about him, the better. Knowing someone meant caring about them. It was bad enough that she'd been bitten by a serious case of the hots for him. She definitely didn't want to add liking him to her list of failings.

"You are up early," Yuriko said.

Raina glanced at her. "Yeah, I'm a real morning person."

"As am I." The other woman seemed to have missed the sarcasm. Just then a soft hum filled the silence. The commander touched her ear and spoke into the com-link that encircled it. "Please excuse me." She rested her fingers lightly on Wizard's shoulder, and their eyes met for an instant. "Reconnaissance only, Wizard. You took too great a chance." She paused, then continued softly, "As did Trey."

"There were"—he glanced at Raina—"circumstances."

"There always are. No chances this run. Understood?"

Wizard said nothing. Yuriko gave him a hard look, then moved off.

Something cold and bitter twisted in Raina's chest, and she knew it for what it was. The wretched worm of jealousy wriggled uncomfortably inside her, and she couldn't figure out how to get rid of it, or why it was there in the first place. The anxiety of the past few days didn't quite cut it as an explanation. Yeah, things had been dicey on the I-pole, but she'd been in worse positions many times, and her emotions had never had her so rolled up in knots. And no man, least of all a mercenary assassin, had ever gotten to her before.

Oh, but he does have his own warped code, an insidious little voice in her head whispered. Yeah, she knew that, but it hardly explained the attraction.

She was about to turn away when his hand shot out, those long, lean fingers closing about her wrist. Not hard enough to hurt her—she could have easily pulled away. Just hard enough to make her stop and turn and bring her gaze up to meet his. Big mistake. His eyes glittered, not cold and distant now but sparking with heat.

A shiver chased along her spine, but it had nothing to do with the frigid clime. He knew it. His lips curved in that dangerous, masculine, knowing smile that made her breath catch and freeze in her throat. For a guy who didn't do it often, he sure knew how to use that smile.

Never one to retreat, Raina held her ground, though every nerve screamed to turn and flee. There was something about this man that reached out and burrowed deep inside of her, making her feel hot and restless, making her want to grab him and pull him down so she could taste him.

His eyes darkened, and she knew he could read every wretched thought. *Frig.*

Retreat was impossible. Attack was her only option.

A soft hiss escaped her as she curved one hand behind his head, taking control of temptation and pulling him down, her mouth open. Their lips touched, and a moan escaped her, low and harsh, fueled by animal need. She tasted him, loving the feel of his lips against hers. He met her thrust, lazy strokes of his tongue and the soft graze of his teeth driving her wild. She tunneled her gloved fingers through his long hair, pressing herself against the hard length of him, the taste of him spinning through her until it seemed to twist into every part of her.

He was lust personified, seduction incarnate. Barely restrained energy, hard muscle, and tightly coiled power.

She longed to tear his clothes from his body, to run her hands over the planes and hollows of his muscled form, to twine herself about his senses as he had about hers. All from just one hot, wet, mindless kiss. And the realization terrified her. Too much. Too fast. One kiss from a mercenary assassin and she was nearly ready to sell her soul for more. It was insanity.

With a soft moan she wrenched away, breathing heavily, feeling as though everything she knew, everything she was, had turned inside out. Deliberately she dragged the back of one gloved hand across her lips, wiping away the feel, the thought of his kiss. But it was not so very easy.

He was watching her, his own need shimmering around him like a halo, and in about three seconds she was going to reach for him and yank him along behind her until they got to her rig and whatever privacy it offered.

The sound of a vehicle caught her attention. Grateful for the distraction, she reined in her thoughts and looked up to see a battered truck driving slowly toward them. The thing was older than the Old Dominion. One door was missing, and the trailer was little more than an open cab with a broken fence barely clinging to the sides.

Wizard hesitated for about a millisecond; then he strode to the truck. "I will take point," he said to the driver, gesturing at the snowscooter as he spoke.

She blinked, stunned at how quickly he had dismissed her, dismissed the molten attraction of seconds past.

Then he turned to her, and she saw that his cool tone belied the heat that still pulsed between them. He had forgotten nothing, and something in his expression promised that he was coming back to finish what they'd started.

TEN

Wizard sped across the frozen terrain, attuned to every nuance of the environment as the runners of the snowscooter glided over the solid layer of ice and snow that covered the earth as far as the eye could see. His gaze automatically scanned the horizon, watching for any subtle hint that they might soon have company, but all was quiet.

Not so his thoughts. They clamored within him in an uncharacteristic cauldron of confusion. She had done something to him, something intangible and inexplicable. Raina Bowen was a beautifully packaged blizzard that roared around and through him, and left him in a state of perplexity.

Unacceptable. He was used to compartments. Here was the place for memories. And here the place for the task at hand. And here the place for sexual release. He had only one compartment for emotion, only one place he allowed another sentient being to enter, and that corner was reserved for Yuriko. Once it had included Tatiana, but now she was locked in the

149

compartment reserved for memories. Dark, powerful memories laced with guilt. He rarely opened that compartment, refused to allow himself to feel the pain of her loss.

He pressed one fist against his forehead, then dropped it back to his side. What was Raina Bowen doing dancing through each and every one of his compartments, wiping out all logical thoughts and strategies?

No, not dancing. More like stomping, with a ten-inch blade in one hand and a plasgun in the other. He couldn't help smiling at the image, surprising himself with his reaction. He'd smiled more in the days since he'd met Raina than he had in the past several years.

Maybe *that* was the attraction. He kept searching for reasons, but found none.

No. Not accurate. He found too many reasons, too many dangers to his calm resolve. When he thought of Raina, he thought of all that was brave and valiant and, yes, even good, though she hid her kindness behind a tough shell. He knew about the kids at Dorje Station, about the sacrifices she'd made for a sister she didn't even know.

He was far too good a strategist to fail in his research of his quarry. And she *was* his quarry, his best means to the end he sought.

Raina was an attraction that should never have happened. One kiss and he'd been ready to lay her down beneath him and take her there in the snow. More than ready. But the worst of it was, he'd sensed that she, too, had been awash in a tide of desire, dragged by the current of need that rippled between them.

He would have used it if he had to, used the desire

he read in her eyes to trick her into going where he wanted. But there had been no need. In the end, Raina had followed her own instinct and ended up exactly where he wanted her to be, here in the Waste, surrounded by Yuriko's rebels.

Raina was the bait. Wizard was the trap.

The idea had seemed perfect before he met her, before he slept on her floor and listened to the sound of her breathing, inhaled the scent of her. Before she'd kissed him, and he'd kissed her.

Desire. To want something very strongly. Like he wanted Raina. A strong wish to have sexual relations with somebody. He wanted more than sexual relations with her. An unsettling thought, but a necessary truth. He could not fight that which he did not acknowledge.

Desire. He could name a half dozen definitions for the word, but none of them would be enough. Those definitions were too mild to describe what he felt for her.

But if not desire, then what?

Wizard shook his head and turned the scooter due south. In the distance he could just make out the shape of Bob's Truck Stop. A matter of minutes and he'd do something so uncharacteristically odd that he couldn't explain it even to himself. Those ragged kids had stayed with him long after he'd left them here with a fistful of his interdollars clutched in their hands.

He'd been fixated on coming back for them, making sure they were taken somewhere safe.

Because it was what *she* would do, given the first opportunity. She would return to save them.

Raina Bowen. She had muddled his mind.

Less than twenty-four hours ago, he'd been covered

in blood, killing ice pirates before they could kill those refugees he and Trey had stumbled upon. Killing was something he knew, something he understood.

He was an assassin. He *took* lives.

He didn't save them.

So what was he doing here, rescuing a bunch of hungry orphans?

"What the hell am I doing here?" he whispered. And then louder, "What the *frigging hell* am I doing here?"

A short, pudgy man with thinning brown hair stood just inside the doors of Duncan Bane's office in Port Uranium. He kept a respectful distance, his eyes darting nervously about the room, settling for the briefest of instants on the shelf, then the desk, then the floor.

"The first delivery has been made, Mr. Bane. Taggart Rales. A Janson man," he said.

Duncan Bane took a sip of black tea, savoring the flavor as it rolled over his tongue, a perfect finish to his morning meal. A woman, curvaceous and rather pretty, hurried forward to take his dirty plate. He'd forgotten her name, or perhaps he'd never bothered to ask. Her right cheek was purpled and swollen, evidence that she had been too slow in her duties the previous morning.

Silent, hulking guards flanked the double doors that led to his inner sanctum. They had stepped aside to allow his underling entry, and they stood now, two frozen statues, ready to give their lives at his word. Amazing how powerful one could be when one held wives and children hostage in the endless tunnels that twisted through the bowels of the earth.

Setting his teacup carefully back on the delicate china saucer, he glanced at the man before him. His shirt was stretched tight across his belly, the edges gaping as he breathed. Duncan made no effort to hide his distaste.

"The first to reach Gladow Station . . . So the race is won. Was Taggart Rales suitably rewarded for being the first trucker to arrive with his load of grain, Mr. James?"

Harlan James shifted nervously. "He was, sir. The mayor of Gladow awarded him the fifty-million-interdollar prize. There was a twelve-piece band. And a pyrotechnic display. Magnetic flares. Everyone in the vicinity was there to celebrate."

"Excellent. And then?"

"Mr. Rales went out to continue his celebration on his own, sir. He was drinking rather heavily. Unfortunately, he was set upon by thieves on his way back to his rig. Beaten to death."

Duncan smiled. He felt truly happy when things went according to his design. "Tssk. Beaten to death. Shocking. Truly shocking. And the interdollar reward?"

"Missing, sir. Obviously taken by the thieves."

"How very distressing. Send my condolences to the man's family. A Janson man, you said. Eligible for pension?" Turning to the com-station on his desk, Duncan called up his private numbered account. It showed a deposit for fifty-million interdollars made just that morning. Untraceable, the account led back to a dead trail of phony businesses and people who did not exist.

"No, sir. No pension. A week shy of eligibility. He leaves behind his wife and twin baby daughters."

"Shame that we won't be able to send them a pension. But we cannot make exceptions. He was not in our employ for the full five years. A week shy. I'm certain they will understand."

Harlan James nodded. His cheeks were flushed, and a sheen of sweat sparkled on his upper lip.

Lifting his cup from the saucer, Duncan took another sip of tea. Cold. The stuff had gone cold. With a snarl, he dashed the antique china against the wall, watched it shatter into tiny fragments. "Clean that up," he barked as the girl hurried forward, stumbling in her haste to obey.

Returning his attention to the man in front of him, Duncan asked softly, "What has you nervous as a cat, Harlan James? You've brought me only pleasant news. So what secrets are you keeping?" He rose, circled his desk, and crossed the room toward Harlan. His steps were slow, careful. He enjoyed the other man's discomfort, reveled in the taste of his fear as it permeated the air in the room. "Tell me," he whispered as he stopped directly in front of him.

"The man called Wizard has disappeared. His truck was rigged to blow, and at first he was reported dead in the explosion. But Ljubisa claims he may have seen him in a truck on the I-pole."

Duncan circled around Harlan, a predator playing with his prey. "Ljubisa," he repeated the name. "Second in command of the Srgeina group? Mongolian ice pirates. Yes?"

"Siberian, sir. Reavers." Harlan swallowed, the sound infringing on the silence of the room.

"You dare correct me?" Duncan whispered.

"No, sir. No. *Mongolian.* Mongolian pirates."

Duncan smiled as Harlan shifted nervously. "And Ljubisa did not kill Wizard because . . . ?"

Harlan brought his hands together, clasping them tightly, although his action did little to mask the shaking of his limbs. "Because you want his companion alive."

"And his companion would be?"

Swallowing convulsively, Harlan said nothing.

"Raina Bowen." Her name left Duncan's lips on a whisper of air. A curse. A caress. He spun and strode back to his desk, black rage curling inside him like bilious smoke, mingling with sexual excitement as he thought of the ways he would like to hurt her. "Get out," he snarled.

Harlan James backed toward the door.

"No." Duncan stared at the wall of glass before him.

Harlan froze at the softly spoken command.

"Arrange for my plane. Have it ready in twenty minutes. The Northern Waste cries out to me, and I would answer its call."

"Yes, Mr. Bane. Yes, sir." Harlan James inched back toward the door and fled the room.

Duncan closed down his com-station, taking care to change his password as he did. His plane would leave in twenty minutes, and it would take less than four hours for him to reach Gladow. Luckily, he would encounter no traffic as he flew. A low laugh escaped him. His was the only aircraft in the entire northern hemisphere.

For a moment he thought of Earl, the man he had given three days to find Raina Bowen. His time had not quite run out, but even if he rode a snowscooter through day and night without stop, three days would not be long enough to reach the Waste and find her. Pity. Duncan made his decision. He could trust no one but himself. He should have taken care of it personally from the first.

Just one small task to complete before he left. He would consult his oracle, the woman whose genetic enhancements had created an unusual and unsettling gift. He wondered if she would be more cooperative this time, his little Tatiana, locked away in her luxurious cell. She had offered him so many tantalizing glimpses into the future, but when it came to his questions about Raina, she was always so unpleasantly vague.

Running the tip of his finger along the edge of the patch that covered his missing eye, he allowed himself the pure pleasure of picturing her, Raina Bowen, naked, broken, chained at his feet. The image was unspeakably delightful. A quiver of excitement radiated through him.

He pressed the button on his direct satellite line, and gave the order for Earl to be terminated. Really, the man should have worked faster.

"Good afternoon." Yuriko stood on the ground beside Raina's rig, a cloth-wrapped bundle held carefully against her chest.

"Is it afternoon?" The sky was pitch-black, but that didn't mean it wasn't afternoon. Raina glanced at her watch, then back at Yuriko. Pulling open the door to the cab, she made a sweeping gesture with one hand. "Come on in."

Company was almost welcome. Talking to someone

beat sitting in the dark wondering when her funds would clear. Wondering where Wizard was.

Okay. That wasn't exactly all she'd been up to. Sitting on her duff just wasn't her style. She had taken to training with the rebels, taught them a few new tricks and picked up a couple herself. She wasn't just sitting around waiting; she was *integrating.* And wasn't that just too strange.

Raina moved aside as Yuriko clambered nimbly into the truck, her bundle cradled in the crook of her arm.

"I made stew. Your recipe." Raina headed toward her living quarters, thinking that she'd had more people in her rig in the last week than she'd had in the past year. Wizard. Now Yuriko. Two more than usual. Oh, and Big Luc, but he didn't count as a person. "You hungry? There's more than enough for both of us."

Pulling another bowl from the cupboard above the sink, she set it beside the one she had taken out for herself earlier. For a second she just stared at the two bowls arranged side by side. She was so used to eating alone.

Yuriko moved up beside her and set her bundle on the counter, unwrapping it to reveal a small clay pot, which she pushed directly beneath the lumi-light. Dark leaves spilled over the sides, and two small pink flowers balanced on thin stalks amidst the tumble of greenery.

It took a moment for Raina to understand, and when she did, she raised her eyes to meet Yuriko's, feeling confused and grateful and a little afraid.

"For you, Raina Bowen. You must keep the plant beneath the lumi-light, but not all day and night. Half the time light. Half the time dark. Add water to keep the earth moist. And use the same fertilizer you add to your hydroponics grow tube."

"I don't think so." Raina took a step back, shaking her head. "I'll kill it."

Yuriko tipped her head to one side, studying her quizzically. "You will not kill it. You haven't killed your hydroponics vegetable garden."

"It takes care of itself. The thing's programmed to be self-sufficient." Raina blew out a breath. "I'm no good at taking care of anything."

"How do you know?"

How did she know? Because no one had ever taken care of her; no one had taught her how to take care of anything—or anyone—else. Glancing back at the plant, Raina was drawn to it despite herself. It looked so perfect there on her counter, adding a warmth to her rig that she hadn't even known was missing. With a tentative touch, she stroked the smooth, shiny leaves.

"You're giving me a gift."

"Yes."

Nothing in life was free. "Why?"

Yuriko smiled, a quick turning of her lips—there, then gone. The subtle expression reminded Raina of something, but exactly what she couldn't say.

"There is no reason, Raina. You admired my plant. Appreciated its beauty. I wanted to gift you with a cutting so you could carry a little bit of warmth with you wherever your travels may lead."

Not knowing how to respond, Raina turned away and began doling out servings of sim-stew. She set two bowls on the table and gestured awkwardly for Yuriko to sit.

"Tasty," Yuriko said after a moment. "Carrots from your greenhouse?"

"Yeah. I bought the potatoes last time I was in New Edmonton. This is the last of them." Without missing a beat, Raina continued. "So, what do you want, Yuriko?"

The commander didn't pretend to misunderstand. "You. Why not stay? Share your knowledge? Work with us?"

Raina gave a startled burst of laughter. "You come right to the point, don't you?"

"I never learned the art of subtlety," Yuriko admitted.

"I work alone. I live alone. And I never stay in one place more than a few days."

"Why?"

Raina blinked at Yuriko's question. Why? Because staying in one place meant that Bane had a better chance of finding her. Staying in one place meant getting to know people, caring about them. Missing them when they left. Or died.

Staying in one place meant trying to build friendships, and no one had ever been her friend. Cynna, the girl she'd roomed with for a short time in Freemont Station, had tried to drug her and sell her to three ice pirates for a stack of interdollars. Old Beatrix, the woman whose home she'd stumbled into days after she'd run from Bane, had let her live in the tiny, damp basement for a while in exchange for cleaning, cooking, and other household chores. But then she'd sold her out. Bane circulated Raina's image on the satellite networks, and the next thing she knew, she saw his goons knocking at Beatrix's door.

Raina had slunk in late that night to recover her

meager possessions, and the old woman had sworn it was just happenstance, that she hadn't given Raina up to them. But Raina knew better. Life had taught her a little bit of caution by then. The next day, all the satellites carried the story of old Beatrix, dead, her throat slit, with Raina's name thrown out there as the prime suspect. It had left Raina wondering whether Beatrix had been telling the truth. Problem was, she could never be sure.

"I'm not a real people person," Raina muttered.

Yuriko cocked her head to one side. "What, no friends?"

For some reason, the memory of the girl she had known only briefly when she had been a prisoner in Bane's camp skimmed the surface of Raina's thoughts. Ethereal and waiflike, Ana had held her hand in the dark, whispered that everything would be fine. She had sounded so certain, as though she knew it for fact. At the time, Raina had thought that Ana was strong, brave, fearless. But looking back on it, she figured that she had just been another terrified child, that holding hands in the dark had given them both strength.

The fact that she hadn't been able to go back for Ana, hadn't been able to save her, haunted Raina when she let it, which wasn't often. Truth was, it was all she'd been able to do to save herself. Still, it was Ana's face she saw when she looked at orphans like Ben and his crew. It was her guilt at leaving Ana behind that she recalled when she thought of her sister, Beth. She hadn't saved Ana, but maybe, just maybe, she could save Beth.

"Think about it," Yuriko said, breaking into Raina's

thoughts, bringing her back to the moment. "Think about staying."

With a start, Raina realized that she *wanted* to think about it, wanted to stay here just a little longer. She'd never had a friend, and now, for the first time, she actually felt as though she was in a place where people liked her, welcomed her, valued her. It was nice. Especially because the rebels were tough enough to take care of themselves.

She'd hated the way she felt after Beatrix and Cynna betrayed her. She'd hated it when Beatrix turned up dead the following day and Bane circulated the story that it was Raina who'd killed her. Raina had quickly learned that it was too dangerous to leave a trail, too frightening to drag someone else into her muck.

The worst of it was, she'd hated the fact that she'd betrayed Ana, left her behind to suffer the fate that she herself had managed to escape. She'd left Ana with Bane. The guilt of it had lessened over the years, but when she let it out, it still slithered to the surface, wet and slimy and stinking like rot.

But Yuriko could more than take care of herself, which made her offer of friendship so very appealing. Raina almost let herself dream—dream of getting Beth and bringing her here and building a life with Yuriko and Jake and Sawyer . . . and Wizard.

Her meal finished, Yuriko rose and cleared away her bowl. She looked over her shoulder as she strode toward the door. "He'll be back. Stay at least until then."

Raina opened her mouth to tell the other woman

that she didn't care. That she was not going to sit around and wait for Wizard. That he meant nothing to her, and that she couldn't care less if she never saw him again.

But she couldn't get the words out. Maybe she was losing her touch. *Damn.* She'd thought that after all this time she'd finally learned to be a pretty good liar.

ELEVEN

Raina stamped her feet to get the circulation going as the first paltry rays of sunlight skimmed the ground. Her shift was almost over. She had spent the night on guard duty with Sawyer, who, despite his running conversation pretty much the entire time, was a vigilant sentry.

"So she figures there's no one in there, right? But I'm hiding behind the crate, just waiting to jump out and scare her," Sawyer said, his voice tinged with laughter, his body shifting as he scanned the perimeter. "So she backs it up and lets rip the biggest, loudest fart I ever heard."

"What?" Raina couldn't help the snort of laughter that escaped. "She didn't."

"Yeah. She did. And I'm standing back there, nearly knocked off my feet, wondering if I jump out and literally scare the shit out of her, or if I crawl into the woodwork and pretend the whole thing never happened."

"Oh, God. I'll never look at Alba the same way again. So what did you do?"

Sawyer grinned. "I spent the next three weeks making farting sounds every time I saw her, and the funny thing is, she never caught on. I had to *explain* it to her."

"You know, Sawyer, you deserved whatever you got." Raina shook her head. "Hiding in the dark like that."

"Yeah—" He broke off, and his gaze shifted, hardened. "We have incoming."

Raina squinted at the horizon, tension knotting in her belly. She focused on the dark shape, a tiny speck that grew in size as it drew nearer the encampment. She couldn't stop the hope that swelled inside her.

Within a few moments she recognized the battered truck that had followed Wizard when he left the rebel camp. Raina swallowed her disappointment as she realized that the black snowscooter wasn't anywhere in sight. From the corner of her eye, she watched the arrival of the truck even as she searched the horizon for some sign of Wizard.

She murmured the appropriate salutation to Sawyer when Jake and Alba came to relieve them, sent him a jaunty wave as he walked off. Her gaze slid to Alba, then away, and she bit back the laughter that surfaced.

After taking a few steps toward her rig, she paused to scan the flat plain, and then turned toward the center of the enclave. The driver of the truck, a man she recognized from the day of her arrival at the camp, climbed out from behind the wheel and strode around to the back. He was lean, handsome, tough, his face scarred by a jagged line that marked his jaw.

Trey. His name was Trey. She remembered that now.

He'd been gone most of the time that she'd been here, so she hadn't had a chance to get to know him at all. His brown eyes swept her, flat and hard. She shivered, wondering what had scarred his face—and his soul.

He pulled down the tailgate, and a small horde of rag-swathed children tumbled out onto the frozen ground, a lop-eared mutt racing between their feet, barking sharply. Raina stared at the dog. She knew that animal. It belonged to the vagabond children they had left at Bob's Truck Stop. She shook her head in amazement.

The leader of the ragged little group, Ben, stood off to one side scanning the perimeter of the camp, watching, assessing. Always on the lookout for danger. His gaze settled on Raina, and he strode toward her. She kept her features neutral, but it was an effort. The kid looked like he'd been shot through a plasma cannon face-first.

He jerked his head in the direction of the truck. "You sent them for us. That guy Trey, and the other one, Juan." He wasn't asking.

"Nope. Not me." She noticed that he didn't mention Wizard, and she didn't mention the fact that she'd thought of these lost children, that she'd intended to return to Bob's and search for them once the rebel funds were in her account. It seemed that someone had beat her to the rescue, and she had a feeling she knew exactly who that someone was.

Assassin, mercenary, bleeding heart . . . Wizard was one strange combination, and he'd earned a big fat bonus point going back for these kids, she thought ruefully.

"Not you? Thought it had to be you . . . you left us

that crate of food and all. No one ever done nothing nice for us before." Ben eyed her sharply for a second through his right eye. The left one was swollen shut, and the skin was a mottled mélange of purple, yellow, and brown. Then he shrugged. His lip was split, and his right arm was curled around his side as though he was babying his ribs, and as he moved he winced.

"So, what rig did you jump in front of?" she asked, keeping her tone light, though her insides twisted at the thought of the pain that had been inflicted on him. She'd been beaten more than once herself, and she wasn't sure what was worse: the physical pain or the agony of being too weak, too helpless to stop it.

"The Janson got me." He turned away, his gaze fixed on the dog as it ran between the children's legs, barking and leaping excitedly. "But not a rig. A fist. Or two." He paused. "And a couple of boots."

Raina sucked in a breath, hoping that Ben hadn't suffered on her account or on Wizard's, but suspecting he had.

"They were looking for you," Ben said softly, confirming the worst. "Raina Bowen. That's you, right?"

They were looking for her. She hadn't expected that, hadn't been prepared for it. *Frig.* The Janson were a lot more tenacious than she'd expected, and that boded ill for her.

Sam had taught her never to give information away for free, so she let Ben's question slide by unanswered, neither confirming nor denying her identity. "I'm assuming they ended up looking worse than you," she said instead. "What did you do? Break their heads, or just rough them up a bit?"

Ben looked at her incredulously. "There were six

Janson. Big bastards. They took turns. Wouldn't have caught me in the first place, but Rui"—he jutted his chin in the direction of the group of kids who stood by the truck, wincing as he moved his sore jaw—"Rui wasn't fast enough. It was him or me, and he's my responsibility. You know. My crew. No one whacks my crew."

So Ben had sacrificed himself for one of the other kids, the little one. She nodded. "So you took on six Janson."

"Yeah. And nearly beat 'em too," he bragged. But there was a catch in his voice, and Raina knew that this episode had decimated his carefully cultivated bravado. Ben glanced at her, his expression stark. "There was another guy with them. He had this patch over one eye and a big scar right down the side of his face. *Slag*, it was bad enough, all those fists and feet knocking me around. But that guy . . ."

Raina's heart twisted in her chest, and she lost her breath. A patch over one eye. Duncan Bane. He was here, in the Waste, and he was looking for her.

"He never raised a finger. Just stood off to one side . . . But he liked it, that guy. He really liked it when they hit me. Every time they landed a punch I could hear him laughing . . . soft . . . low." He paused, and then continued in a whisper. "He liked it, got off on it. You know?"

She understood, and the thought made her sick.

"How'd you get away?" She didn't need to ask if he knew that they would have beaten him to death if they'd had the chance, just for the sport of it. He already knew. A kid like him definitely knew.

Just as she'd known all those years ago, Duncan

Bane's hand shoved down her pants, his other arm tight around her throat, choking her. She'd been twelve years old, and she'd known, even though he'd promised to let her go when he was done. Yeah, he'd have let her go—straight into a hole in the ground, her throat slit from ear to ear. Only he'd have had his fun first. Beaten her. Cut her.

Exactly what he'd do if he caught her now, only this time he wouldn't make it last a single night. He'd make it go on and on until night blended into day and day into night, and all she would ever know was suffering.

The breath left her in a rush as she tore her thoughts away from that dangerous path. There was nothing to be found in her memories, and even less to be found in guessing at what might be.

"I pretended I was out for the count," Ben said. "They wanted me awake. Awake and screaming. Slag, the second their attention wandered, I was up and running. I live and breathe that territory. I'm fast. And I'm skinny. Lots of places for a fast, skinny mouse to hide."

"Yeah. You did good." She glanced at him, and he shrugged at her praise, though she sensed that he was pleased.

"Do you think they'll find that girl they were looking for?" she asked, tense.

"Oh, yeah. I told them exactly where she went." Ben nodded sagely. "I took my time. Like they were forcing it out of me. Then I told 'em. South. Raina Bowen went south. Said she was heading for the Equatorial Band. Something about wanting to see sunshine."

Raina blinked, and then she smiled at him. He

started to grin back, stopped short, and winced as he pressed his fingertips to his swollen lip. "Not my fault I have a lousy sense of direction. Never could tell my right from my left. North from south."

The yippy little dog darted over and wove between their ankles, then tore off again as one of the kids summoned him. "Come on, Spike! Time to eat."

"Spike?" Raina laughed.

Ben stared at her for a minute, then punched her lightly in the shoulder, a gesture of camaraderie. Turning away, he swaggered to the front of the pack and led his crew inside, out of the cold, as Trey enticed them with offers of hot food and warm shelter.

Huddled in her parka, Raina let the wind swirl about her body and watched them go. She was not ready to follow the group indoors. She still needed time. Time to feel. Time to think. Duncan Bane had come to the Waste, and he would not rest until he found her.

Terror was an endless, frigid pit, and she refused to let herself fall in.

Swallowing, she let her gaze roam slowly across the horizon again. The time of reckoning for a long-ago night had finally arrived. So many years she had spent watching over her shoulder, knowing that he was out there just waiting for the moment of his choosing. But why now? Why search her out now that Sam was dead?

"Ah," she said aloud, her thoughts clearing. Yes. That explained it. *Now that Sam was dead.* Bane was a dichotomy, a man with an impatient temper, but he was also a master of strategy. If the idea took him, he would plan and wait and watch, then enjoy every minute of his revenge. Closing her eyes, she remembered his face, the horrible feel of his rough hands, the too-sweet smell of his breath.

She remembered the blood, the sharp metallic tang, the warm spatter of it across her own cheek, and his howl of pain and rage, animalistic in its intensity. The sound had followed her into the night as she fled his luxurious chamber, a twelve-year-old girl running half-naked into the darkness to escape the fate her father had traded her into.

Sam hadn't been much of a father, but he'd been all she had. Now, with him dead, she was truly alone.

Alone. Bane would like that. It was why he had finally come for her.

"Straighten. Turn. Throw." Raina rose from her crouched position, spun, aimed, and tossed her knife all in a single fluid motion. Her blade sank into the large rag-filled sack that rested on the crumbling wall.

Ben whistled through his teeth, shaking his head as he strode over to pull her knife from the heart-shaped target they had drawn on the sack. "You ever miss?"

He handed the knife back to her, hilt first.

Raina thought of her own years of training. For each miss she'd been rewarded with Sam's slap. "I try not to."

"Try not to? We've been going at this for hours and hours every day this week. You haven't missed once." Ben rubbed his nose with the back of one gloved hand.

You miss, you die. Sam would have cuffed her for a miss, and he'd have done a lot worse to see her here, hanging around the rebel camp training a group of snot-nosed kids, even though her funds must have cleared days ago. Hell, she hadn't even checked . . . it was almost as though she was latching on to an excuse to stay. She couldn't explain why she was still here, not to herself and not to anyone else.

Pathetic. She was pathetic.

She thought of Yuriko's plant, a gift from one friend to another, thought of Yuriko's request that she stay, at least for a little while. At least until Wizard returned.

Was that what she was waiting for?

Frig. She was letting these people break down her wall, and she knew, she just knew with icy, gut-churning certainty, that it was a really bad idea.

"Again," she told Ben as she crossed to the sack and settled it in place on the low wall. He sent her a mutinous glare, and she thought he might argue, but after a second he trudged back into place and hunkered down with his back to the target.

Raina's gaze flicked to the horizon, searching the stark, frozen line. Nothing stirred, and she turned away, moving to safer territory lest Ben throw his knife wide and carve a chunk out of her hide. She squelched the feeling of disappointment that surged in her breast. No sign of Wizard. Maybe he was never coming back.

"You looking for him again? Don't you ever get tired of watching the same boring, flat plane?"

She turned and found Ben facing her, watching her. The bruising around his eye had faded to a nice shade of puke green, and the swelling on his lip had gone down. He looked almost normal, especially now that his swagger had returned and the chip on his shoulder had grown back to boulder-sized proportions.

"Looking for who?" Raina asked, immediately realizing that it was the wrong answer. She should have told Ben to drop and give her twenty for daring to move off subject. The topic of the day was how to throw a knife through a man's heart. It was a handy skill to have. She frowned as the kid grinned.

Then his gaze flickered and focused on a point over her shoulder. Raina felt her heart constrict, then swell, and she knew that if she turned she would see it, a black snowscooter flying across the rimed tundra.

"That's enough for today." Her voice was a hoarse whisper.

Ben's grin widened as he crossed and handed her the knife. "Wanna go wait for him over there?"

She followed his gaze to where Yuriko, Trey, and Juan stood talking and waiting, their attention fixed on Wizard as he rode steadily closer.

"I'm not waiting for him." She thrust the spare knife into the sheath in her boot.

"Okay." If Ben grinned any wider, his lip would split open again.

Raina turned away and headed for her rig. She kept her eyes focused straight ahead, refusing to turn and check on Wizard's progress, refusing to acknowledge the tiny thrill that blossomed inside of her. He was back. And he was dangerous. Not to her physical self, but to the emotions she'd worked so hard to bury all these years. He made her *feel*. He made her *want*.

She keyed in her code and slapped open the door to the rig. Pausing, she let her gaze wander to where the others stood, let herself watch as Wizard rode into the camp and pulled the snowscooter into a tight arc before stopping directly in front of Yuriko. The woman's face lit up in a smile of welcome. Raina's insides twisted, wringing envy in fat, heavy drops that puddled and spread until she thought it would make her retch.

Wizard's attention was riveted on the commander as he climbed from the scooter. Raina knew what it felt like to be the recipient of that studied, intent concentration. His eyes were focused on Yuriko as though he saw nothing else. Together they strode into a nearby building.

Well, there you go. He hadn't even spared a glance to check whether she was around. Raina turned away, pulling off her parka with short, jerky movements, angry with herself for feeling things she had no business feeling. Angry with Wizard because he obviously didn't feel them.

She was losing her frigging mind.

TWELVE

Unable to sit and do nothing, Raina wrapped herself in two layers of thermal gear, which, according to the ad-vid, was designed to wick moisture from her body while keeping her toasty warm. *Right.* Like she ever felt warm here in the subzero zone. She closed the zip-seam on her insulated joggers, focused her thoughts on a workout, and left the rig.

An inky, star-flecked saucer of sky hung over the camp. Legs pumping, arms moving in synchronized rhythm, she began to run. Three laps, five. Now her mind was emptying, the emotions she didn't want to deal with fading away as the physical sensation of working her muscles took over. She forced herself to think of nothing but the smooth flow of her limbs as she ran, let herself forget time and place.

Made herself forget the man who haunted her every thought.

One more lap, she told herself, even though she'd told herself the exact same thing five laps ago. Maybe if she worked herself to the point of complete physical exhaustion she'd be able to exorcise the weird bug that had taken over her rational thought processes and made her jealous to the point of actual pain.

She wanted Wizard in the worst way, but that wasn't the problem. The problem was that she'd missed him. Missed talking to him. Missed seeing the tiny hint of a smile that she managed to drag out of him. If she just wanted him in the physical sense, she could see her way clear to spending one raunchy night in his arms and then leaving without a backward glance.

Yeah, she wanted to jump him, but she wanted to just be with him too. The thing was, she couldn't bring herself to strut into Yuriko's territory to take him. *Frig.* The first real friend she'd ever had, and the woman just had to have a prior claim on the man Raina wanted.

As she rounded a corner, she saw the two of them from a distance. They walked the perimeter of the camp, heads bent close, joined in whispered conversation. Whatever they discussed, Raina wasn't privy to it, and a cold blade of resentment sliced through her. She'd bet anything that Yuriko and Wizard shared history, though neither of them had given any hint about whatever was between them. Still, the aura of tension that hovered about them like a swarm of nasty little blackflies in the spring gave it away. Forcing herself to keep moving, she ran on, aware of Wizard turning slowly as she passed, his eyes locked on her.

She meant to just run. She meant to ignore him, to not even turn her head the tiniest bit. But she betrayed herself, her gaze sliding to his, and she lost her breath as she saw her own hot need mirrored in his expression.

What the hell? He was walking with one woman, lusting after another. And absolute idiot that she was, she felt glad that he'd stopped midconversation and turned to follow her movements with harsh yearning etched on his face.

Then she felt guilty because she didn't want to hurt Yuriko.

Frowning, she realized that the other woman was watching the exchange with what could only be described as outright amusement. So *would* it hurt Yuriko if Raina hooked up with Wizard? Wasn't it Yuriko who had urged her to stay put until his return?

Maybe, for Yuriko, whatever the two of them had been to each other really was buried in the past.

Her concentration lost, Raina gave up on her run. She slowed to a lope, and then stalked to her rig. Her chest was inflating and deflating like a bellows, and she could feel the sweat trickling down her back. With a frustrated sigh, she climbed up and headed straight for her shower and min-dry, stripping off her clothes as she went, wanting the pounding spray on her skin. She'd wash her running gear afterward.

Turning on the water, she stepped under the steady stream and sighed as the spray sluiced over her. She reached for the soap, working a thick lather in her hands and then on her body as she rubbed her belly, her breasts, the curve of her buttocks, all the while wishing it were Wizard touching her, stroking her, making her throb and ache.

A soft sound, no more than a breath of warning,

made her gasp. He was here. She could sense it. Wizard had broken into her rig.

Again.

"Raina." He said her name, just her name, but his tone, rasping and low with lust, made her shiver.

Slowly, so slowly, she turned to face him. He stood just outside the shower stall, his hair hanging straight and thick about his muscled shoulders, his eyes glittering in the glow of the lumi-light as he stared at her. Eyes like molten silver, bright against the dark fringe of lashes, intent, hungry, heavy lidded with primal need. He was frightening in his beauty, the marcasite beads woven in his hair, the forbidden tattoo circling the lean, sinuous muscle that corded his arm.

"How did you get in here?" she asked. Did it matter? Did she care? He was here, naked, the hard, thick length of his erection jutting forward, and all she wanted was to touch him and rub herself against him.

"There is no lock that can hold against me, no barrier I cannot breach." His words, spoken in that delicious, low, masculine tone, were no braggart's claim, but a simple truth.

He was very good at that. At penetrating barriers. At telling the truth.

She stared up at him and in that moment she knew exactly what she felt. Not love. Oh, no. What fairy tale was she drifting through? It was hot, heavy, raunchy lust. She wanted to curl her fingers around the solid strength of his body, sink her teeth into his warm flesh, taste him, lick him, bite him, fill herself with him. And from the look on his face, he was feeling it in equal measure.

Eyes never leaving hers, Wizard stepped into the

small shower stall, filling the space, the heat of him coming over her like a mist. The corners of his mouth kicked up in a hard, masculine smile. Knowing. Hungry. That smile drew her, puckering her nipples, twisting the knot of desire in her belly until she gasped and lurched at him to press her lips to his, frenzied, wet. Angling his head, he opened his mouth on hers, took her lower lip between his teeth and bit her just hard enough to make her moan, hard enough to make her clutch his shoulders and sway against him.

He ran his hand along her arm, leaving a tingling path of sensation in his wake. In a brief and subtle tease he clasped his fingers with hers, and then dragged the soap from her grasp.

The weight of his body pressed her against the cool tile, and the tips of his fingers trailed over her lips, her chin, her breast. He took her nipple between his fingers, pulling, twisting gently, then harder, and he kissed her, openmouthed, deep. The taste of him— clean arctic air. Cool, fresh.

A sigh of disappointment escaped her as he pulled back and dropped his hand to work the soap in his blunt, strong fingers, raising a lather that she expected he would rub on her heated flesh. But he didn't touch her. Instead, he braced one palm against the shower wall and, eyes never leaving hers, he wrapped his free hand around the hard, heavy length of his erection, working the soap along the broad crown and thick shaft in slow, smooth strokes.

Wanting—no, *needing* to touch him, she reached out, tracing her finger along the soapy tip of his cock, the contact sending a sharp twist of desire biting deep, so intense it bordered on pain.

He jerked his hips, and she closed her hand around his, her fingers gliding between his, slick, hot, her breath coming in shallow huffs, in and out, the tempo matching the slide and stroke of her hand on his shaft. A raw groan dragged from deep inside of him, the sound making her shudder.

Too much. She wanted him so badly it was crazy, scary. Everything in her screamed that this was a mistake. There was no future in this.

No, that was *good*. No future. Just the *now*.

She would get her money. She would leave. He had to know that.

Breathing hard, Raina reached out of the shower stall and yanked open the drawer beside the sink. She pulled out a small oblong instrument, jammed her thumb into the hole at the top, and waited impatiently for the light to flash green. "Blood-borne pathogen and STD detector," she muttered, pretty sure he had to know what it was. "I'm clean."

She handed the instrument to Wizard. He pushed his thumb into the hole, and the light flashed, declaring that he, too, was disease free.

Narrowing his eyes, he tossed the thing aside and slapped the flat of his palm against the smooth tile at her back. She turned to the opposite side, only to realize that his hand was already braced against the shower wall. She was trapped, and she liked it. Liked the feel of his hard body pressing down on hers, liked the way he watched her with a scintillating intensity that promised ecstasy.

Anticipation ratcheted through her.

"What would you have done if the light had flashed red?"

"Killed you," Raina whispered. And she half meant it.

"Fertility?" he rasped.

"Not for nine more days. We're good to go." Thank God for modern science.

She caught his wrists, pressed them back and down until she held them tight to the wall, low at his hips, the warm water pouring over them like a curtain. He made no protest. Leaning his head to hers, he pushed his tongue in her mouth, sucking, biting, leaving her feeling shivery and hot and darkly excited.

Rearing back, she licked her lips, catching beads of water. She wanted to lick *him*, suck him, taste the salt of his skin, feel the velvet weight of his shaft in her mouth. She wanted to breach his icy wall, to splinter his cool control. If she were going to steal the pleasure of this one encounter before she left, she was determined to make it memorable.

She kissed his neck, his chest, sinking to her knees to press her lips to the ridged muscle of his belly, all the while holding his hands pressed to the wall, though, in truth, she knew it was only anticipation that bound him in place. He rocked his hips, up and forward, and she took his cock in her mouth, sucking him inside, wet, liquid, slathering him with her tongue, scraping her teeth along the sensitive skin. And each time he thrust toward her, the power, the pleasure, spiraled up. A thrill arced through her as she realized that she had brought this cool, controlled man outside the boundary of his natural restraint.

Letting his head fall back against the wet tile, Wizard closed his eyes and groaned, lost in the pleasure of her mouth, sensation driving him, making him shudder as his balls tightened with the effort of holding himself back.

He caught her wrists, dragging her up until she stood facing him. He was desperate now to have her, and uneasy with that desperation. She made him ache, made him *feel*, not just the throb of his cock but the beat of his heart and the swell of something warm and unfamiliar. Confusing.

Affection. Tenderness. He shoved at those emotions, thrusting them toward the compartment he had assigned them. This was sex. Just sex.

With a groan he pulled her against him, shoved his fingers up into her, primitive, crude, the heel of his palm pressed against the sensitive nub of her desire. She cried out and bucked against him, rocking into his touch and squirming, wet and slick, her passion enhancing his own.

She ran her hands over his body, raking her nails along his skin. With a growl he caught her hips, lifting her and pulling her against him, sliding his hand along the tender skin of her thigh and wrapping her leg around his waist. She read his intent, braced one hand on his shoulder, pushing herself up until she was the right height. He guided his penis between her legs and thrust up into her, a rough motion, into the slick, hot core of her body. She hissed as he palmed her breast, kneading it, squeezing the nipple between his thumb and forefinger until it puckered and swelled. Dipping his head, he took her in his mouth, drawing on her hard, and all the while he moved inside her, his hands on her hips shifting her against him, adding to the friction and heat in a way that made her gasp and cry out.

Wizard gritted his teeth, focusing on the feel of her. He hooked his arm under her knee and gripped her buttocks, pumping slow, long strokes as he set the pattern. She was trembling, shuddering, tilting her hips to pull him deeper, hold him tighter, and it took everything he had to set a slow, rhythmic pace.

"Shhh. There's no rush," he whispered, kissing the hollow of her throat.

"There is." She gasped. "A rush. God, I'm so hot. You're so . . ." A shudder rippled through her frame, and she thrust against him. "You're so hard. . . ."

Breath panting from between parted lips, Raina pressed the sole of one foot against the slick wall of the shower, seeking purchase as she squirmed against him, her hands clutching the steely muscles of his shoulders. He seemed content to take his time, his pace meant to tease and torment and feed the dark lust that burned inside her. She was so close, poised on the edge, and still he drew out their pleasure, each deliberate stroke dragging her deeper into a mindless, clawing hunger, holding her prisoner to her own frantic need.

Her vision blurred, and in a frenzy she sank her teeth into his neck, sucking, biting.

His rhythm unraveled, collapsed, and he gripped her buttocks tighter, drove into her faster, harder, taking them both into a sharp, swift spiral. A low cry tore from her throat, her muscles trembling as she convulsed around him, her fingers curled into his shoulders, her head thrown back as she screamed her release.

The feel of her convulsing around him drove him to the brink, and he crashed over, great, surging waves radiating from his loins, ripping away the layers of his control as he came with a primitive groan.

For a long time he stood there, holding her with her back braced against the wall, and he was still shuddering, jerking. Finally he let her slide down along his body, her weight coming to rest on her own limbs.

"I think I need a shower," she whispered, her lips moving on his neck.

Startled, he laughed.

"I love your laugh." She kissed him on the mouth.

I love your laugh. Wizard blinked, shocked by the way her casually tossed words made him feel, and he had the irrational urge to drag her against his chest, hold her tight, and explain everything.

If he did that, she would likely try to kill him.

He frowned. He had built his plan on solid logic. She was the only thing in the world that could draw Duncan Bane from his fortress. She was the key to justice. If he told her who he was, what he was, she would see only betrayal. She would hate him. That end was certain.

The fact that he had never meant to hurt her would not matter.

Raina turned, reset the temperature of the water, and retrieved the soap. "Yeah. I definitely need a shower."

She sent him a jaunty grin over her shoulder, and he felt a sharp twist in the center of his chest. Emotion. Dangerous emotion.

He had no idea what to do with it.

But the spark she ignited with that grin and the wicked twinkle in her eyes . . . he knew what to do with those.

Reaching past her to close off the faucet, he took the soap from her hand, set it aside, and caught her about the waist. He swung her around, opening his mouth on hers in a deep kiss that spilled through him, through her, taking his time as he moved her to the bed and tumbled them both onto the sheets. His need was building as though they had not just made love, emotion inspiring his every touch.

"I'm wet," she murmured, though as a protest it lacked conviction. As he reached down to stroke between her legs, she gave a strangled laugh. "I meant I'm wet from the shower."

"So am I." He bit the side of her neck, gently, so gently, touching her with unhurried caresses, building her passion in a slow climb that made her moan and sigh.

He worked the broad head of his penis into her. Smooth. Tight. Slick. So hot and wet, he was undone. He thrust deeper, faster, feeling her approaching climax in the tightening of her body, and the panting gasps that tore from her lips. She gave a low cry, and he felt the contractions of her release pulsing through her, through him, dragging him with her, the pleasure ramping through his veins to his cock. He clamped his teeth together, thrust into her once, deep, and held still. He lost his breath, his sight, his grasp of reality. There was only the pleasure, the endless pleasure of her.

With a sated sigh, Raina wrapped her arms around him, holding tight as he lowered his weight full against her, nuzzling her hair, her cheek. Rolling to one side, he pulled her against him, cradling her in the warm curve of his body.

Eyes closed, she sucked in a slow breath, let it out, and realized that she was *warm*. Blissfully, beautifully warm.

It was a long time before she opened her eyes, and when she did, she found him watching her. For an instant she wondered exactly what she saw etched in the sculpted planes of his face, the glittering depths of his eyes. He tugged the quilt up to cover her.

"Thank you," she whispered.

"You're welcome." There was smug satisfaction in his voice.

She slapped his arm. "I meant for covering me with the quilt."

"I would be happy to cover you anytime."

Glad to hear it, she thought, and smiled. "A joke," she murmured.

"One that made you smile." She could tell he was pleased by that. The guy didn't ask for much.

She lay there, incredibly relaxed, and then reality slunk within the circle of her contentment. She had lowered her barriers, opened a tiny corner of her emotions to this man, and she didn't even know his name. *Hell.* Her brain was fried.

"Um, Wizard . . . what . . ." She took a breath. "What's your name? Your real name?"

He studied her, looking faintly baffled.

"Your *real* name . . ." she prompted.

"Wizard is my name."

"Your parents named you Wizard?"

A small hesitation. "No."

"So you changed your name to Wizard? Legally?"

"No."

Pushing herself up on one elbow, she stared at him. "I can keep asking questions. And you can keep grunting one-word answers at me. Or you can just tell me. I'd like it better if you just tell me."

This time the hesitation was longer, long enough that it left her feeling deflated and a little sad. Then he said, "My assigned registration number is WZRD839. I chose the name Wizard. It seemed appropriate." He shifted so his tattoo was in her line of sight. "If you look carefully, you can see the original letters and numbers. Though I took time with the design, I could not eradicate the remnants of my registration number."

Appalled, Raina lifted one hand to trace her fingertips over the tattooed pattern that circled his arm. "You mean that you didn't have a name? That you were only a number?"

He nodded once. "Affirmative." His tone held no rancor, his expression no self-pity. She marveled at his composure.

"What about your parents?"

"I know nothing of my progenitors. I was one of several experimental progeny in a lab of the Old Dominion. The testing was inconclusive, the experiment terminated under unexpected conditions."

Raina stared at him, uncertain that she had heard him correctly, unable to process what he was telling her. He was an experiment. *God.* She couldn't wrap her thoughts around it. Still, something nagged at her, a story she'd heard here and there over the years about an Old Dominion experiment gone wrong. She'd thought it a tall tale parents told their kids to keep them in line. "What unexpected conditions?"

"War." He shrugged. "When Sam Bowen found us, he instructed us to choose names in order to more effectively integrate into society."

"You said 'us.' Who is 'us'?" She shook her head. "And you said *Sam*. What the hell does Sam have to do with this?"

"I was one of three subjects who survived."

She shivered, feeling faintly ill. One of three subjects. He talked about himself as though he weren't even human. But she knew he was. Whatever his origins were, whatever lab he'd been grown in, he was still a human being. She had seen him treat those vagabond children with kindness. She knew he would do anything to protect the rebel camp, even from her. She had lain beneath him, felt the desire rise in him, known the tenderness of his touch.

She had seen him bleed.

He was a human being.

But she understood the unspoken undercurrent that she sensed he held inside. She truly did. Sometimes, when the nightmares got too real, when she had to do things she could barely face just to survive, she doubted her own humanity.

In a way they were kindred spirits. Wizard showed no emotion, and maybe he truly didn't feel any, but she thought he did. She was adept at Sam's teachings, adept at masking her feelings. That didn't mean she didn't feel; it meant only that she'd been trained not to acknowledge it. Was Wizard like her?

Too hard to ask those questions. Instead she whispered, "And Sam? What does Sam have to do with this?"

"Sam Bowen was the commander of the squad that found us in an underground government facility in the desert region of a place once known as Nevada. With the Second Noble War came nuclear destruction and the fall of the Old Dominion. The facility was buried. Forgotten."

Buried. Forgotten. Like the crazy, outlandish stories she'd heard. "Frigging hell. Are you telling me the stories are true? That you grew up in a lab, raised by a computer?" She choked on the next words, because she knew that he was telling her exactly that. "That you were buried alive and the corpses of your siblings were stored in the freezer?"

"Affirmative, with one correction. Not all of the original subjects were my genetic siblings, although all three who survived share genetic material."

Raina sat up, raising her knees to her chest, clutching the quilt about her throat as though it would protect her from this horror. She reached out and laid a tentative touch on his forearm. He looked down, staring at her hand, his expression puzzled.

"Ah," he said, raising his eyes to meet hers. "Do you offer comfort?"

"Do you want my comfort?" She felt completely ill at ease, uncertain how to proceed. Emotional interactions were not her forte. Normally she'd be the last person to offer solace to anyone, but for some reason she wanted to offer it to Wizard.

"There is no need. I merely relay historical facts, Raina."

She shook her head and began to pull her hand away, but he stopped her, placing his large, square palm on top of her smaller one. He watched her warily, subtly shifting away from her and sitting up to rest his back against the wall even as he held her hand in place. It was as if he didn't know whether to withdraw or to draw near, to seek comfort from her or to push her aside. Damn, but she could swear that he was as confused as she was.

Wizard tapped one finger rhythmically on the back of her hand. Raina watched the subtle movement, noticing it, and wondering why she did. He'd done it before, when the ice pirates had first arrived and their rigs had shown on her radar. And another time, perhaps, though she couldn't place it.

"The New Government Order told Sam to leave us. That resources should not be wasted repairing errors of the Old Dominion."

"Leave you?" Raina thought she would be sick. Someone had ordered Sam to leave those children, to leave Wizard, in a nightmare cell. A hell of the government's making. "Who would do that?"

"Duncan Bane."

She sucked in a breath. *Yes, I have something against Mr. Bane.*

Well, no frigging wonder.

"Sam refused." Wizard met her gaze, his gray eyes flat, distant. "I remember hearing his words through the wall, muffled. There was something in his tone that was foreign to me. I had never heard anger, but now I know that Sam was angry. And afraid. He dug us out and paid a heavy price. I am sorry, Raina. It was the events of that day, and everything that followed, that turned Sam Bowen into the father you knew. I should have explained sooner. Before we . . ."

She felt him withdraw, felt him pull away and seal himself behind a wall as surely as if he had removed himself physically. He shifted and her hand dropped away, landing on the quilt, breaking the connection.

"Don't you do that. Don't you dare do that." She

couldn't bear for him to pull away, and she couldn't understand why. Normally she preferred to maintain a healthy distance, but with Wizard she wanted to touch him, to feel the warmth of his skin.

He made her glad to be alive, glad to be human, to be able to feel and think. And make love. Glad just to be with him.

Frigging pathetic. A man who was almost a machine made her feel human. There was something so wrong with this picture.

He stared at her for so long that she wondered if he even understood what she meant. And then he took her hand in his and said, "My apologies."

"I don't want apologies. I want some kind of explanation. What price did Sam pay?" She wiggled her fingers, lacing them with his.

"The New Government Order did not take kindly to a commander who refused to follow orders. Sam took us out of there, brought us into the world." Wizard shook his head. "In one sense he saved us. In another, he condemned us to a hell more terrible than the one we were living. In order to achieve our full potential we were subjected to—" He stopped and shook his head.

"Tell me," Raina insisted, feeling that she had to know. There was something here that was significant to her . . . the price . . . Wizard . . . Sam . . . There was something here. "Tell me."

"We could not integrate. Could not find our place in the world we were thrust into. Our emotions were not developed. We could not understand human interaction. We were raised by a computer after the scientist in charge of the experiment died, and each of us functioned as an entity driven by logic. Duncan Bane initially saw no value in us, and so Sam Bowen paid the price of his disobedience."

"What price?" Raina whispered, her eyes fixed on his.

"He paid for our lives with the lives of those he loved. Your mother's life." She felt as though he had punched her, her gut clenching as he said the words. "And Bane intended to exact payment of your life as well."

"But I wasn't there that day, so I survived," she whispered. "So why didn't they try again? Why didn't they kill me? Kill Sam?"

"Once the Order realized our value as assassins, killing machines—no conscience, no remorse—Sam was spared, though he received a dishonorable discharge from duty."

She'd thought her father had gone mad, chased by demons after her mother's death. But now she understood there had been more to it than that. Wizard's words explained so very much. Suddenly her world shifted, tilting wildly on its axis and leaving her with more questions than she had started with. The worst of it was, she no longer felt certain that she wanted the answers.

"I am . . . sorry, Raina." Wizard's voice was low, and the words sounded hesitant, as though wrenched from deep inside him.

"You called yourself a killing machine with no conscience and no remorse." She felt the tears creeping down her cheeks, and she raised her gaze to find him watching her. Everything he had told her, everything she knew about him collided inside of her with a resounding crash. "When I first realized you were an assassin, I thought that. But I know now it isn't true. So don't say it. Don't you ever say that. You are not a machine. You have emotions. You *do* have a conscience."

"I am an assassin."

"Who have you *assassinated* lately? Not killed in self-defense or protecting the innocent. *Assassinated*. Killed in cold blood for personal gain," she demanded. "There's a difference."

He said nothing.

A hollow laugh escaped her. "We make a fine pair. A man who has a computer chip instead of a heart, and a woman whose emotions were beaten out of her." She rubbed the back of her hand across her eyes, dashing away her treacherous tears. What the hell was wrong with her? Great sex had turned on an invisible faucet and she was watering worse than a leaky pipe.

"You know something? I've never killed anyone." She shrugged. "Not even Sam, though for a long time I felt like it was my fault he died. I guess he believed that making me tough was the only way to keep me alive. In the end, he gave his life for me. He acted as a decoy so I could escape. Ice pirates. Reavers. They caught him and killed him. I've been living with the memory, with the belief that in a way, *I* killed him. If I'd been faster, or stronger, or smarter . . ." She trailed off, uncertain of exactly what she had been trying to say. "I just ran when he told me to, like I did in every training exercise we ever did, and then he was dead."

Wizard tapped his fingers on the quilt. "Emotions are foreign to me, yet I find that I do not want this to cause you distress. Raina, I have some . . . some *attachment* to you. There is no logic in it, but I find that . . ." He paused, took a breath, then said, "I like you."

He liked her. *Frig.* She liked him, too. More than liked him, and that scared the heck out of her. She reached out with her free hand, stilling the tapping of his finger. Raising her gaze, she let her eyes meet his.

"Commander Yuriko has the same habit," Raina whispered. "Tapping her finger when she's thinking. The only outward show of nerves I've seen from either one of you."

Gray eyes.

Thick black hair.

Right. The pieces clicked together like the finest Equatorial Band locking gear. She exhaled a short puff of air. "Let me guess. She's got the same tattoo as you. And her call numbers were . . . ?"

"YRKO339."

Jealous. A snort of laughter escaped her, and then another. She'd been jealous of his relationship with icy, cool Commander Yuriko. She laughed harder, unable to stop. Of all the moronic, half-witted things . . . She'd been jealous of his relationship with his *sister*.

"She's your sister."

"Our maternal and paternal gametes originate from the same subjects."

Raina's breath hissed from between her teeth.

Wizard slid down the wall to lie fully beside her. "She is my sister," he confirmed.

She swallowed. "I'm really glad to hear it." No wonder Yuriko had been so amused by the calf eyes she kept sending at Wizard.

He wrapped one arm across Raina's chest, pulling her close, holding her. For a guy who had no grasp of emotions, he could sure read hers.

"Sleep," he whispered. "Time enough in the morning to face your demons."

Her instinct was to argue, to tell him that she did not need his opinion or advice, that she was not tired, could not possibly sleep after the revelations of the past tension-fraught moments. She wanted to tell him that she'd never let a man sleep in her bed.

Sex was one thing. Letting him stay in her bed was quite another; it implied an intimacy that she wasn't sure she was ready to face. But the steady rise and fall of his chest told her that he was already halfway gone, and after a moment she surprised herself by closing her eyes, the warmth of his body, the strength of him, the weight of his arms wrapped around her leading her into dreamless slumber.

THIRTEEN

Raina awoke to the realization that something was holding her down—a solid, heavy band pressed across her chest. Panic surged, hot and dark, like blood welling from a wound. Forcing herself to take shallow, even breaths, she opened her eyes to mere slits. Sunlight dappled the walls of her cabin. She was home, and it was day.

Memories flooded her, and she realized that the band across her chest was a masculine arm. The insight made her panic swell.

Wizard. He lay on his side in her bed, his forearm tossed across her chest, his breath ruffling her hair. Emotions cascaded through her, and she grappled with the urge to turn in his embrace and enjoy all the hard parts of him that pressed against her. With a sigh, she realized that she had an equally strong inclination to toss him out in the snow, to clear her space and leave it uncluttered by any entanglement.

She bit her lip to stifle a moan, not wanting to wake him just yet. How had he ended up in her bed?

He was in her bed because she'd invited him to be there.

No, not true. She hadn't just invited him; she'd insisted.

The heat of passion warmed her as she remembered the erotic magic he had wrought with his hands, his mouth, every part of him. Oh, this was anything but good. What the hell was she doing hooking up with a New Government Order assassin?

The breath left her in a rush. She was honest enough not to even try to pretend that she could use that as a protective barrier. He wasn't an assassin. Not anymore. He was a man with morals and ethics, with a sense of honor that made him go back for a group of ragtag orphans with no future and no hope. She swallowed, feeling confused and more than a little afraid.

It was bad enough that she'd tumbled into bed with him. It only made it worse that she liked him. Really, really liked him.

Carefully, inch by inch, she moved his arm away. She wanted space, wanted to be far away from him and the temptation he posed. There were too many things that needed sorting out before she could face whatever it was she felt for this strange man who turned her blood into a boiling vat of sheer lust. Despite her morning-after jitters, she smiled at the memory of their lovemaking, unable to stop herself.

At least he'd kept her warm.

She stood for a long moment, watching him, the rise and fall of his chest, the relaxed set of his features. Beautiful . . . he was so beautiful.

And she *so* needed to put some space between them.

Gathering her clothes, she tiptoed to the tiny shower,

making quick use of the pounding water and her blessed min-dry. Dressed, she retrieved her knife, belted it in place, and slipped into her parka.

The fresh morning air felt invigorating as she stepped from the truck. She turned her face into the wind, hoping its frigid bite would help clear her thoughts. That lasted about three seconds, and then she thought better of her plan and pulled her hood close about her face.

"Someday I'll live in the Equatorial Band," she muttered as she strode forward. "And the only wind on my face will be a southern breeze."

Reaching into her pocket she withdrew the dehydrated fruit-and-vegetable bar that she'd grabbed on her way out of the rig. She took a bite and chewed thoughtfully as she crossed the encampment toward the remains of a building from the last century, jagged and broken from years of war and neglect. Finding a sheltered niche, she clambered onto a low wall and leaned back against the cold concrete.

As far as the eye could see there was snow. Ice. And more ice. Raina sighed, finishing the last of her portable breakfast. She really wanted to go somewhere warm. *Yeah.* Somewhere sunny and warm. The heat generated by Wizard in her bed didn't count, because it wasn't permanent.

Okay. Where had that thought come from? She didn't want permanence. She was a loner. The last thing she wanted was someone she'd have to answer to, someone crowding her space. Worse, someone to nurture and care for; hell, even a plant scared her.

Permanence meant ultimate disappointment, and that she could do without.

She chewed, swallowed, the dehydrated bar lodging uncomfortably in her throat.

Glancing up, she found Yuriko standing a few feet away. The commander wore the same amused smile that had tugged at her lips every time she'd watched Wizard and Raina exchanging searing glances. Only now Raina was finally in on the joke.

"How does the plant fare?" Yuriko asked. "Is it flourishing?"

"I haven't killed it yet." Raina patted a place at her side, and Yuriko accepted the silent invitation, gracefully shimmying onto the cold stone.

Raina stared at the horizon. The Waste stretched endlessly in all directions, open, free. She swallowed, thinking of Wizard and Yuriko trapped in a tiny lab for so many long years. "What was it like? How did you manage to . . . to survive without going mad?"

Oddly, Yuriko did not ask what she was talking about. She answered as though Raina's question hadn't simply flown out of nowhere. "Children all over the Northern Waste scrabble and claw for every crumb, fight for their very lives in the harshest of situations, perform surgery on one another or even on themselves, and you ask how *I* survived? I was warm, dry, well fed. The human spirit is bold, Raina. In some, it is nearly unbreakable. Every hardship, every tragedy serves only to forge a stronger being. Such was the way for Wizard, for me."

Forge a stronger being. Was that what hardship had done for her?

"He said there was a third. . . ."

Yuriko looked at her sharply. "He told you of Tatiana?"

"He said very little. Only that there was another child in the lab with the two of you."

Yuriko hesitated, then said, "The story is his to share, Raina. I will tell you only that Tatiana is dead, and her suffering was long and terrible." She sounded infinitely sad, as though the memory of her sister's suffering were imprinted on her own soul.

"I wish . . ." Raina shifted and stared down at the icy ground, uncertain of what she wished. There was no way to change the past, no way to lessen the misery of bereavement.

"Raina Bowen," Yuriko's smooth voice brought her from her painful reverie. "We have visitors."

Her head snapped up, and she followed Yuriko's gaze to a dark smudge that broke the clean, cold line of the winter landscape. Far in the distance—trucks. More than one. More than a dozen, if she read the size of the mass approaching them correctly. Janson? Maybe, but her gut said no.

"Reavers. Twelve trucks. Scaled outer shell. Gun turrets. Plascannons on the lead three," Yuriko said, and for a moment Raina thought she was speaking to her. Then she realized that the Commander was talking into a small lip-com, communicating with her team of rebels.

Reavers. It just had to be frigging Reavers.

Raina felt the sick bite of guilt. In all likelihood, she and Wizard had led them here.

She blinked and stared hard at the horizon. All she could make out was a small, dark blob. The trucks were still so far away that she couldn't even decipher individual shapes, let alone scaling and armaments. Yet Yuriko could see every tiny detail. Her distance vision was unbelievable.

The wind stilled for an instant, and Raina noticed the silence then. The subtle sounds of the encampment—a child's laugh, the tread of the guards' feet on the solid snow—were gone. She looked around and saw no one, no sign of living beings. Even the dogs had vanished from their pen. The rebel camp was locked down, stripped of any observable human presence. Obviously she and Yuriko weren't the only ones to notice the arrival of their uninvited company.

Raina glanced back at the horizon. The dark blob had doubled in size. She suspected that it would be only moments before she would be able to discern the differentiated shapes of the ice pirates' trucks. Her thoughts slid to Ben, his young cohorts, even the dog that was with them, Spike. She remembered the faces of the rebel children she had seen here in the encampment and the faces of their mothers. With a shudder, she pictured them dead.

"Frigging hell. I brought them here. Me. They must have followed my trail. That makes me responsible." Fury welled inside her—at herself for being careless, at the pirates for following her.

Yuriko held up her hand for an instant, barked orders into the lip-com, and said, "Your concerns are acknowledged, but we have been attacked before, when our camp was in a different location." Raina couldn't help but notice how much she sounded like Wizard. "Sometimes, despite our best attempts, the ice pirates find us."

Raina sucked in a breath, weighing the other woman's words. If what Yuriko said was true, then this was not her fight. She ought to just get the hell out of here.

Again an image of Ben's battered face shimmered at the forefront of her thoughts. He'd taken a beating to protect her, a woman he didn't even know. Brave kid. So how was she supposed to live with herself if she did less? She was here in this rebel camp and she'd fight with them, because if she left, and if they died, she would see the children's faces every night in her darkest dreams. Damned if she didn't already have enough demons biting her butt without adding a pack of dead kids to the mix.

With ruthless honesty, she thought of Sawyer and Jake and Alba. They were her friends. She couldn't just walk away and leave them to face this threat. Somehow, without her noticing, these strangers had all become her friends.

She broke into a slow lope, sensing Yuriko's presence just behind her.

"Talen, get the children and elders to safety," Yuriko ordered into her lip-com. "Juan, sniper formation, B-squad, take it to the west quadrant. Robert, Trey, C-squad to me. We have weapons to unload." There was a brief pause, and then she added, "Advance guard, go. Follow sigma protocol." Her voice was tight as she finished, "Live to see peace."

Raina wondered what that was all about as she reached her rig and banged one fist against the side. "Get up, Wizard," she called as she caught hold of the bar on the side door and swung up onto the running board.

"Wizard is no longer within." Something in the other woman's tone made a chill creep up her spine, and she thought of that odd sentence Yuriko had said earlier. *Live to see peace.* As in . . . don't die?

"So, uh, where is he?" Raina asked, feigning non-chalance, though her gut felt as though someone had driven a hot poker right through her center.

"He leads the advance guard."

"The advance guard?" Raina turned slowly to look at Yuriko, disliking the sound of that. The knot in her belly twisted even tighter, and she fought the urge to double over and wrap her arms around herself. It wouldn't stop the pain. And it wouldn't stop Wizard from getting himself killed. Every instinct whispered that he was headed for trouble.

Yuriko stood on the ground just below her, studying the incoming threat. Raina followed her gaze. There were a handful of snowscooters whizzing across the tundra toward the ice pirates. The riders wore no body armor, were offered no protection on the treeless plain, no shelter from the massive gun turrets of the pirates.

Live to see peace. But they wouldn't, Raina thought. Not a single one of them could possibly survive, not mounted on scooters against metal-scaled rigs.

Great. Just great. Talk about a love-'em-and-leave-'em scenario. Before she even had time to decide exactly what the hell she felt for Wizard, he was going to go and get himself blown into tiny blood-drenched shreds.

"Why the hell don't you just call it the suicide squad?" she snarled.

"We do." Yuriko met her gaze, her gray eyes so like Wizard's, cool as polished tungsten.

"And let me guess . . . It's made up exclusively of volunteers." Raina closed her mouth with a snap. In the distance she watched as a group of rebels, guns in hand, ammunition belts strapped across their chests, jogged past. She thought she recognized Trey in the lead, his scarred face set in a resolute expression. C-squad moving to the front line. Would any of them live to see tomorrow?

Her gaze returned to the lethal group of pirate rigs drawing relentlessly closer. The suicide squad—or advance guard, as Yuriko had called them—flew across the ice, just begging for a quick and painful end.

Stupid man. Stupid, stupid man. Wizard was about to get himself blown to shreds. Either that, or he'd be gutted and his intestines fed down his throat. But wait, hadn't she had pretty much these exact thoughts before? *Oh, yeah.* That fateful night when she'd decided to step in and save Wizard from the Janson.

Only he hadn't really needed saving that night.

So why, oh, why did she think he needed saving today?

Because she couldn't just stand here and watch him die. At least if she was out there with him, she could watch his back.

Trying to get yourself killed? Not your fight, girl. Run away. Now.

"Shut up, Sam. You're dead. The least you could do is stop messing with my head," she muttered to herself.

With a low growl, Raina stalked over to the line of rebels that snaked away from a large crate where weapons were being unloaded with ruthless efficiency. She cut in at the front, and when Gerhardt tossed an AT950 at her, she ran a checklist faster than she ever had in her life, slung the huge plasgun over her shoulder, and bolted toward the side of her rig. Hitting the button for her hydraulic lift, she tapped one foot against the hard ground. Her snowscooter took an eternity before it lowered to the ground. She vaulted into the seat and revved the engine.

"Raina."

She looked up to find Yuriko watching her. Raising one hand, the commander made the universal sign of peace. "Be safe, Raina Bowen. Live to see peace."

"And you, Yuriko." Raina smiled ruefully as she returned the simple hand gesture. Imagine that. She'd come this far for her dreams of home, her fantasy of a place to call her own, but instead of the interdollar reward that was supposed to buy it for her, she'd found a man who made her willing to risk her life for a cause, and a whole camp full of people who had offered her a home. She supposed those were rewards in their own right, if she lived long enough to collect them.

Frigging hell.

She swallowed. "Yuriko, if I don't come back . . . if you survive this day . . . send my money to Beth Bowen. She's at the Sheppard School. Tell her . . ." She shook her head. "Tell her nothing." Raina sighed. "You're like Wizard, right? You can break any code, any lock, right? So . . . you find my money, all of it, and you take care of Beth."

"You have my word," Yuriko said, pulling her lip-com off and setting a frequency. She tossed the gear to Raina. "You'll need to communicate if you're to be of any help at all."

Catching the lip-com, Raina slipped it on and tucked the receiver into her ear. She gunned the engine and, leaning low on the scooter, she rode for the horizon and the trucks that loomed like dark beasts against the stark white backdrop of endless frozen plane. Her gaze remained fixed on the leader of the advance guard, the snowscooter way out in front. He was too far away to make a clear identification, but she knew who he was.

Until she resolved exactly what was going on between them, she wasn't about to let Wizard go and get himself killed.

She'd beat him back to life if he did.

Wizard sensed her arrival. His gut clenched with an unfamiliar emotion, and it took him a moment to pinpoint exactly what it was. Anger. Anger at Raina for putting herself in danger. Anger at Yuriko for letting her. Anger at himself for . . . for being angry.

He rubbed one clenched fist against his forehead. Not good. There was no place in the immediacy of his current task for unnecessary emotion. He recognized worry and the sharp hum of excitement. With cold resolve he took his anger and the rest of the unwelcome emotions that bubbled from some dark well inside of him, folded them into tidy rectangles, and filed them away in the appropriate compartments in his mind. He would revisit them at a more appropriate time.

Right now, there was room for only the task at hand. He rapidly calculated trajectories and probabilities even as he tracked Raina's progress across the Waste from the corner of his eye.

He narrowed his eyes in confusion, because a part of him was *glad* she had his back. And that emotion refused to be put in its place.

The other snowscooters were far ahead, having gotten a solid head start. Raina squinted against the sting of the bitter wind and jammed one hand in the pocket of her parka to pull out her antiglare lenses. It was pure dumb luck that she'd taken them with her when she first left the rig that morning. She hoped that luck would hold.

Her speed only made the temperature feel even colder, and her cheeks stung as though hit again and again by a brutal hand. She was close enough now that she could count the trucks, an even dozen of them, barreling forward on thick caterpillar treads, their outer shells reinforced by heavy plates of metal scaling. The steady drone of the massive truck engines thrummed through her body, blending with the beating of her heart.

Her mouth felt dry, and the sick ball that always formed in the pit of her belly right before a fight was there, twisting in a tight little knot.

Reaching back over her shoulder, she grasped the AT950, letting the butt of the gun fill her hand. For a moment she regretted not taking the time to run inside the rig and get her own modified AT850. Hers was a slightly smaller gun, a little older, but her modifications cut the recoil and the delay.

She fought the urge to lick her lips, knowing that if she did, the moisture would freeze instantly and only make the uncomfortable sensation worse. And she fought the acidic urge to puke. She had to be crazy, tearing across the frozen tundra, chasing after . . . what? A man? The dream of glory? Neither option was her style.

Whatever her reasons, they were buried deep enough that she couldn't find them right now. Time enough to ponder her innermost soul later. If she survived.

Sam's voice rang in her head, reminding her that everyone felt fear, but what separated the coward from the hero were knife-edge smarts and the ability to control that fear. Of course, he also taught her that only fools fought battles that weren't their own. Shaking her head, she focused on the first thought. She'd chosen her path today, and she'd see it through to the end, even though her little snowscooter pitted against the hard-shelled tanks was the equivalent of a mosquito against a genetically engineered shaggy-haired mastodon.

Maybe that made her a fool. Or maybe it made her brave. Or maybe it just made her human.

The ground to her right erupted in a spray of jagged ice shards, each one the size of a man's fist. Raina leaned hard to the left and wove the scooter back and forth in an evasive pattern. Plasgun fire. The frigging Reavers were giving them a less than friendly welcome.

"Raina Bowen," Wizard's voice came to her through the com—cool, even, devoid of inflection. "Position left."

He was imperturbable; she'd give him that. No comment on why she'd come flying after them or what she thought she was doing. Just the order, position left. She slid smoothly into place at his left flank, noticing that the other scooters paired up in a similar fashion.

The final scooter hung back, its driver sending carefully aimed plasgun blasts from the double-fisted shooters he held, offering them what paltry cover he could.

"We want the three plascannon rigs," Wizard explained. "The plan is straightforward. Pair up. Each lead driver is responsible for the explosive device. Dive under your assigned rig, snap a mine on the undercarriage, and roll out the back. Flank drivers, you will then go in and retrieve the lead driver assigned to you. On my mark."

So those were his orders. Dive in and get killed. No time for contemplation or explanation. Raina swallowed. Wizard was going to leap off his scooter, roll under the armored beast, and try to snap a phosphorous mine on the underbelly. Then he was going to try to roll out from beneath the rig without being crushed to death by caterpillar tires the size of entire buildings.

Okay. That part of the plan could work. But then he expected her to dart in and grab him, then get the two of them the hell out of there without getting blown to high heaven.

She glanced at the other pairs of snowscooters and saw that they were already peeling off, heading for their assigned trucks. This was madness. Suicide. Her gaze strayed to Wizard's broad back. She might never have a chance to tell him . . . to tell him . . .

"Wizard—" she began.

"Com silence. Now," he ordered, his voice colder than the air that cut her lungs with each breath, and she shut her mouth, uncertain of what she had intended to say even if she'd been given the chance.

They wove and darted closer to the massive trucks, barely evading blasts of plasgun fire. More than once Raina felt the edge of a shot against her side or her back, but always it missed her by a hair's breadth.

A flash of blue light followed by a wild burst of flame erupted to her right. One of their scooters— gone, its driver incinerated in a massive plasgun blast.

The rider who'd been covering their backs moved forward, taking the lost man's place. There was no time for sorrow or regret. No time to think of a man she had known only a short while. If she was alive at the end of the day, she would allow herself the luxury of mourning a comrade.

Fingers curled so tightly they ached, Raina held on as they careened across the snow, easy targets for the pirate gunners. Their odds for success were minuscule. The only way they could get worse was for the teams to split, for each lead to have to work alone. Another flash of blue death exploded, this time on her left, and she swallowed a cry as the tortured screams of her companions erupted, then died abruptly. Only four of them left now, and they'd accomplished nothing. Nothing except getting themselves killed.

Of course, the odds had just improved considerably—in favor of the ice pirates.

Wizard slowed almost imperceptibly, allowing her to draw alongside him. He tossed a phosphorous mine at her, and she caught it with one hand.

The breath left her in a rush. Unlike cytoplast, which was extremely stable, phosphorous mines could detonate with the smallest provocation. She was lucky that her arm hadn't been blown off at the shoulder.

"Take the center truck, Raina." He looked at her then, and as she met his gaze, she thought she saw an instant of regret. "We each work alone now."

"Piece of cake, Wizard," she said into her lip-com. The man was insane. Or he had a death wish. Maybe both. She was supposed to dive under an armored truck the size of a mountain and blow it to the sky. The fact that she wasn't running in the opposite direction made her about as crazy as him. "Get in. Get out. I'll meet you back at base for lunch."

A plas-shot ate the ground directly in front of her, and she swerved hard left. By the time she righted herself, Wizard was zipping away.

Fixing her gaze on the truck in front of her, Raina did a quick calculation of her options. There was a winch in front with a thick cable attached to a massive hook. Great for helping the pirates drag themselves out of slippery spots. Not so great for her. It lowered the front of the rig and hung down over the edge, making it impossible for her to just drive right underneath and do her drop-the-mine-and-go trick.

She could snap the mine on her scooter, and send the whole thing under the rig. Glancing around, she figured that option signed her death certificate. The radius of the explosion would be large enough that the chunks of debris would get her, and even if they didn't, she'd be on foot, easy pickings for the remaining trucks.

The horizon called to her. She should gun her engine and go. Get the hell out of this mess. There was no one to stop her, no one to make her give her life for a bunch of strangers. Yeah, she'd have to leave her rig behind, but she had funds hidden, places she could go to lie low and lick her wounds. At least she'd be alive.

Frigid air burned her throat and tore at her chest as she dragged in a deep breath. There was no one to tell her to stay.

Only she'd jumped in head first of her own free will, and she wasn't one to turn tail and run. She blew out a breath, clouding the air as warm hit cold. Turning her face to the mammoth black-and-chrome grille of the pirates' plascannon rig, she felt her heart accelerate to a near painful speed, each beat pounding in her chest. One chance. She flexed her fingers and focused on the winch, her gaze fixed on the pointed talon of the metal hook. The roar of the engine filled her ears. She cut the sharpest turn she could, drawing right alongside the winch and matching her speed and direction to that of the truck.

Grabbing the massive coil of cable she hauled back on it, enormously glad that she'd been blessed with amazing coordination and strength. She pressed the insides of her thighs against the smooth seat of the scooter, desperately struggling to maintain her precarious hold. The hook swung free with jarring force, the sharp metal point catching the sun, glinting evilly as it swayed out and then arced toward her, gathering speed.

She tried to duck, to swerve.

Too late. Too frigging late.

The hook pierced her parka, her shirt, her skin. Pain exploded along Raina's side, swallowing her, choking her. Nausea rolled up her chest into her throat, bitter on the back of her tongue. And then the hook fell away, catching on the edge of her clothing, its descent slowed by happenstance.

She didn't dare look at her side. No time. No frigging time for this. Lurching awkwardly, she caught the hook, her movement leaving her light-headed, the pain screaming, her side on fire, her left arm half-numb.

With a mad shove she anchored the hook to her scooter, slapping her palm against the ignition to kill the engine. The cable uncoiled slowly, and the momentum of the truck towed her snowscooter in a frenetic and unsteady swaying rhythm. She had seconds. Only seconds.

With a wild cry, she threw herself under the pirates' rig, ripping her gun from across her back and swinging it flat against her chest. She hit with a force that made her scream, made her head swim with the agony of it. Rolling faceup, she lay for a second, breathing heavily, fumbling for the phosphorous mine. Her hand shook as she slapped it against the underbelly, snapped it in place, set the firing pin. Thirty seconds.

She lifted her head, watching as the massive rig rode on top of her. At the far end she could see the light of day, and then uncoiling like a fish on a line, her snowscooter.

The rig passed and the blue sky spread above her. With a single hard thrust, she twisted her body to the side and up, the sound of her agony torn from her throat, mingling with the roar of the truck's engine. She closed her gloved hands around the cable—the right far stronger than the left—and let the thick line feed through. It burned her gloves, leaving tattered runnels. The scooter bumped her booted feet, hard.

Reaching up, she grasped the steering column and pulled herself upright, swinging one leg over the seat, holding her left arm tight against her body. The scooter was pulled along behind the rig, tethered by the cable, dragged toward the explosion that was mere seconds away. One glance at the cable told her it was too thick for her to cut through with her knife.

Twenty seconds.

Her heart felt like it would burst from her chest. For once she didn't feel the cold. Sweat trickled down her back, her sides. Or maybe that was blood. Red, red blood, and the Reavers would win, would kill her just as they had killed Sam.

Not in this frigging lifetime.

She closed her thighs tight on the scooter, freeing her right hand. Her left arm was useless to her now. She whipped the plasgun up, aimed, and fired.

Missed.

Oh, God.

She fired a second shot, severing the cable. The thick line snapped upward with ferocious speed, and she twisted to avoid being caught in its recoil.

Burning acid and sour fear churned inside of her as she pressed her fingers to the ignition. The thrum of the engine sprang to life, a sound that made her want to laugh out loud. Panting, she spun the scooter north and gunned the engine.

A wall of heat and wrenching sound beat on her back as she tore up the ground, and a quick glance over her shoulder confirmed that she'd taken out one plascannon rig. *Well, hallelujah. Score one for the rebels.*

Raina circled back, leaning low on the scooter, weaving madly as the plas-shots of the other trucks rained down on her like deadly hail. She spun an arc around the back of the rig that Wizard had assigned to himself. No sign of him.

Her breath came in short gasps, the pain in her side a wretched fire. Her vision shifted, blurred. She hoped she could hold it together long enough to find him. Where the hell was he?

Then she saw it. The charred and twisted remains of his snowscooter sat in the center of a blackened patch of snow. The sight sent a jagged pain slicing through her, an ugly wrenching that hurt more than her frigging side. She sped toward the still-sparking wreck. Nothing stirred. No sign of life.

"Wizard," she roared.

He was *not* dead. She would not *let* him be dead.

FOURTEEN

A dark shape—so insignificant against the vastness of the Waste and the magnitude of their enemies—moved fast across the frozen ground.

Wizard.

At the sight of him the tightness in Raina's throat gave way and the invisible bands that held her ribs eased. Clean, cold air filled her lungs. On a tight turn, leaning so low she could smell the snow, Raina tore after him, swerving madly to avoid the enemy fire. *Frig*—he was fast.

She pulled ahead of him and felt him settle with a solid thump on the scooter at her back. The engine hummed with the added weight. A wave of relief crashed over her. Wizard was there, his hard body pressed tight against hers, confirming that they were both alive. Exhilaration pumped through her system, leaving her giddy.

Zipping across the frozen ground, Raina kept her focus on the rebel encampment. An enormous ripple of hot air hit them from behind even as a harsh surge of sound warped and twisted around them. She glanced over her shoulder to see two of the pirates' rigs mushroom outward in huge balls of fire that grew and melded, showering them with debris.

As they approached the camp, the rebel plascannons shot over them, taking out yet another pirate rig, upping the odds that the rebels would survive to see the setting of the northern sun.

Trey raised a hand in welcome as they whizzed past, and Yuriko nodded at them from her post near the shell of the bombed-out building where she and Raina had shared more than one conversation. Sawyer sent them a jaunty salute from his perch high in the ancient column of crumbling concrete and twisted steel that had long ago been home to hundreds of people. With a loud whoop he sent a barrage of plasgun fire down on the remaining pirate rigs.

"Yeah, I'm happy to see you, too." Raina grinned, riding high on a heady mix of victory and adrenaline, feeling as if she were sitting on top of the world and Wizard were sitting right up there with her.

She waved a greeting, then huffed in a short gasp as her side screamed in protest. Turning the snowscooter toward her rig, she intended to restock her dwindled supply of ammunition and get back out in the fight. As she drew to a stop, she closed her eyes, focusing on the thud of Wizard's heart against her back.

Alive. He was alive. And his heart beat in rhythm with hers—or not.

Frowning, Raina focused on his heartbeat. Hers was running like a jackrabbit's, pounding with a tempo so erratic it left her feeling faintly nauseated. His was slow, steady, one beat for every three of hers. With her left arm pressed tight against her side, she climbed off the scooter and faced him.

"That was some run," she said, her lips wobbling into an attempt at a smile. With her adrenaline high starting to crash, the pain in her side made it an effort just to stay upright.

"Affirmative. I am pleased by our success."

She blinked. He sounded like an automaton. No emotion. No fear. Just cool command and action. She had been so worried, so desperate when she thought he might not have survived, and she was still reeling from the intensity of her emotions.

Wizard, on the other hand, looked like he'd just taken a casual stroll. She doubted that he'd even broken a sweat. His emotions, his psyche, were apparently unaffected by their near escape, untouched by the loss of the others in the advance guard. He was as frozen and stiff as the hard-packed ice beneath her feet.

"You are injured." He stared at her, a sharp gaze that cut deep inside her. Slowly, so slowly, he reached out and touched his gloved fingers to her cheek. No change in expression, no word of comfort, just that fleeting touch. He climbed off the snowscooter, his expression remote. "Report to the med-tech," he said, and then strode away.

Raina sagged against the scooter, letting it bolster her weight. One minute to catch her breath, get her bearings, and she'd do as he said. Anything else would be just plain dumb.

Halfway across the camp he stopped, turned. Her heart banged against her ribs. He gave her a long, hard stare before spinning and continuing on his way.

"Of all the morons in the frozen north," she grumbled, and staggered off in the direction of the med-tech.

Ben bounded up beside her. "That was great," he said, bouncing up and down on the balls of his feet in his excitement. "You and Wizard, you showed 'em."

In a bizarre and unexpected act, he threw his arms around her in a brief hug, and then jumped back, laughing nervously.

Raina bit back a groan of pain, swallowing the lump of emotion in her throat.

"I'm really glad you didn't die, Raina. Really glad."

"So'm I," she mumbled, concentrating on staying upright.

Ben's brow furrowed in concern. "You're not okay." He pressed up against her good side, grabbing her arm and slinging it over his shoulder, using his body as a strut. "But you will be. Soon as we get to the med-tech, you'll be fixed right up."

Leaning on him, Raina felt a rush of gratitude. The kid cared about her, actually cared about whether or not she would be all right. The realization was discon-certing.

Together they stumbled forward, one step and an-other, until Ben stopped, his attention focused on the opposite end of the camp. Raina followed his gaze, wet her lips, a quick, nervous roll inward and then the swipe of her tongue.

Wizard. He was standing, frozen, watching them. Her breath caught and held as she watched him mount up. Throughout the remainder of the day she snagged the occasional glimpse of him, and each time her heart did that treacherous flip-flop inside her chest, leaving her cursing the Waste, cursing the Reavers, and cursing Wizard loudest of all.

* * *

The flaming wreckage of the pirate rigs dotted the plain. Hydrogen didn't usually explode, but it did provide enough fuel for a bonfire that would last a week.

Clean, though still too tired to claim that she was refreshed, Raina crossed to her bed. With a tug she dragged the quilt up and over her shoulders, trying to ward off a chill that was slowly consuming her from the inside out. She rested her hand lightly on her wound, bound now with biotech sealing agent. Not as bad as she had first thought. But it still hurt like slag.

The thought made her smile. That was Ben's word, *slag*, and he'd said it so many times today she must have it branded on her brain.

They had won the day, this small band of rebels. Friends. Comrades.

Her smile faded. She had risked her life for them. For Ben, for Yuriko. For the rebel children whose names she had learned over the past weeks and whose faces had dogged her thoughts as she rode out to meet her fate. For Sawyer and Juan and Trey and every other rebel who had come to be more than a nameless face that she would leave behind without a thought.

She had risked her life for Wizard.

Frigging hell.

She didn't want to care about any of them, and least of all him. She did just fine on her own. The last thing she needed was to give her half-frozen heart to a man who didn't have one of his own.

A shiver coursed through her. Today she'd seen what Wizard was: ruthless, focused, brave. And what he wasn't: emotional. She didn't think there was a single warm emotion in that computer chip of a brain.

But what the hell had she expected?

Sucking in a breath, she irritably shoved a strand of hair back from her face. She had no business feeling this way. It was stupid. It was dangerous. She wanted to be as cold, as dispassionate as he was. That was safer. Cool, clinical, controlled—that was what she'd aimed for most of her life. It was what other people believed her to be . . . what she'd believed herself to be.

But it was a lie, because deep inside she still had those dangerous feelings that could affect her decisions and cost her her life. Mostly, she managed to bury them deeper than an Old Dominion garbage pit, but somehow Wizard had burrowed way down inside of her. He'd made her care. And she was mightily pissed off at herself for that.

Turning, she caught sight of her reflection in the darkened window glass, and she stepped closer, staring at the pale oval of her face. She tugged the quilt tighter around her shoulders, feeling incredibly weary.

She needed to leave. Soon. Before her emotions got any more tangled with the people in this camp, before her heart got any more tangled with Wizard.

With a sigh, Raina crossed to her small sink. Tea. She needed something hot, because the chill inside of her was growing.

"Do not ever do that again." The words were low and rough, spoken against the shell of her ear. She gave a squeak of surprise as Wizard's hands closed about her waist and he spun her so she was backed to the wall. Chest heaving, she stared at him as he stepped back. His jaw was darkened by a day's growth of beard, his face etched in lines of tension. He looked raw and powerful. Male. Beautiful.

The quilt sagged down one shoulder, and she

grabbed for it, this last vestige of protection. Her hand closed over nothing, and she felt the soft swish of the cloth as it slid to the floor.

He leaned in close, breathing her in. His jaw rasped along her cheek, and his hands were warm on her waist, tunneling under her shirt, skin to skin.

"Do not ever do that to me again," he repeated, terse.

"Don't . . . I . . ." She shook her head. "Do what?"

"Do not make me know fear." His eyes glittered in the meager glow of the single lumi-light, and his voice was harsh with barely leashed emotion. "I *felt* fear. It was . . . unpleasant."

For a moment she just stared at him, confusion clouding her thoughts. Then she realized he was talking about her coming after him, her participation in the mission. He'd been *afraid*. For her.

Not for himself. Never for himself.

A man who was incapable of emotion *feared* for her.

His hands tensed around her waist, not hurting her but holding tight. Like he never wanted to let go. He moved his hand a little higher, tracing his fingertips along her wound, his expression dark.

She'd thought him detached. Disconnected.

She'd been wrong.

Anger, aggression, pent-up adrenaline from the events of the day . . . all that and more throbbed just below the surface of his restraint. She could feel emotion emanating from him in pulsing waves.

"I—"She wasn't even sure what she'd been about to say. This was as new, as confusing, as strange for her as it obviously was for him. Then words didn't matter, because he cut her off with a hard kiss, letting the weight of his body pin her back against the wall.

He was anything but gentle, slanting his mouth over hers in a wild, hungry joining that left her breathless.

A dull ache exploded at the juncture of her thighs, and she was suddenly desperate to have him inside her. She lifted up on her toes, pressing herself against the hard ridge of his erection, wanting him so badly it was a physical pain.

Inexplicable confusion welled up inside of her. She didn't just want him; she wanted to wrap herself around him and keep him warm and safe.

He'd been afraid for her. That meant he cared about what happened to her. Enough to storm in here all bristling male aggression and throbbing passion.

"Fuck," he snarled. The word shocked her, and told her much.

He yanked her against him, kissed her deeply, rough, hot, with a raw need that told her everything his words did not. Lifting her mouth to his, Raina arched against him, her nipples hard, pebbled by the cold air and by the hot wave of desire that spiraled through her, replacing her uncertainty. She moaned as he deepened the kiss, his body hard under her hands, and she twined her fingers in the thick length of his hair, dragging him closer, taking his heat and strength and making them her own.

A sound escaped him, low in his throat, a dark groan. He slid his body against hers, hard, rubbing his chest against her sensitive nipples as he pushed his tongue into her mouth. That kiss lived inside her, wet, deep, teeth and tongue and the taste of him stealing her breath until she gasped air through his open mouth and her own, his knee pushing between hers.

He shucked her out of her shirt, her pants. With an abrupt speed that left her gasping, he parted the moist folds of her flesh, pushed his fingers up into her, a little rough, scraping over her clitoris as he moved. Sensation pounded her, harsh and unyielding, and she screamed, her cry caught in his mouth, her limbs shaking with the abrupt, powerful release of her climax, his strength the only thing holding her upright.

"Oh, God," she moaned, her body still convulsing with shock after shock. "Frig, that was fast." She laughed, a shaky sound, half laugh, half groan, her orgasm leaving her limp and breathless.

He let her go, and she slid down the wall, a tangle of limbs, staring up at him as he wrenched his thermal shirt over his head, off his arms, muscles rippling, outlined in gorgeous contrast of light and shadow. Holding her gaze, he moved his hands lower, sliding them along his ridged abdomen, shoving his pants down over lean hips.

"Wizard." His name was a plea as he came fully atop her, there on the floor, his weight covering her, glorious heat and heaviness pressing down on her as he pushed her knees wide.

The broad head of his penis nudged the opening of her body, and then he drove into her, slick, wet, a smooth thrust that made her gasp. There was no delicacy, no control, just hard, pounding need, beyond her control, beyond his.

She felt stretched, filled, hugely, darkly excited, so sensitive. She hissed, the pleasure spreading through her as he pumped deeper, again, and again, each thrust pushing her closer to the edge.

He took her nipple in his mouth and sucked, a hard

tug. Pulsing, crying out, she came as he jerked and trembled, his body taut above her own, their release coming upon them almost as one.

Raina closed her eyes, letting her head fall back against the floor, Wizard's weight pressing down upon her. She wet her lips. "What was that?" she breathed, the effort of speaking almost too much for her.

"I can't lose you," he whispered, burying his face in the wildly tangled strands of her hair. "Everything depends on your staying safe."

She opened her mouth to ask him what he meant, but he turned his face to hers and kissed her as though they hadn't just made wild, crazy love. Wrapping her legs tightly around him, she let him lift her and carry her to the bed. She sucked back a gasp as her side twinged in protest. Together they fell onto the soft mattress, Wizard cushioning her fall.

For a time they lay in a tangle of limbs, touching, caressing. "I'm cold," she whispered.

His hot hands covered her, stroking the skin of her thigh, the curve of her waist. The length of his hard, rippling body came against her, warming her to her core. With a low moan, she rolled him onto his back, straddling him, taking him deep inside of her once more.

Gray eyes glittering, he watched her as she moved, letting her take her pleasure of him, meeting her every thrust.

"I thought you were cold." He moved his hips to bring her tighter against him, the movement drawing her dangerously close to the edge.

"You make me warm." *You make me happy.* She pushed the thought aside. Happy was scary. But sex . . . well, sex was great.

Only it was *more*. *Damn, damn, damn.*

She bucked against him as he increased the tempo and dragged her with him into a mindless spiral of pleasure until they both shattered, the sounds of their release mingling in a single harsh cry. Collapsing against his chest, she closed her eyes, wishing that this moment could be her eternity.

And they would live happily ever after . . .

A bubble of self-mocking laughter welled up. She had a sudden vision of Wizard as the fairy-tale hero of the stories her mother had read her when she was a small child. *Oh, God.* Was that what she thought she wanted? With him?

She didn't trust him.

Did she?

What the hell did she know about trust?

She rolled off him onto her side, and found him watching her. His expression was as cool and remote as always, and she felt a pang of regret. What had she expected? Old-style gallantry? Pretty words and an undying declaration of affection?

"Of all the morons in the frozen north," she muttered, irritated with herself at the turn of her thoughts.

"I do not comprehend. Please clarify," he said, looking at her quizzically, head tilted to one side.

"A girl has a right to dream of a little romance." As soon as she said the words, she realized how silly they sounded. The urge to bury her face in her hands was strong, but she toughed it out, holding his gaze. She wasn't a little girl anymore, dreaming of ancient fairy tales, and Wizard was anything but a romantic hero. She didn't think there was a single sentimental chromosome in his body. Computer boy just wasn't programmed for it. And up until this very moment she would have sworn that neither was she.

He stared at her, saying nothing, his gray eyes narrowed in thought. "Romance. Compliments. Gifts." He gave an abrupt nod. "Understood."

Running his fingers through the long strands of her hair, he leaned in close. His pupils were dilated to deep, dark pools surrounded by a thin gray rim. God, he was gorgeous. "Raina . . ."

She licked her lips.

He trailed his hand across the curve of her collarbone, down along her chest to the tip of her breast. Her nipple puckered and swelled.

"Your eyes are appropriately spaced," he whispered. She blinked.

"And your ears are proportional to your face. The collagen fibers of your integument have maintained a wrinkle-free and youthful appearance." He looked at her earnestly. "Compliments."

"Ummm . . ." She frowned. "My integument?"

"Tomorrow I will order you a set of titanium body armor. Lightweight and impenetrable." The corners of his mouth kicked up just a bit, and he looked incredibly pleased with himself. "Gifts."

A startled gasp of laughter escaped her. He was wooing her with titanium. It was definitely a novel approach.

Wizard tugged on the edge of the quilt, bringing it up to cover her. Raina stared at him, torn between laughter and tears. He looked so honest, so sincere. Then he tossed one arm carelessly across her shoulders, and let his mouth curve the rest of the way into that too-rarely-seen masculine smile.

"Romance," he said, rolling so that his front was tight against her back.

She felt the steady rise and fall of his chest as she waited for him to say something more. The pattern of his breathing remained steady, and after a few minutes she realized that he was asleep.

She couldn't help it. She laughed. Softly, so as not to wake him. Snuggling closer, she closed her eyes. Compliments. Gifts. Romance. And then her dream lover rolled onto his back and let out a light snore.

"Hey!" Someone banged against the side of the rig. Raina bolted upright, knocking her head against Wizard's cheek as he did the same.

"You in there? Raina?" Sawyer's voice.

Bang, bang, bang. "Come on!" Yuriko called.

What the hell were they slamming against her truck?

Someone howled like a dog, setting off the real dogs until the night was filled with noise.

"We're doing the two-fifty club! Move along, little doggy!" Sawyer yelled.

Dragging on her clothing as she went, Raina stumbled to the front of the rig and opened the door of the cab. Sawyer stood grinning up at her, and behind him was a large group of rebels, including Yuriko and Trey.

"Come on, girl." Sawyer motioned for her to come closer. "Get on down here and join the party. It's minus-fifty out here, and if you don't put a move on it, you're going to miss all the fun."

Bewildered, Raina sniffed the air. "What have you been drinking?"

Sawyer turned and slung an arm around Trey's shoulder. "Haven't been drinking anything. Yet. Wouldn't be safe. But once we're done . . . well, then I just might indulge. . . ."

Turning to Yuriko, Raina shook her head. "Care to explain?"

"The current temperature is minus-fifty degrees Celsius. The Russian stone sauna will soon reach a temperature of two hundred degrees," Yuriko said, her eyes sparking with merriment.

"And your point is?" Raina moved her hand in a questioning gesture.

"The two-fifty club."

"Okay." She looked back and forth between a stupidly grinning Sawyer and a somber Trey, who looked like he might crack a smile at some point if she waited long enough. They had all gone stark raving mad. No other explanation for it. "What's the two-fifty club, and why would I want to join?"

"We'll sit in the stone sauna until it reaches the full two hundred degrees. We will then do a lap to the guard post and back." Trey turned to look at the guard post, and then back at Raina.

She stared at him. "Excuse me? Outside? In minus-fifty-degree weather?"

"You got it. The sauna, then a lap around camp in the fresh air." Sawyer chortled. "Naked. Come on."

"Naked?" Raina squeaked. "Out there? In the cold?" She backed away, shaking her head from side to side and holding her hands up as if to ward off an attack. "No, thanks. Not me. Not happening."

"Happening," Yuriko said, and swung into the cab to link her arm through Raina's. "But you may wear undergarments if you wish." She pulled aside the edge of her shirt to flash a strap of her bright pink bra, and then laughed as Raina made a choked sound.

"Come on, Wizard," Yuriko called over her shoulder. "Cold doesn't bother you, so you have no excuse not to join the club. It isn't as though we haven't been inviting you for years. And it's about time we socialized you. Isolation is unhealthy."

She dragged Raina from the rig, letting her stop only long enough to retrieve her parka and boots.

Laughing, the group half sprinted, half skipped across the compound, Raina pulled along by Yuriko. After a moment she felt a hand wrap around her waist and she turned to see Wizard beside her.

"This is crazy."

"Affirmative."

But crazy or not, they ran with the others to the building across the camp and tore off layer after layer of clothing until only their underclothes remained. As she stripped out of her thermal shirt and pants, Raina allowed herself a few covert peaks at Wizard's broad shoulders, his muscled back, the hard, round curve of his buttocks outlined beneath the smooth material of his drawers. That view alone was worth the run in the frigid air.

Laughing and talking, the group tumbled into the large stone sauna. The success of the day made for a jovial mood, and Trey finally cracked that smile, his gaze a little wistful as he looked at Yuriko, who was tugging playfully at Sawyer's briefs.

"Thought you said we should do this naked," she teased.

Sawyer glanced at Trey, who loomed behind Yuriko with a warning clear in his gaze. "Briefs'll do," he said.

Steam swirled around them, wrapping them in heated tendrils as Raina and Wizard climbed to a bench near the top. It was hotter up there, and within moments she was cocooned in the moist, sultry air of the sauna, feeling warm and drowsy. And happy.

She turned her head, her eyes seeking Wizard. Reaching out, she twined her fingers with his.

He frowned, examining their clasped hands. Then he looked at her and smiled. "Hand-holding. A courtship ritual."

"One ninety-eight . . ." Trey intoned, leaning forward to read the thermometer. Murmured conversations died, and a moment later he said, "One ninety-nine . . ."

A hum of excitement shimmered through the group.

"Two hundred! Go! Go!"

Whooping and shouting, everyone bolted from the sauna, stumbling over one another and laughing as they searched for boots. Raina clambered down from the upper bench as Trey and Yuriko made a dash for the door and ran nearly naked into the frigid night air.

Trey roared as the chill hit him, and Yuriko laughed, pirouetting with arms outstretched.

Raina whirled to face Wizard, who stood directly behind her. "Um, I don't think so." With a wave of her hand she shooed him away. "The sauna was nice, but I'm not going out there."

"The club is identified as the two-fifty club. The objective is to expose the body to the full two hundred and fifty degrees." Wizard bent and closed his fingers around her ankle, forcing her foot into her boot.

"No, really," Raina continued, trying to pull away.

"I'm not fond of the cold. I'll settle for the two hundred club and leave the extra minus-fifty for everyone else."

Her breath left her in a whoosh as Wizard bent, angled his shoulder against her belly on the side opposite her healing wound, and lifted her clear off the ground so that her arms dangled along the backs of his legs and her legs draped over his chest. He pushed her second boot onto her remaining foot, then set her upright.

"You are afraid?"

Raina narrowed her eyes at him. "Of a little cold air? Not hardly."

"Then trust me. I will run by your side."

Trust him. She sucked in a breath.

"Ready?" he asked, one dark brow quirking upward.

She shook her head and laughed. "No. But I guess I'm doing this anyway." Spinning, she sprinted out into the cold.

"This is not healthy," she yelled, gasping, feet pumping as she ran after the others, glacial air lashing her exposed skin. "It puts a strain on your heart going from somewhere really, really hot to somewhere this cold. I could have a heart attack."

Wizard jogged at her side. "The probability of your suffering a myocardial infarction is—"

"Stow it," she interrupted, shooting him a quelling look as she poured on speed. "It's too frigging c-c-cold to talk!"

Of course Wizard didn't quell, and he didn't look cold. He looked as though he could happily stroll out here in his skivvies for the rest of the evening.

She was beyond frozen as she rounded the guard

post, beyond icy as she sprinted the last few feet back to the building that held the sauna. It was a miracle that her limbs didn't just crack and fall off.

"S-s-s-sauna." She tumbled into the building, kicked off her boots, and stumbled toward the room that promised blessed warmth.

Pushing the door open, she jerked to a halt. In front of her sat a group of people who looked so damned happy to see her. Yuriko. Sawyer. Trey. Ben. Juan. All the friends she had made among the Northern Waste Settlers Committee, a fancy name for rebels. And she supposed that made her a rebel, somewhere deep in her heart. These were people she cared about. People who cared about her.

She grinned, unable to help it, elated by the realization that for the first time in her adult life, she was not well and truly alone. These rebels had become her friends.

The joy of belonging flooded her as she laughed at their antics. She had a place here. She was one of them.

"Hey, Raina, how's your side?" Sawyer called.

"I hardly know it's there." She glanced down, surprised to find the wound pink instead of the angry red it had been earlier. The biotech was already doing its job, sealing her skin. She'd always healed quickly, but this seemed fast even for her.

Wizard grabbed her hand and tugged her along as he climbed to the highest bench of the sauna. As they settled on a spot in the corner, she turned to stare at him and thought about every moment of their love-making, every whispered tender word. He'd said that he couldn't lose her, that everything depended on her staying safe, and she knew with absolute certainty that he had meant those words.

Wow.

She felt humbled.

"Do not be concerned. Your body temperature will quickly acclimatize to the change."

Raina winked at him and smiled. "I'll trust you on that one."

FIFTEEN

With the coming of the new day, reality intruded, dusting aside the high spirits that had followed the rebel win over the ice pirates. They had buried the remains of their dead at the rising of the sun, no mean feat in the tundra. They'd needed titanium attachments to dig out the graves.

Now, seven rebels sat in a windowless, airless war room around a scarred and warped round table, discussing choices. Raina was invited to join them, though she viewed her role more as observer than participant. She leaned back in her chair, thinking that their options were few, and those they did have barely warranted debate.

Run like hell. That was her advice. But she wasn't used to being a part of group discussions, so she kept silent, musing on the crazy reason she couldn't begin to explain that kept her sitting here. Her gaze slid to Wizard, then away.

They'd made love. They'd played in the snow with their friends. They had gone back to her rig and made love again, slower, sweeter, long into the night. But this morning he'd been gone when she opened her eyes, leaving no opportunity for even a brief conversation. Then Yuriko had come for her, led her here, and she wasn't about to have a delicate discussion concerning the future of their relationship with this many witnesses.

The future of their *relationship? Oh, man.*

Blowing out a short huff of air, she focused on the debate that swirled around her, the discussion of the future of the entire camp.

Back and forth it went.

They must stand and fight.

No. They couldn't remain here. The ice pirates had found them once, and that meant others could come. They needed a new home base.

Again she looked at Wizard, and she couldn't help wondering where he'd gone that morning and what had been important enough to drag him from her bed. She shouldn't feel hurt. What the hell had she expected . . . a set of leg irons that would join them at the ankle?

But he had promised compliments, romance, gifts. . . . So how long did it take for titanium body armor to be delivered?

"I say we stay and fight." Trey leaned forward in his seat, his movement emphasizing his statement. His beautiful, scarred face was tense, his jaw set.

Juan slapped both hands on the tabletop, half rising as he spoke, his dark eyes moving slowly to encompass each of his comrades. "We lost nine men and women to the ice pirates. Lives stolen by a terrible, senseless war. Let us leave this place. Wizard has suggested we find a new camp where our children will be safe. I am in agreement with him."

After considering the other man's words, Trey shook his head. "No disrespect, my friends"—he inclined his head first to Juan, then to Wizard—"but I disagree. If we run, we will never be free. What life will the families of our settlers have, fleeing like scared arctic hares?" The comparison was Yuriko's from an earlier comment. Trey arched a brow at her, as though challenging her in some way, leaving Raina wondering just what was going on with those two. Last night she could have sworn they were intimate. But today she wasn't so sure.

"Our children can never be safe in a world led by men such as Duncan Bane," Yuriko said.

Raina tensed at the sound of Bane's name. "I thought we were fighting Reavers. Ice pirates. What does Bane have to do with this?"

Yuriko made a soft sound, and Raina narrowed her eyes at her, finely honed internal alarm clanging. Something wasn't right.

For a long moment no one said a word.

"I support our original plan." All eyes turned to the speaker. Gerhardt was a man of few words, and when he spoke he commanded attention. "Draw Bane out. Break his hold over the Northern Waste and carve a place for ourselves and our families." He paused, lips drawn in a taut line. "Kill him if necessary."

Kill him. Kill Bane. Raina had dreamed about doing exactly that for just about forever. Problem was, he never left an opening for anyone to get at him. He was as well guarded as the Interdollar Production Facility in Neo-Tokyo.

Trey looked at Wizard. "Did you contact him as planned?"

"Affirmative."

Raina's stomach did a slow roll. Affirmative? They had contacted Bane? What the hell? This was all news to her.

"Then we stick with the original plan," Trey said, resting one hand on Juan's shoulder. "Remove the threat Bane poses and make the Waste our own. There is no other way. For every pirate rig we destroy, they have twenty waiting to move. We cannot continue to dismember a monster that will only grow longer and more dangerous arms. We must cut off the monster's head. We must draw Duncan Bane from his well-protected tower. Without him, the Reavers will lose focus. They will war amongst themselves as they did years ago."

Juan turned to face him. "And the Janson?"

"Janson Transport exists only because of Bane. Without him, the company will fail. Other, smaller, legitimate operations will have an opportunity to fill the void."

"Circumstances have changed since the inception of our plan." Yuriko spoke to the table at large, though her attention was focused on Raina. "We may need to rethink our strategy for drawing Bane out."

"Strategy? For drawing Bane out?" Raina let the words tumble free, every instinct screaming that danger was about to jump up and bite her in the ass. "And just how do you propose to do that? How do you plan to entice a man who hides behind the safe veneer of respectability, who pretends to be a man of honor? Just what the hell do you intend to use as bait?"

There was nothing that was important enough to Duncan Bane to force him from the safety of his impenetrable tower, nothing he wanted badly enough except for—

She sucked in a sharp breath as she turned, her gaze locking with Wizard's. His fingers tapped rhythmically on the tabletop in that rare gesture that hinted at unease. And she knew. *Knew* what he had done. Disbelief swamped her, followed by a cold, hard rage that was sickening in its intensity.

The only thing Duncan Bane wanted badly enough to leave the safety of his fortress for was *her*, which meant that she knew exactly what they intended to use as bait.

Frig. They hadn't just *intended* it; they'd done it. Bane was here. Looking for her. She was the lure. She was the frigging arctic hare.

"I understand that Wizard now has a stake in the outcome, but there is no reason that Raina must be put at undue risk. She can be protected," Gerhardt said firmly.

"Protected? Are you crazy? You think you can protect anyone from Bane?" Slowly she laid her palms flat on the table, making the simple action the focus of her attention, desperate to hold on to her control. God, she couldn't breathe, couldn't think straight.

Looking around the room at the faces of the people whom only last night she had thought of as friends, she tried to regain her equilibrium. Friends! What the hell was she thinking? Their betrayal sank sharp talons of misery deep into her heart.

Of all the morons in the frozen north, she had to be the biggest. She'd trusted them. All of them. She, who had faced betrayal all her life and who should have known better.

Oh, frig. The pain was horrific. Wizard. Betrayed. He'd betrayed her.

The agony of it stole her breath, made her clammy and sick. Everyone she'd ever trusted in her entire life had betrayed her. But it had never hurt this much. *Wizard.*

She swallowed, willing herself not to throw up.

Suddenly Wizard's every comment took on a new and forbidding meaning. *Everything depends on your staying safe,* he'd rasped, as though his entire being depended on it. She'd thought it was because he cared for her. Moron. Of course he'd wanted to keep her safe. Keep her alive. You kept a worm alive until you stuck it on the hook. Live bait wriggled and squirmed, attracting the biggest fish.

"You used me." Her voice was barely above a whisper. Closing her eyes for a moment, Raina struggled to order her muddled thoughts as they whirred inside her head like a spinning top.

She opened her eyes and found Wizard still watching her, his gaze as inscrutable as ever. If she had hoped for some warmth, some affection to shimmer in his eyes, she was sadly disappointed. There was nothing mirrored there but cool control.

She had trusted him, believed in him. Frig, how could she not have known better?

The hard knot in the center of her chest grew, pushing outward until every breath was a monstrous effort. Wizard's betrayal was worse than Sam's had ever been, than anyone else's had ever been. Because she was older. Wiser. Because she knew that monsters really did lurk in the dark.

Because she was at fault here. She had allowed herself to trust. She had facilitated this treachery. Which meant . . . what? . . . that she couldn't even trust herself?

Drawing on every ounce of her self-control, she centered her thoughts, dragged herself inward. If she let her restraint slip even the merest fraction of a yuale, she would become no better than a berserker, mindlessly lashing out at anyone within reach.

She glared at Wizard, and thought in that instant that if she let herself, she could kill him. He watched her with his impassive stare, no expression marking his perfect features. Except there, in the depths of his eyes, she thought she saw regret. . . . No! She would not believe in him. She would not play the fool again. Loyalty was a wispy dream, blown away by the slightest breeze.

Betrayal was something she knew well, something she understood.

She carefully pushed her chair back, away from the others. Their faces turned toward her, their expressions wary. *Frig.* Had they all known?

"You used me to get to Bane. Which makes me the bait." She rose to her feet, backing away, her gaze roaming the faces of the men and women she had risked her life to save. "And it worked. Bane's here. In the Waste."

Wariness skittered across Juan's features. *Good.* Let him sweat. Hell, let them all sweat.

"We were unaware of his arrival." Yuriko. Her voice

was calm, mellifluous. Another sick wave washed over Raina. She'd thought she had found a kindred spirit, a woman she could call friend.

"What is his location?" Wizard asked, and Raina bit back a scream of frustration and pain. No connection, no emotion. Frigging computer chip for a brain. Why had she ever thought different?

"Here and there." She forced the words past bloodless lips, the muscles of her jaw drawn tight.

Damn Wizard for making her believe in fairy tales and dreams. He was a tumor, and the faster she hacked him out of her heart, the better. She gritted her teeth. She had used Wizard to scratch an itch. That was all. He meant nothing to her. Nothing.

Maybe sometime in the next millennium she'd learn to believe that.

"What numbers did he bring with him?" Yuriko asked, exchanging a look with Wizard. Something in her tone assured Raina that Yuriko really hadn't known Bane had arrived. Young Ben had obviously chosen to share that information only with her. It might have been ammunition for her if she'd been smart enough not to blurt it out like that. What the hell was wrong with her?

"You orchestrated this." Raina glared at Wizard, nearly choking on the admission. "Every second since we met. You planned it, and I fell into it." Time enough to crawl into a hole and lick her wounds later. Right now she wanted answers. Right now knowledge might be the only thing that would keep her alive. "How did you know Bane would come after me?"

"Raina, please sit." Yuriko's voice was smooth, cool, controlled. "We will explain."

"Frigging right, you'll explain." Raina could feel anger and bitterness clawing their way free, and she tamped them down with ruthless control. "What right did you have to play with my life?"

"A moment of privacy, if we may?" Yuriko looked at the others seated around the table, and Raina realized that in the intensity of the moment she'd almost forgotten they were there. One by one they rose and filed toward the door. Each had to pass by Raina in order to exit, and she was careful to meet the gaze of every one of them, marking them. Payback might be a long time in coming, but when it did come, it would be sweet.

Trey hesitated, his expression drawn. "Raina . . ."

"Please go." Yuriko gave him a tight smile. "All will be well."

After a moment he too left the room.

Alone with Wizard and Yuriko, Raina slammed the cage door on her feelings. A writhing ball of rage threatened to break free and consume her, but she was determined to control it long enough to get some answers. Then she'd take her money and get the hell out of here. Head for greener pastures . . . or if not greener, at least less frozen.

"What the hell is going on here? What do you know about me, and how did you know that Bane would come after me?"

"Please. Sit." Yuriko gestured to the chair that Raina had vacated.

Resentment churning in her gut, Raina shoved the chair aside with one booted foot, and instead perched on the edge of the table, looking down on the two of them.

Yuriko nodded in acknowledgment. "A master strategist," she said.

"No." The sound of Raina's hollow laughter echoed off the barren walls. "But obviously I'm in the presence of masters. You figured out the only way to get Bane to leave his protective compound: me. I want to know how. Why."

"We do owe you an explanation. And Wizard will tell you." Rising, Yuriko rested her hand lightly on Raina's shoulder, and then she, too, left the room.

Raina swallowed the urge to call her back, because as angry as she was at Yuriko, those feelings were nothing compared to the roiling cauldron of hurt and pain and rage that was directed at Wizard. She didn't want to be alone with him, didn't want to hear what he had to say.

"You were my target." Wizard rose and paced to the far end of the room.

That was all he was going to say? Not another word?

"I was your target." *Frig.* That hurt worse than frostbite. "So in my rig that day, when we were listening to Lissy Abbott interview Bane, you asked me about him, wanted to know the connection." Her breath hissed from between her teeth. "But you already knew. Damn you, somehow you already knew."

Wizard crossed the room, stopping directly in front of her. She could smell the soap he'd used in her shower, and the subtle, warm scent of man.

"You are aware that I was an assassin for the Order. Even after I left their employ, I took the occasional assignment. Those that held a specific appeal."

"Killing holds appeal for you?" Even as she said it, she knew that the reason he'd taken this assignment—hell, probably every assignment—was to help the rebels, but she didn't want to credit him for any honorable motivation. She wanted to paint him the villain. *Frig.* He'd done a damn fine job of painting himself.

He sent her a hard glance. "You were my next target. Only I wasn't to kill you. I was to bring you in alive. Unharmed. An unusual directive for Duncan Bane." His tone was calm, even. He could have been discussing the workings of a hydrogen pump instead of the fact that Bane wanted to torture her, break her, and eventually kill her.

She squelched the urge to land a neat kick right between his legs. Maybe he'd show some emotion then.

Raina blew out a slow breath. Bane wanted her brought in unharmed because hurting her was a privilege he would reserve only for himself. A sliver of dread pierced her, but she crushed it, refusing to show anything to Wizard, the man who had gotten under the razor-sharp wall of her defenses. The man who had betrayed her.

What was she thinking? She'd known him for a few days. They'd done the wild thing, had a couple of deep conversations. Not exactly the basis for a bond of trust and faith. He probably didn't even consider it a betrayal. He'd made no commitment to her. Even if he had, life should have toughened her up enough that she should have regarded him with a healthy dose of skepticism. So why hadn't she? And why the hell did it hurt so much?

"But you didn't bring me in," she said. "You're here with sister Yuriko and her crew, and so am I, which means what? That you've openly broken with the Order? No more dual allegiance?"

Wizard opened his mouth to answer, but Raina held

out her hand, palm forward. Suddenly she felt so very tired, and she knew that whatever answers he gave, it wouldn't change a thing. She was as alone as she had always been. Maybe even more so, because for a few golden hours she'd thought . . . what? That she'd found her place in the world with her instant family of rebel settlers?

That she'd fallen in love with a Waste-trash assassin?

"Forget it. I just want out of here." She shifted, ready to rise.

Wizard's hand shot out, and he closed his fingers around her wrist. The shock of his touch made her jerk as though she'd been wrapped in a live plasma line.

Why did it have to be this man—this dishonorable, lying, mercenary swine—who turned her blood hot and made her wish that he'd been something different?

"Raina, you cannot leave. He will hunt you down." His voice was low and rough. He almost sounded as if he cared what happened to her. But she knew now that was a pipe dream. He'd used her to get to Bane. Period. "Remain here where I can protect you."

"I don't need you to protect me," she snarled. *I just need you to love me. Frig. Kill that thought.* With a sharp tug, she tried to yank her wrist free of his grasp.

He took a slow breath, held tight. "Understood."

"I can do whatever I damn well please." *Okay.* That was about as petulant as a girl could get.

She wanted to hate him. For messing with her head. For making her feel things she'd thought herself immune to. For making her wish she could feel them still. With him.

"Bane's never found me before. Not in all these

years. And I'm not about to hang around here and let him find me now."

"He has never really looked before," Wizard pointed out calmly. "But whatever his reasons, he has now determined that the time is right to pursue you."

With precise movements she hooked the tips of her fingers under his and pried his hand from her wrist. "I can take care of myself."

"Unacceptable."

"Do not"—she leaned in and locked her eyes on his—"try to tell me what is unacceptable. I answer to myself, Wizard. You'd do well to remember that."

To her surprise, something bright and hot glittered in the depths of his eyes. If she didn't know he was close to being a frigging machine, she'd have thought it was frustration, maybe even anger that she saw there.

"Hear my explanation. You cannot fathom my logic if you do not have the tools to work with."

"Oh, that's okay." Raina sent him a too-sweet smile. "I've already encountered your tool, Wizard. It wasn't all that great."

He blinked, then tipped his head to the side. "A joke?" he asked.

"No. An insult. To you." She rolled her eyes.

"Ah." He shrugged. "Insults have no place in this discussion." And just like that, he let it go, as if her denigrating comment about his manhood were beneath his notice.

And maybe it was. For an instant Raina felt small, even petty, at having baited him like that. Then she reminded herself that he had used her to entrap a snake like Duncan Bane. She remembered what was at stake—her life—and her remorse evaporated like steam from a hot exhaust pipe.

"Okay, Wizard. Talk." Not that she was buying anything he was selling, but he might slip up and provide some useful information. One never could tell.

He nodded slowly, opened his mouth, closed it again. After a second he stalked to the door, yanked it open, and beckoned someone inside. Yuriko.

"You have learned to use language more efficiently than I have, Yuriko. You explain."

"Nuh-uh." Raina slapped one palm against the tabletop with a sharp crack. "*You* talk, Wizard. You're the one who lured me here, who tricked me, who used me. You just try to explain that."

Yuriko folded her arms across her chest, pushed the door shut from the inside, and leaned back against the wall. There was a pained expression on her face that hinted at her discomfort, but Raina wasn't willing to spare any sympathy for her.

"We meant no harm to you," Yuriko said softly. "It was never our intention to turn you over to Bane, only to use you to lure him closer to us."

"So I should be thankful that I'm only the appetizer and not the meal?" Suddenly weary, her anger evaporating into quiet desolation, Raina shook her head. "It doesn't matter what you meant. Harm was done. And I doubt you even know just what you've unleashed. He'll stop at nothing now that he's finally decided to hunt me. He won't care how many lives he takes, how many families he destroys. Hell, he'll enjoy it." She rubbed her hands up and down her arms. Beth. He'd find out about Beth. *Frigging damned hell.* "Bane will kill every man, woman, and child in this compound, just because he can." She turned to Wizard. "How many years did you work for him? Kill for him?"

"I killed those who were above the law. Men who carried out crimes against humanity and could not be made to pay. Murderers. Warmongers. I have never killed an innocent."

"How do you know?" she whispered. "How can you be sure?" But even as she asked the question, she knew he was telling the truth. Wizard would have made sure. He was programmed to be sure.

"So you're telling me that Bane sent you after criminals cloaked in the guise of respectability? I have a hard time believing that. More likely he would have wanted to ally himself with them."

Wizard drummed his fingers on his thigh. "Bane wanted to be the supreme commander, the leader of a broken world. Any other with the same vision was a threat to him, and I was the weapon he thought he wielded against them," he said.

"Why? Why would you allow him to use you as judge, jury, and executioner? There are still laws that govern this world, and contract killers aren't part of that picture."

"Laws set by the New Government Order?" Wizard's smile was cold. "I did not allow him to use me. There are reasons that I killed, and they have nothing to do with the Order, or with Bane."

"So you killed for your own reasons. Your own justifications. Because they were *bad* people? And that makes it right?"

"I make no claim of moral rectitude. I make no excuses for what I am." His gray eyes glittered. "You knew that from the start, Raina."

She had known that, and she hated that he was right, hated that she couldn't see him as a murderer. She had so wanted one more thing to detest him for, and the image of Wizard slaughtering innocents was what she had hoped would break his hold on her emotions. But she couldn't believe it of him no matter how hard she tried.

He had a code of honor, and it was very important to him. He would never break it, which made his betrayal of her that much more painful. Had she meant anything at all to him, he would not have done this to her.

"So you killed to help make the world a better place? And just where would you fit into that new world?"

He blinked, and she sensed that she had struck something inside him. "There is no place for me in that world. I am a monster, bred to be a soldier, a killer."

"So what? You're working here for the greater good? Nice and noble? I'm having trouble with that picture." She paused for a moment and when he made no reply she continued. "Why break with Bane now? Why dangle me in front of him at this exact time?"

"He chose the time," Yuriko said, reminding Raina that she was in the room. She'd almost forgotten, so intent had she been on Wizard and his reactions and statements. "Because Sam died and you were alone."

Alone. Alone. She'd always been alone, even when Sam was alive. The only time she'd ever thought she

had found a place had been here with—*No. No. No.*
She was better off alone.

"Yuriko, she needs to be told."

"Told what?" Raina frowned as Yuriko pushed herself from the wall, shaking her head.

"We are not certain. The knowledge may do harm rather than good," Yuriko argued.

Raina prowled across the space that separated her from Wizard, circling him slowly, using her body to physically cut him off from Yuriko. "Tell me what?"

"Duncan Bane was the man responsible for what happened to us," Wizard said. "Not for the experiment that spawned us. But he was the commander of the unit that found us. And he was the one who gave the order to leave us there, buried alive in a forgotten laboratory with only the frozen bodies of our siblings for company. I knew nothing of emotions then. They were foreign to our upbringing by AI465."

Despite herself, Raina felt a tug of heartbreak at his words, empathy for what he had suffered. The emotion angered her, and she focused on anything but the way his description of his barren childhood made her feel. "AI465?"

"The computer that was responsible for our training and upbringing after the death of Dr. Graham."

He was silent for a moment, and Raina almost prodded him, asked what happened next, but she steeled herself against giving him even that small advantage. Instead she stared at him and waited. She could sense Yuriko behind her, sense the tension that radiated from her. Well, that was new.

"After we were found, Duncan Bane ordered that

we be left in the lab and monitored. Essentially, he wanted to continue the experiment. Later, when he learned of our special qualities and the means to enhance them, Bane had us—"

"No." Yuriko cut him off. "You must not. It will serve no good purpose. We do not know it for a certainty."

Raina kept her attention focused on Wizard. "Know what for a certainty?" she prodded.

"We believe there was a reason for Sam's harsh treatment of you. We believe—"

"No!" Yuriko said again, her voice sharp.

Raina almost laughed. A reason? They thought they knew the reason? There was nothing they could tell her that she didn't already know. Her mother's death had driven Sam mad, but he'd quickly discovered that no matter how many times he hit her, he couldn't exorcise the demons from his own soul. Afterward there were always the tears and the days he'd get so drunk he couldn't stand. Eventually he'd stopped, and then he'd just pretty much acted as though she didn't exist.

Over the years she got quicker at dodging him, healed faster when he did manage to catch her, until the day she got old enough to leave, thinking she'd never look back. Then there'd been that job that went wrong, and Sam, there, leading her out, dying in her place.

Now that she knew of the link between Bane and the Reavers, she thought that he had planned to catch her then. Sam had saved her from more than just the ice pirates.

"There's nothing you can tell me about Sam that I don't already know."

"Are you familiar with the physiology of the human immune response? Specific resistance?" Wizard asked.

She tipped her head in confusion. "That's standard grade-three science. There are two arms of specific resistance to disease: T-cells and B-cells. Also known as cellular immunity and humoral immunity. I don't see the relevance."

"You recall the pandemic diseases of the late twentieth and early twenty-first centuries . . . AIDS. SARS. Ebola. Asian bird flu."

"Wizard." Yuriko's tone held a hint of warning.

"MOFS. Multiple organ failure syndrome," Wizard continued, ignoring her, staring hard at Raina as though willing her to listen.

Raina nodded. "That killed my grandmother. Those diseases wiped out half the world's population before they were eradicated. But what the hell does that have to do with me and Sam?"

"What is the basis of immunity? Of immunization?" Wizard asked.

"Frigging twenty questions," Raina muttered. "Memory. The B-cells and T-cells develop memory of any pathogen they encounter and on subsequent exposures they mount a massive response." She was a little surprised that she remembered all of this. It was as though she had typed in a request and her mind were scrolling the information for her inner eye to read. *Weird*. "What's your point?"

"My genetic capacity to withstand physical damage is based on a similar template," Wizard explained. "Upon exposure to damaging agents—a physical blow, poison, an open wound—my body responds in much the same way that the average person's immune system responds. With each exposure to physical damage, my body retains a memory of that damage and on subsequent exposures I am able to heal more rapidly."

"But you heal almost instantaneously." Her gaze swiveled to Yuriko, read the pained expression on her face. "Oh, my God," Raina whispered, feeling ill. "He did that. Bane. He what? Beat you? Stabbed you? So you would develop some kind of immunity and heal faster each time? You and Yuriko?"

"I was subject to Bane's training process, as was Yuriko." He watched her carefully. "And you."

"Me?" His words made no sense to her, but something about the way he was looking at her made her mighty nervous. "I don't get it."

"The day your mother was killed. What do you remember?"

She shook her head. "Nothing. I don't remember anything until . . . I don't know . . . maybe weeks later."

"Do you remember being injured?"

"I wasn't injured. I wasn't there." Her head pounded, and for a second she thought she remembered an explosion and blood and pain. Shaking her head, Raina took a step back. This was all too much. He was hinting at things and telling her things that she couldn't bear to know. "I wasn't there."

Wizard said nothing, just watched her with that polished-tungsten gaze, waiting for her to get there on her own.

"Are you telling me I *was* there? That I was hurt?"

"I owed Sam my life; I paid him with yours. Bane had instituted his training process by then. Sam knew about it, knew about me. When you were injured there was little hope you would survive. He came to me, and I donated my blood to save you, something I had not done before or since. There was no guarantee, but it seemed logical that my capacity to regenerate would aid your recovery."

Oh, man. This could not be happening. "And it did?"

"Yes. We were unaware at the time that the capacity would remain with you permanently. That you would be able to process injury and retain memory of it in the same manner that Yuriko and I were capable of, although to a lesser degree." He watched her intently. "That elements of my genome would become incorporated with your own."

She thought of the times that she'd been faster than her opponent, stronger, smarter. Not by a lot. By just enough to keep her safe.

"This is frigging crazy," she muttered. Her world spun. "So you're saying Sam wasn't a drunken ass. He was . . . God, what? He was making me stronger. Every time he hit me, he was . . . *immunizing* me? That's frigging impossible."

The pieces of the puzzle clicked into place, and an unexpected calm swept over her. There. She had her answer. For so many years she had wondered what had happened to the man she barely remembered, the father who had played with her and tickled her and laughed with her. She had wondered what had turned him into the monster who had driven her to be faster, braver, stronger, smarter. As if her life had depended on it. Because it had. Her life had depended on it, and Sam had tried to protect her in the only way he could—by teaching her how to protect herself.

"If you're telling the truth, then why'd he leave me

with Bane when I was twelve?" Her head pounded so hard that her vision blurred. "Why'd he leave me with that monster?"

Yuriko stepped forward, hand outstretched as if to offer comfort. Shooting her a warning glare, Raina held her off.

"Bane took you. And he lied." Yuriko dropped her hand to her side.

Wizard spoke with cold conviction. "Sam never gave you over into Bane's keeping, but he blamed himself always for failing to keep you safe."

Reeling from information overload, Raina swallowed the lump that clogged her throat. What if he was telling her the truth? Did she dare trust him? The thought made her snort with derision. Easy answer there. No.

Frig. It was all hydrogen through the pump . . . she couldn't change any of it. Her gaze shifted to Yuriko. No sense pondering Sam's motivations, and no sense hanging around listening to explanations. The walls closed in on her. She had to get out of here.

Trust no one. She'd broken her own golden rule. And worst of all, by trusting them she'd created a situation where she was afraid to trust herself.

But the worst thing was, despite everything they'd done, a part of her still wanted to stay.

There were no words for this good-bye, so she settled for a quick glance at Yuriko and a mumbled, "I'll take care of your plant."

Raina pushed herself to her feet, refusing to look at Wizard.

Oh, she didn't deny that he had his reasons for what he'd done, didn't negate the fact that he had an ax to grind with Duncan Bane. She just couldn't forgive him for dragging her into it and tearing apart her small, relatively safe world. Worse, she couldn't forgive him for making her care about him, about the people in this camp. One more argument for leaving—because if she stayed, Bane would find them, and he would kill them all.

She did look at Wizard then, at those eyes, liquid silver touched with a thread of blue, framed in dark, dark lashes, at the fullness of his lips, sensual, his mouth almost too beautiful for a man, and she had to fight not to allow herself to soften. He had betrayed her, and she still wanted to kiss him. To climb on top of him and stick her tongue in his mouth, run her hands over his body and rip his clothes off him. She wanted to wrap herself in the shelter of his arms, to have him at her back in a fight.

But that was so wrong. He'd never had her back. He'd had his own motives all along, and she'd followed him like a lamb to the slaughter.

Frig.

Tearing her gaze away, she fisted her hands at her sides. Wizard was a lowlife snake. She strode across the room toward the door.

"Raina." Wizard's voice, low and rough, touched a chord deep inside her even though she didn't want it to. "Stay."

She yanked open the door and took a step through, paused long enough to whisper, "Live to see peace."

Taking a deep breath, Raina stared at the long, dark corridor that led to her lonely future, and wondered if the pain in her shattered heart could kill her. Putting one foot in front of the other, she started walking.

SIXTEEN

Keying in the pay code for the Sheppard School, Raina loaded enough interdollars to cover five years' worth of tuition, and some spending money on the side. In five years Beth would be nineteen, too old to stay at the school any longer. But five years of safety, security, the environment she had always known . . . that had to be worth something.

The money was pretty much all Raina had. Everything. All the security she could afford to buy for her sister. She had to hope it would be enough.

She sucked in a slow breath, blew it out. If she survived this, she'd have to start over, build a life from scratch. That was fine. She could do it. If she survived.

And if she didn't . . . well, it was better the funds go to Beth than sit unclaimed in a series of numbered accounts.

Raina frowned as the school account flashed its balance. More than she had loaded. Much more.

"What?" she muttered, fingers keying in the access

code to query the balance. Again it flashed, the number unchanged. More than double what she had put in.

Sam? Had Sam managed to find the money to pay for Beth's care before he died? She didn't think so. With his last words he'd begged Raina to take care of Beth. He hadn't acted like a man confident of his daughter's care.

She typed the inquiry, sent it, and then her gut clenched as she read the name on the account report. *Wizard. Frigging Wizard.* He'd paid Beth's tuition, but how? Why?

How did he even know about her?

Staring at the screen, Raina felt her belly do a slow, sick roll. If Wizard knew about Beth, did that mean that Bane knew about her too?

Her resolution hardened. She might not frigging survive this, but if she died, she was taking Bane to hell with her.

Either way her sister would be safe.

Glancing up, she checked her appearance in the mirror, smoothing her hair one last time, practicing her smile.

She wanted the kid to know that someone had cared. Someone had wanted her safe. Someone would have loved her if she'd lived long enough to be given the chance.

Her fingers curled, tightening into fists, and Raina focused on her breathing, calming her racing heart. She was going to create a holopic. That was all. Just a holopic. She forced her shoulders, her hands, to relax as she directed the feed to Beth's school, ensuring encryption and safety codes for the eighteen transfers the feed would follow before it reached her. And then she pressed the start button.

"Hello, Beth," she said softly, her eyes burning. "I'm your sister, Raina. I'm so sorry I never had the chance to meet you in person, to talk to you, to know you. . . ."

Raina ran, booted feet pounding on the frozen ground. Jagged shards of frigid air scored her lungs with each labored breath. Her heart pounded, slamming against her rib cage. She focused on the rhythm of it, the solid thumping that kept her moving at a steady pace. The shouting behind her grew louder, closer, and she concentrated on the horizon as she ran.

There was nowhere for her to go. She knew it. They knew it. But she needed to keep up the pretense that if she ran long enough, she might escape. They thought her a terrified arctic hare tearing across the tundra. Of all the morons in the frozen north, this time she would make certain that Duncan Bane was the biggest, because this time the hunter had become the hunted.

Only he didn't know it yet.

Her legs wobbled and her vision blurred, obscured by the tears that leaked out as her body tried to moisten eyes burned by the bitter wind. She'd run for hours. They would easily believe that she could run no more. Actually, she still had some life left in her, which left her wondering if maybe, just maybe, Wizard had told her the truth.

She glanced over her shoulder, sensing Bane's minions close at her heels. They thought they'd run her to ground. She figured her ruse was believable, so there was no point in continuing. Flopping forward, she rested her hands on her thighs, allowing herself a precious moment to drag in a harsh rasp of air.

"Hello, pretty." The voice was low, and it came from directly behind her. The timbre, the pitch . . . Her skin crawled. She had thought she was ready for him, had known he would come, but all the mental preparation had not lessened the impact of this meeting.

She swallowed back the bitter bile that curdled in her gut. Slowly she straightened and turned to face her nightmare.

"Raina always brought a snack," Ben grumbled. He surged to his feet, spun, and aimed the plasgun, firing off a round without hesitation. The shot went wide of the mark. Glancing at Wizard, he shrugged. "So why'd you let her go?"

"She was not mine to keep," Wizard said. The words sounded hollow, even to him. Not his to keep. But perhaps she might have been his to . . . to what? To make love to? To laugh with? To *feel* emotion for?

He should have found a way to keep her with him, to keep her safe. That was the issue here. He had failed again. Failed Raina as he had failed Tatiana, his little sister, the trusting one, the one so ill prepared to leave the sheltered world of the lab that had been their home. He had not kept her with him, had not kept her safe, and she had paid for his failing with her life. Was that the fate that was to be Raina Bowen's?

He had intended to follow her, to guard her safety, but the very day she left the rebel compound was again attacked. Torn between conflicting loyalties, he had assessed the situation and calculated probabilities. The correct choice was to remain in the rebel camp, but for the first time in his life he had been inclined to pursue the alternate choice, the one guided by his heart.

Yuriko had pointed out that Raina would not welcome his interference—that, in fact, his presence could endanger her. If she was focused on trying to get rid of him, she might miss a threat and fail to protect herself. That possibility was unacceptable. Too, if Bane knew that Wizard left the camp, he would know that Raina had left as well. Wizard's best intentions could easily have the opposite effect.

No, he thought ruthlessly. *At least admit the truth.* He had been afraid to go after her, afraid she would refuse him, turn him away. Afraid she would not forgive him. That was the ugliest truth, the one he needed to face.

Again, she had made him know fear, a terror of a different sort.

Unwilling to face his regrets, he filed them away and concentrated on Ben. "As you turn, visualize the target in your mind even before your arm swings into position." He rested his fingers on the top of the boy's plasgun and pushed it down. "Again."

"We've been doing this for two hours. I'm hungry. You never bring any food," Ben complained. He followed Wizard's instructions anyway, positioning himself for the next shot. They had been practicing together every day, with Ben clearly determined to master the weapon and learn how to defend his comrades. "You make it look so easy," he grumbled. "Like you don't even have to think about it."

Wizard shook his head. "I don't." If he let himself think, then his mind filled with images of Raina and with raw and bitter regret. The emotion was new to him. Unfamiliar. Unpleasant. And it was leaking out of the compartment he had assigned it to, permeating his every thought.

Even the loss of Tatiana had not eroded his control in this manner.

"That's exactly what Raina said when she was showing me how to throw a knife. She said she didn't have to think abou—" Ben cut himself short and stared at a point behind Wizard's shoulder.

Turning abruptly, Wizard found Yuriko striding toward him across the compound. Her expression was set, her gait brisk. At the sight of her he felt a cold frisson of unease skitter along his skin. The feeling grew until he recognized it as the same kind of insidious fear that had come upon him the day the ice pirates had attacked the encampment. He had been afraid that day that Raina would be wounded, even killed. His fear had had nothing to do with losing the bait he needed to draw out Duncan Bane and everything to do with the safety of the woman who had found a way to unlock his emotions. She had taught him to laugh. Taught him to feel.

Right now, looking at the dark horror in Yuriko's eyes, the wellspring of his emotion erupted, and he almost wished he could go back to the way he had been before Raina had blasted apart his control.

"Bane has her," he said, never doubting it.

"Affirmative."

At her confirmation he felt as though a haze had been lifted from his mind. He stopped his futile struggle, and instead opened himself to the fear, the anguish, the worry, using the emotions to strengthen himself, to solidify his goal. He was a warrior bred to the task, a finely honed fighting machine. And this battle was the most important of his life. "How long?"

"Approximately four hours. He is holding her at Bob's Truck Stop."

"I will retrieve her. And I will terminate Bane."

Yuriko nodded sharply. "He has a force of sixty men. Two squads of ice pirates travel to join him from opposite trajectories. If they reach him, his position will be significantly reinforced."

"Send intercept teams for the pirates. I go to retrieve Raina Bowen."

"She may not be alive."

Wizard turned to his sister, his conviction never wavering. "She is alive. Bane would not grant her the peace of death. He will prolong her suffering." He took a slow breath. "And thanks to me, she will survive almost any horror he inflicts upon her."

"You do not know that, and you should not have explained before she left. It is too—"

"Explained what?" Ben asked.

"—dangerous," Wizard said brusquely, his gaze locked on Yuriko. "Had she not known of her status, she would have—"

Ben looked back and forth between the two. "What do you mean, Raina's status? You mean, like, she's pregnant or something?"

Fertility? He had asked her. She'd shaken her head, smiled. *Not for nine more days.* "No. She is not pregnant—"

"—run headlong into danger perhaps?" Yuriko demanded. "In what way would that have been different from the present circumstance? But armed with the knowledge of her unique physiology, the fact that your blood allowed a molecular transformation of her nucleotide sequence—"

"There is no proof of any physiological or genetic modification in Raina Bowen," Wizard said.

"Then what are you two talking about? Her nucleotide sequence? You mean, like, her DNA?" Ben asked.

Wizard bent and retrieved the two plasguns that lay on the ground at his feet. "We waste time."

Ben stepped forward and took a deep breath. "I'm going with you. I know that truck stop better than anyone . . . every nook and cranny. Every hidey-hole. I can help."

"Understood," Yuriko said. "Trey is assembling three teams. He heads to the east, Gerhardt to the west. I am for the truck stop. We leave in one hour. Ben, you are with me. Wizard—" She stopped abruptly.

Wizard was barely aware that she was still speaking. He was already striding across the encampment, his focus constricting into a narrow field with two essential goals: Find Raina Bowen. Execute Duncan Bane.

"Five minutes," he said over his shoulder, never breaking stride. "Be ready, or I leave alone."

Duncan Bane ran his fingers along the edge of the patch that covered his ruined eye. Raina had been lovely as a child, but now she was so much more than that. For years he had pleasured himself while he fantasized about Raina Bowen. He had pictured her beaten, tortured, her skin oozing blood from a thousand carefully placed tiny cuts, and he had stroked himself while he imagined the pleasure of making her suffer.

He had long remembered the silky fall of her golden hair, the incredible blue of her eyes, the lovely terror that had made them go wide and dark as he touched her.

But his memory had been of a helpless twelve-year-old girl in a woman's lush body. This was so much better. He preferred the woman to the girl. How much more satisfying to decimate a strong opponent than a weak one. And here was Raina grown strong, tempered by the buffeting storms of life. He ached to dominate her, this resilient and bold woman Raina had become. He wanted to break her. But slowly, so slowly, so he could relish each stage of her collapse, watch her recover from each session, only to face the next and the next.

Soon he would go to her, but not quite yet. He would leave her in the dark hole he'd thrown her into for just a little longer, let her fear fester and grow.

Duncan crossed the expanse of the huge insulated dome that had been set up for his convenience. Heaters the size of turbine engines blew warm air into the interior. It was unthinkable that he, Duncan Bane, would house himself with the whores and thieves who frequented Bob's. Instead he brought his own accommodation, and servants to see to his needs. He glanced at the dark-haired young woman cowering in a corner, clutching the edges of the clothing he had torn from her body. She sobbed softly, wrapping her arms tightly about herself.

With a snarl he sent her away. Again his body had failed to heed his will, and he had been unable to per-

269

form despite the fact that he had beaten the girl first. Mewling creature.

Raina had done this to him, made him unable to function in that manner, but his time, his moment of pure and deserved vengeance had come. He would use her until she begged for mercy, until she begged for death. But, oh, he would not grant that. No. Instead he would grant her time. Time to heal. Time to live with the knowledge that he would return again and again to do worse than she could imagine in her darkest nightmare. He owed her for the loss of his eye, and for other losses less obvious to the casual observer. He would take his payment in thin strands of flesh peeled from her naked body.

The thought brought untold delight, akin to the feeling that had pounded through him when he had caught her, so exquisite as to be indefinable. If the fantasy was so delightful, how much more perfect the reality would be.

Duncan picked up his tea and took a sip. He had expected a prolonged and tedious search, but mere days into his northern sojourn he had found her. Foolish woman to pass so close to Bob's Truck Stop. Did she not realize that his spies were everywhere?

Still, one piece of his ultimate pleasure was missing. Wizard. No one walked away from Duncan Bane. No one. Least of all a genetically mutated mercenary tramp.

Raina had remained unexpectedly long in the rebel camp. With Wizard. Had they formed an alliance, Wizard and Raina? An attachment? If he killed Wizard in front of her, would she suffer?

Duncan smiled. His men were searching, and it was only a matter of time before the assassin was found.

In an empty storage room in the basement of Bob's Truck Stop, Raina shivered uncontrollably, naked in the darkness of her prison. *Frig*—she really hated the cold. And Bane knew it. So of course he'd ordered his thugs to strip her naked and chain her here in a room so cold that it left her shaking. But not cold enough to kill her. *Oh, no.* Bane wanted her alive. Demoralized. Afraid. Desperate. But alive.

So much for Wizard's assertion that she was modified, just like him. *He* didn't feel the cold, while she was still subject to its icy chill. *Wizard. Frig.* She would *not* think about him.

Shivering so hard she could barely think, she shoved back the gnawing doubt that ate at her. A tide of panic battered her control, but she refused to allow it to gain ground. She'd known exactly what Bane would do if he caught her. Had counted on it, in fact. She had chosen her course. Plotted it. Charted it. She would not let fear destroy her now.

She was smarter than Bane. Tougher. Maybe she always had been. So why had she run for more than half her life? Why hadn't she realized that she should take a stand and fight long before now?

An image of Wizard shimmered through her mind, frustrating her efforts to hold it at bay. He'd believed her capable of handling anything. He'd assigned her as his partner when they'd carried out their near-suicidal mission against the ice pirates. He'd let her steer her own course against the Reavers and the Janson, never trying to intervene or take over. He'd treated her as an equal. He'd treated her with respect.

Was it his confidence that had rubbed off on her? She didn't like to think so, preferring the idea that he had simply acted as the catalyst that finally allowed her to fully trust in herself. Except she didn't. That was the problem. And maybe this decision to go after Bane instead of waiting for him to come for her was her way of reviving her sagging sense of self.

She gritted her teeth. Wizard had made her trust *him*. And he'd betrayed her. But it was a betrayal set in motion long before he knew her. Did that lessen the depth of his duplicity? Weeks ago she would have said no, but she had had so many long, lonely days with nothing to do but think, and now she wasn't so certain.

Raina lifted her hands, testing the bonds that held her. Metal cuffs. Thick chains. No half measures for Duncan Bane. Everything was progressing exactly as she had hoped. The cuffs and chains fed her confidence. A rope would have posed a problem, but a metal lock was easy. She'd come prepared.

Focusing on her task, she ran her tongue along the roof of her mouth, pressing as hard as she could. The thin, cylindrical ridge under the tissue of her palate shifted. She ignored the sharp pain that accompanied the movement. Again, she worked the area with her tongue, patiently wriggling the thin metal pin free of the mucous membrane that lined the roof of her mouth.

She was a prisoner because she had chosen to become one. Enough of her life had been wasted on frantic glances over her shoulder, always waiting for the day that Bane would catch her. Somehow the day she had walked away from Wizard had become the day she decided that she would wait no more. She would go after Bane and end this game of cat and mouse. She'd been strong enough to turn her back on Wizard, the man she was willing to die for, the man she could never forgive.

Surely she was strong enough to defeat one sadistic bastard.

Of course, she'd made sure that to all appearances she was unwilling, that she'd been caught off guard. She'd run as if she thought she might escape. When Bane had caught her, she'd fought as though she thought she might win. And he had bought into the vision because it was exactly what he'd wanted to see.

He'd had his thugs drag her here, to Bob's. One bit of luck to add to her escalating tally. She'd hidden clothes and weapons nearby in the hope that he'd bring her here. A calculated risk. Bob's Truck Stop was the only place that even hinted at civilization within a three-hundred-yuale radius. Duncan Bane viewed himself as nothing if not civilized.

She winced as a particularly firm push of her tongue dislodged the thin metal pin from where she'd rammed it into the roof of her mouth. She'd known Bane would strip her naked, that he'd take any protection, any hope of escape away from her. He wanted her terrified, cowed, vulnerable. So she'd let him see exactly that, while she'd hidden the pin that would grant her escape in the only place she could—inside her body.

Bane hadn't come to her yet. Not his style. He wanted her to sit, and stew, and dream up terrifying scenarios of what he would do when he finally arrived.

Surprise. She didn't intend to wait around.

Clamping her teeth around the newly freed pin, she ignored the metallic tang of blood that pooled in her mouth, welcomed the throb of pain that reminded her she was alive. She bent forward, willing her shivering to subside lest she drop the pin and lose her one chance. Her fingers shook, but she managed to clasp the small metal pick and angle it slowly until it slid into the lock of the manacles that held her wrists.

Slowly, so slowly, she turned it this way and that. Her fingers were numb with cold. She could barely feel the thin sliver of metal.

She tightened her grip. Too late. The soft clang of metal on stone told her that the pin had hit the floor. Tears of anger and desperation stung her eyes.

Frig. She'd known this was not going to be easy, but the reality of the situation jeopardized her ability to maintain her control. She was naked, frozen, chained, and her one chance for freedom was somewhere on the floor, hidden by the darkness.

Lowering herself to the ground she wriggled carefully across the floor, her fingers lightly sweeping an arc in front of her, feeling for the pin.

Stupid, clumsy girl. Sam's voice, there in her head. She hadn't heard it for so long, she half believed that he was gone. The sound of her chains dragging across the floor as she slowly moved her hands grated in her ears.

Not gone. Sam would never be gone. He was the reason that she was tough, strong, brave. Hell, he was the reason she was alive. She supposed she could forgive him for everything else. Maybe. If she lived through this, she'd have to think about it.

The breath hissed from between her clenched teeth as her fingers closed around the errant pin. She'd found it.

Time had no meaning for her. There was only the lock and the pin that she manipulated painstakingly until at last she heard the soft snick of the catch giving way. For an instant the memory of Wizard and how he had bypassed her state-of-the-art lock system snaked through her thoughts. She thrust the recollection aside, trying to focus only on the present.

Her time with Wizard was nothing more than a fantasy. A hot, writhing memory to carry with her for decades. And she *would* carry it. She would take it out and savor it and remember what it had felt like to believe in the fairy tale even for a few days. But not now. Now she had a mission to complete, and an enemy to kill.

Taking a slow, calming breath, she laid the manacles carefully on the ground. No sense giving her captors a warning by tossing the metal onto the floor with a loud clank. She spit out a mouthful of warm, blood, disgusted by the metallic taste of it. Her palate ached with a dull intensity, and she couldn't stop her tongue from running across the sore flesh. Raina shook her head. The pain was a small price to pay for her freedom.

After wiping the back of one hand across her lips, she bent and retrieved the pin from the lock. Palms pressed flat to the frigid walls, she worked her way around the room, feeling carefully in the darkness until she found the door. No light leaked into her tiny cell, so she assumed that either the door had been sealed or that there was no light in the area beyond her prison.

So cold. She was so frigging cold.

No. She refused to allow herself to focus on anything but the task. For this moment the cold did not exist, her fear did not exist. There was only the need to free herself from the tiny room that served as her cell. Closing her trembling fingers around the door handle, she slipped the pin into the lock.

Hello, luck. The lock proved a poor challenge, giving way on her first try. Of course, she was held in a storeroom in the basement of Bob's . . . there was no reason for a sturdy lock on this door. She eased the door open and peered around the edge. The hallway was almost as dark as the room that had served as her cell. There was no sound, no smell other than the faint stink of something rotting. No sign of a guard.

She shook her head. It appeared that Bane had assumed she'd be an easy target, but she was taking no chances. She closed the door behind her just in case someone walked by, then moved along the hallway with silent, measured steps, ever conscious of the fact that she didn't know what monsters lurked in the shadows.

A dim gray light filtered from beneath a door about halfway along the hall, and Raina paused, listening intently. No sound. Closing her trembling fingers around the handle, she tried it. Unlocked. She pushed it open and slipped inside.

The smell hit her like a fist. The garbage room. *Perfect.*

She hesitated. Too easy. It all felt too easy. Glancing around, she peered into the musty corners of the room, searching for a trap. Nothing moved. No one there. She gave a soft huff of relief.

Within seconds Raina reached the opening to the outdoor chute. The chute was supposed to be heated to make certain that waste matter tossed down didn't freeze against the sides and block the entry. Only, for some reason, the heat hadn't been turned on.

Clumps of frozen refuse clung to the metal walls of the shaft. Gingerly Raina tested one. Satisfied that it would hold her weight, she began to climb.

Stifling a cry as one of the clumps of garbage tore away from the shaft, she slapped her feet and her palms against the metal sides, pressing outward with all her strength, barely stopping herself from tumbling back down. Desperately she bolstered herself against the frozen metal walls of the tiny, claustrophobic tube. Her skin stuck to the frozen surface. Gingerly she pulled. Stuck fast, like a fly on flypaper.

With a sharp jerk she tore one hand away from the wall, gritting her teeth against the pain. Tears stung her eyes as she reached up for the next clump of garbage that adhered to the wall, her hand slick with her blood.

Biting her lip so hard that it split, Raina repeated the process, ripping each limb from the frozen metal, inching her way up the tube.

She rolled free of the opening and immediately bounded to her feet, biting back a cry as the bitter wind thrashed her naked skin and the frigid ground tore at her already damaged soles. Minutes, if that, before she froze to death. She staggered toward the bundle she had hidden behind the enormous trash bins that were collected once a month.

Snatching up her clothes, she donned them as quickly as she could, given that her whole body was shaking so hard that she could barely even breathe. With a snap of her wrist she released the heat packs she'd installed front and back. The packs began their slow burn, warming her body back to normal temperature.

Then she removed the syringe from her pocket and injected the therma-chem that she had prepared in advance, wincing at the smoldering ache that fanned out from the injection site. Therma-chem cost a small fortune, but it was an essential component of the emergency kit that all truckers carried by mandatory law of the New Government Order. For her entire career, she'd always thought of it as a cash grab by the Order. And it was. The chem worked for only a short time, and if a stranded trucker actually needed to use it, they'd still be facing death by refrigeration within an hour. Raina smiled. Wouldn't it just stick in Bane's craw to realize that his little moneymaker had actually helped facilitate her escape.

It took less than five minutes to return her body to a normal temperature. No longer shivering, she leaned out and did a rapid perusal of the vicinity.

The night sky was black, overcast, the stars obscured by the blanket of cloud. In the distance she could see the billowing white top of Bane's personal dome, illuminated by two large lights near the front. There would likely be guards set up for his protection, and she imagined there might be a guard at the front door of Bob's.

In the shadowy corner behind the trash bins, Raina

squatted down and checked her weapons. The Setti86 was strapped to her thigh. She had a knife harnessed at her back, one in her boot, and a small spare in the tidy sheath at her wrist. A belt studded with throwstars hung low on her hips.

In the event that all else failed, she had a little surprise for Duncan Bane, one she truly hoped she didn't have to use, because that little surprise just might buy her a one-way ticket to hell right along with Bane. It was a trip she wasn't anxious to make.

Who was she trying to kid? She wasn't likely to live to see morning, but she wasn't going out alone. She was taking Bane with her, no matter the cost.

Beth would be safe. At least then her life would have meant something. Hadn't she always had this thing for orphan kids?

Ben and Spike and Trey and Sawyer . . . they'd be safe. Yuriko. Wizard. Why was that so important to her?

These people had betrayed her, and when she had first learned of it, she had felt as though they had thrust a blade through her soul. But just as she had accepted that she could no longer run from her fate, that she must turn and face Bane, determining the course of her life rather than fleeing from it, she had also realized that in truth, there were layers and gray values of betrayal.

Whatever plan they had set in motion had been done before they had ever met her, before she had become real to them. If she was honest, she knew that in the end each one of them would have fought for her if she had let them.

Hadn't Ben taken a beating to protect her?

Hadn't Yuriko asked her to stay, even though it

meant that Bane would never have rested until he found them? She had been willing to offer protection and the hand of friendship.

Raina swallowed, closed her eyes, and let memories of Wizard course through her. He'd asked her to stay. She could almost feel the caress of his velvet voice as he said that single word. Amazing how hindsight could bring clarity. Maybe, if she made it through the night, she'd go back and see if Wizard had really meant it, see if they had something more than gorgeous, perfect sex. A grim smile tugged at her lips. *Yeah.* All she needed to do was survive the night.

Creeping through the darkness, she hugged the shadows. For the first time in her life she felt true appreciation for the frigid clime of the Waste. It kept people indoors, or at least kept them close to any shelter or warmth. That made her clandestine movements easier. There was no one around to see her.

One step and another. Her pulse hammered in her ears. A lifetime of waiting for this exact moment, waiting for the beast to pounce on her from the darkest reaches of her imagination. Except that the beast was real. He was a flesh-and-blood man whose actions had stolen her childhood, her innocence, her parents' lives. She was sick and tired of waiting for the beast to leap upon her. The time had come to hunt him in his own lair. Kill him.

She'd be doing the world a favor.

Only a short span of flat plain lay between her and Bane's dome. A quick dash and she would be there. So many years of running away, and they had brought her full circle, running *toward* the fiend who had ripped her world apart. How did one evil man gain such power?

Taking a deep breath, she readied herself to leave the relative protection of the building that concealed her presence. Fifteen seconds where she'd be out in the open, she figured. All she needed was fifteen seconds of luck.

She lunged forward, but something caught her arm, whirled her back. A hard hand slapped over her mouth, catching the startled exclamation that flew to her lips. She continued to struggle, and then quickly changed tactics, letting her weight drop like an avalanche, expecting that the guard who held her would react with surprise.

Only he didn't.

Heart pounding, she fought panic as the guard's fingers bit into her arms and he jerked her tight against him.

SEVENTEEN

"Unacceptable," a voice whispered against her ear. But even before she heard the word, she *knew*. His height. The clean smell of his skin. The hard planes of his chest.

Wizard.

Frigging hell. She'd wanted him safe. And *here* definitely wasn't safe.

She turned to face him, feeling a momentary pang as he let the arm he'd held her with fall away. "What are you doing here?"

His eyes glittered in the darkness. "Saving your butt."

It felt like a million years ago that she'd spoken the same words to him.

"Saving my butt for what? Breakfast?" she whispered, half choked by the pain in her chest, in her heart.

God, he'd come after her, knowing that she'd walked out on him and that she hadn't looked back, knowing that if Bane caught him it would mean a slow and agonizing death. He'd come to save her, and she was almost tempted to let him. Except she was used to saving herself. Old habits were hard to break. Combine that with the fact that she couldn't trust him, couldn't be certain that he'd actually come for *her*, that it wasn't just Bane he wanted, and she was left with one big, muddled mess. Maybe she didn't trust herself to decide.

With a soft sound of distress, she stepped away from his inviting warmth. Sticking to the shadows, she scanned the perimeter, instinct making her careful even though her thoughts were so confused. Something kept nagging at her. The ease of her escape. The lack of a guard.

A whisper of air and the subtle shift of his body told her that Wizard, too, was assessing their surroundings.

"I can't leave until he's dead," she said, sure and clear. No more running.

"Understood."

She clenched her fists. A part of her wanted Wizard to stand by her side as she faced her nightmare, wanted him to be her buttress, her support. Another part of her wanted him to run, to escape from what was most likely a suicide mission more dangerous than the one they had joined in together against the ice pirates.

Together they'd beaten the odds on the last one. The likelihood was that one of them would die this time out. And, God, she didn't want Wizard to die. She wanted him to walk free in the sunshine, to know laughter, to know love.

Because, despite his betrayal, she loved him.

She had to realize that *now*? The thought of love

frightened her even as it freed her. *Frig*. She needed this right now like she needed a jammed plasgun.

Trust her to find a way to make the impossible even more difficult.

Dragging in a breath, she leaned forward, let her weight rest against Wizard's solid form. This might be her last chance to feel the warmth of his embrace, and she wasn't about to pass it up. For an instant he seemed startled, stiff, and then he wrapped his arms around her and held her tight.

She didn't dare imagine that he loved her back, though she ached with the wish that it was so. Closing her eyes, she just let him hold her, allowed herself the moment.

Somewhere deep inside of her was a neglected little girl who desperately wanted to be loved, wanted to know she was worthy of that lofty emotion. She fought against the bitter tide of long-buried sentiments and insecurities, and she faced the desolate child she had once been. Her mother dead and buried, her father drowning in his own bitter despair, she had been alone. Forever alone. Man, she had some real issues to work out.

"What is it?" His breath was warm against her cheek.

Her heart twisted. She couldn't tell him; her emotions were too fresh, too raw. But she could not deny him. A part of her wanted him to know, to understand. "I'm thinking that—" She broke off, tried again. "These are not the best circumstances to have this conversation." Only there might never be a second chance.

As if he read her innermost fears, Wizard tightened his embrace, holding her as if he would never let her go.

"You know, emotion is a crazy thing. Despite everything, I loved Sam. Whatever poor excuse for a father he was, he was the only father I had."

"I am unaware of any coherent connection between your statement and your current situation. Please clarify."

Trust Wizard to call a spade a spade. She would have laughed if she hadn't suspected that if she let any emotion surface, it would quickly overwhelm her.

"I failed him. Sam. He died, slit open by pirates because I wasn't fast enough, smart enough, tough enough," she explained softly. "Even though I loved him, I couldn't save him."

"As he could not save your mother." Wizard was silent for the span of a heartbeat, and then he continued. "As I could not save Tatiana."

"Yes." He understood, she realized, and now she faced the possibility that once again someone she loved risked paying the price for her errors. The truth was a bitter pill. Her lack of trust extended even to herself. She could not trust her ability to keep Wizard safe.

"Go," she whispered. "Go now, while you still can. I don't want to fail you." To fail the man she loved. "I want you to—"

"Go where? My place is here."

Why? Why is it here? Because there is a job for you to do, or because of me? The questions clogged her throat, and she was paralyzed with the inability to let them tumble free.

"Damn you, Wizard," she whispered. "I've finally worked it all out, finally stopped running in circles trying to evade the monster in my closet. And then here you are, making everything all complicated."

"Raina." Wizard's voice reached out to her through the darkness. "Do you remember the time we spent in the ice cave? You asked me if I ever feel scared."

"Yeah. I remember. You told me that emotions like fear were unfamiliar to you." God, right about now she wouldn't mind if that emotion were a little less real for her.

"They *were* unfamiliar to me."

She heard the inflection in his voice, sensed the hidden meaning. "Were?"

The wind swirled around them, and Wizard shifted closer, angling his body to block her from the worst of it. So chivalry hadn't died a brutal death.

His gloved hand came up to stroke her cheek through the thermal balaclava that protected her face from frostbite.

"Past tense." His voice vibrated with emotion, and she felt it shimmer through her. "Fear is no longer an unfamiliar emotion. I am afraid, Raina. For you. I . . ." He hesitated, and her heart constricted, her breath catching in her throat as she waited for whatever secret he would share.

A subtle tension filtered through his body, rippled from him to her where their sides pressed together, a silent portent. The shift of his weight away from her warned her that something was wrong.

"I am so pleased to learn of your fear." The oily voice slithering toward her froze the blood in Raina's veins. Bane. He'd found them, and she hadn't even been aware of his approach. "Did you not think I would vid-wire your cell, Raina? That I would not know every move you made, every breath you took? I was rather impressed by your ingenuity." He gave a high giggle that made her shudder. "And so looking forward to watching your face as you realized your escape was all a dream, a farce. I let you get away, just to enjoy your despair as I caught you."

So Bane had known the second she had escaped, had been aware of her every move. A part of her had sensed that, known it was all too easy.

"Let me extend a welcome, assassin," Bane continued. "I had wondered if the two of you might have formed some attachment."

"Distract him." Wizard's whispered words fanned across her skin. "I require ten minutes. I must make the way safe for the others." He moved away, melting into the darkness, leaving her feeling desperate and alone. And more afraid than she had ever been in her life. It was one thing to imagine facing Bane. Quite another to actually do it.

"Tsk . . . have you turned coward, assassin? Slinking away like a rat?" Only the wind answered. Wizard was gone. Bane spoke into his lip-com, alerted his troops to be vigilant.

Ten minutes to do what? And who exactly were the others Wizard referred to? *Frig.* All her life she'd wanted to be respected for her ability to handle things on her own. Wouldn't you know it . . . the one time she wouldn't have minded a little help and she was left to cope all by her lonesome. But then, Wizard had had faith in her ability to handle herself right from the start. That was part of his appeal.

"*Raina.*" Bane's voice, on her right.

Earlier she had blessed the fact that the clouds were

thick as a thermal blanket, heralding a mounting storm and blocking the light of the moon and stars. The unnatural darkness had been her advantage. Now it was her enemy.

Whirling, she followed the sound of Bane's footsteps crunching on the ice as he stalked her.

She was not going to cower. She was a fighter, and it was time for her to act like one. Her hand snaked along her back, reaching for her knife.

Payback.

The air rippled, and pain tore through her wrist as Bane's booted foot hammered skin and muscle and bone. Hand numb, her grasp faltered, and the knife hit the frozen ground with a dull thud. Bane laughed as she gasped and shook out her hand, trying to return feeling to the deadened appendage.

"Night-vision goggles, my sweet," he whispered in answer to her unasked question. "I can see you, but you can't see me. It adds a lovely dimension to the game, don't you think?"

"It'd be better if I had a pair," she muttered, shrinking from the sound of his voice. Where was Wizard? Did he know that Bane could match his night vision, that he no longer had the advantage?

Bane's fingers closed over her arm, biting deep, hurting her. She refused to show any sign of weakness, refused to struggle in his hold. He wanted that. He'd enjoy it.

Squinting, she tried to see how many men he'd brought with him. One? Ten?

The odds had turned against her, but it was a possibility that she had taken into account. One way or another, Duncan Bane's reign of terror would end tonight.

The sound of a scuffle drifted across the windswept landscape. A sharp cry carried on the night wind, and then something heavy fell to the ground. Wizard must have taken down a guard. Using the distraction to her advantage, Raina dropped and rolled away from Bane. She lashed out and felt immeasurable satisfaction as her carefully placed kick slammed against his shin. His hiss of pain was a reward in itself.

"Bitch!"

She rolled again, hoping to evade him. He struck her hard in the ribs, and she cried out against the deep ache that burrowed through her. Bane used the toe of his boot to nudge her over onto her back, then rammed the sole of his foot into her breastbone, pinning her in place.

"I will bargain with you, assassin," he called. "Though you took so many worthless lives, I will offer you yours. If you want your life, and . . . let me sweeten the pot . . . the lives of those pathetic rebels, then let me keep the girl. Walk away, assassin. Walk away, and I will call off the ice pirates. I will let your pathetic band of ragged warriors live to see the weak rays of tomorrow's sun."

Wrapping her hands around Bane's ankle, Raina tried to dislodge his foot, but her wrist was numb from the blow he had delivered earlier. She struggled to drag in enough breath to call out a warning to Wizard. *Don't trust him. His offer is a ruse to get you out in the open, where he can gun you down like a dog.*

But Wizard would know that. He was too smart not to figure it out.

"Assassin, what price the life of your sister?"

Raina felt sick at his words. Was Yuriko on her way

290

here? Was she one of the people Wizard had wanted to protect?

"The life of your sister, assassin. Not Yuriko, no." Bane cackled at some secret joke. "Your *other* sister. Tatiana. Tatiana. Where is Tatiana?"

Tatiana. Raina thought of the girl she had known when she had been Bane's prisoner as a child, the girl she had been forced to leave behind. Ana. Dark hair. Enormous gray eyes that seemed to see more than was there. The gears clicked smoothly into place. *Ana* was *Tatiana*, Wizard's sister. Alive? And Bane knew some secret about her, was dangling it like a frigging rotting carrot.

Frig. Could this get any worse?

Bane pressed down harder against her ribs, then dropped the butt of his plasgun to land a sharp blow to her solar plexus. The breath left her in a harsh exhalation.

Okay. That was worse.

"And you, Raina Bowen, what is the assassin's life worth to you? Surrender now, and I will send him on his way, alive and in one piece. I make the offer once and only once. I am in a generous mood."

She would have liked to believe him, except that she knew he was a lying snake. *Don't be afraid, pretty Raina. I won't hurt you.*

Yeah. Right. And there was no ice in the Waste.

Wrenching to the side, Raina struggled to free herself. Bane laughed softly, dropping the butt of the gun to hit her again.

She'd counted on that. With a rapid jerk of her arm, she deflected the worst of the blow. A flick of her wrist and the knife she had sheathed there slipped free. With strength born of utter desperation she plunged the blade into the instep of Bane's foot, slicing thick boot and tender flesh.

His howl of pain and rage filled the night. "You will pay for that, bitch. In tears and cries, you will pay." He snarled, reaching down to drag the knife free and toss it aside.

Lurching sideways, hand outstretched, Raina fumbled for the discarded weapon, a surge of relief flowing through her as the tips of her fingers brushed the hilt. Almost there. Almost—

With a guttural sound, Bane closed one hand around her ankle and yanked her away, leaving the knife beyond her reach.

"Assassin," Bane called again, breathing heavily.

The wail of the wind was his only answer.

"Find him. Kill him. Bring me his severed, bloody head," Bane spoke into his lip-com, summoning his minions.

So much for playing nice. Wizard was definitely not going to lose his head, not if she had anything to say about it. Pressing the soles of her feet against the ground, Raina arched her back, pushed hard with her palms, forced herself to her feet. Her battered body screamed in protest, her damaged palms and soles flaring with agony.

Gasping, she tried to orient herself, tried to recall exactly where her plasgun had landed when it was thrust aside. If she could only—

Bane lunged to one side, too fast for her, the butt of his plasgun catching her own where it lay on the ground. She cringed at the sound of her hope spinning away across the ice.

Frig. She was running out of options.

Suddenly a tremendous noise rent the silence, and the dome of endless dark sky exploded in a ball of light. If she'd had it in her, Raina would have smiled. Wizard must have hit the munitions site. One small victory.

The light of the fire meant that Bane had lost the advantage his night-vision goggles had offered. She could now see him as clearly as he saw her. Shaking her head, she struggled to focus her vision. Everything looked hazy. Raina swiped one hand across her eyes. It came away wet. Blood. She was bleeding from the place he'd hit her.

She blinked. A second explosion roared into the night, and then Wizard strode through the wall of smoke and flame, eyes locked on her, jaw set. Come to save her.

Swaying, she grinned, and a wash of strength filled her as she watched him. Hell, she was going to save herself. But she might let him help.

A guard ran from the corner of the building and leveled his plasgun at Wizard's back.

Feeling as though she were swimming through sludge, she reached out instinctively, fingers splayed. "No!" The denial stuck in her throat like bitter syrup.

Wizard spun, fired at the guard, then whirled back toward Bane. Too late, too late. Bane turned his plasgun on Wizard and fired. The shot hit him full in the chest, knocking him back against the wall before he slumped to the ground.

Holding her arms tight against her bruised ribs, Raina stumbled forward. Wizard didn't move. No breath clouded the air in front of his face; no rise and fall of his chest gave a hint of life. Gone. He couldn't be gone.

Bane raised his gun again and aimed.

No. Not like this. A high, keening cry, more animal than human, slashed the night. Dragging her last knife free of the sheath in her boot, she lunged at Bane, wanting to tear out his remaining eye, to rip him to shreds. "You bastard! You filthy, worthless bastard."

Her blade bit through the thermal gear he wore, slicing his forearm as he raised it in defense.

He spun, bringing his plasgun full across her face. She would have fallen, but he caught her arm with his free hand, holding her up.

Raina's fingers locked on the edge of his patch and she ripped it away, revealing his ruined face, the gaping, scarred socket where his eye had been. She had done this. She had marked him on a long ago night in a desperate attempt to escape. Only she'd never truly escaped him. She'd spent her whole life trying to run away from the scars he'd inflicted on her, the scars that ran soul deep.

And now he'd taken Wizard.

Her gaze cut to his still form. "Get up!" she screamed, struggling against Bane's rough grasp, every nerve on fire, the agony inside her twisting on itself until she felt sheared in half by the force of it. "You're supposed to be invincible, Wizard. Frigging invincible."

He was supposed to live to see peace. He wasn't supposed to die here in the frigging frozen north with his chest blasted open.

"Get up," she whispered. "Please."

Bane grinned down at her, his ruined face distorted

in an evil leer. "Choose," he said. "Life or death." He jutted his chin at Wizard's limp form. "Alive come morning . . . or dead like your friend."

An icy calm enveloped her, and she knew the only answer she could give.

She'd wanted to send him to hell. She'd wanted to send him alone. But she'd prepared for the possibility that she might be forced to accompany him. There were no more choices.

Bane's grasp tightened, and he shook her like a baby's rattle. "Choose!" he snarled, bringing the plasgun up under her chin.

Shoving her tongue against the back of her jawbone, behind her molars, she freed the small pellet that she had anchored there the previous day.

The lockpick had been her one chance for freedom. The pellet was her last chance at Bane. Carefully she pushed it between her teeth. She'd have about thirty seconds from the time she bit down on it. Thirty seconds to make her peace.

But the rest of the frigging free world . . . well, if she could do this, it would buy them a lifetime. A lifetime without Duncan Bane.

There was the possibility that Wizard had been telling the truth, that somehow her genetic makeup had been modified and she could survive more than the average person. She could hope, but she wasn't counting on it.

There was also the possibility that the antitoxin she'd administered to herself yesterday might prove effective. She wasn't counting on that either. The poison she'd chosen was lethal and fast. Diotoxin based. There was no known antiserum, but she'd researched all related chemical compounds, and she'd dosed against those. A long shot, but the only shot she had.

She so did not want to die. Especially here in the frigging frozen north, never having known the kiss of sunshine on the beach.

Twisting in Bane's grasp she stared at Wizard.

This was a really bad dream. It was the nightmare that had haunted her all her life, only this time it had spilled over into the real world. Again. Just as it had when she was a kid.

"I'm ready to wake up now," she muttered, her heart sitting like a twisted ball of scrap metal in her chest.

And then he moved. Wizard moved. Just the twitch of a finger, but enough to tell her he was alive. Hope flared brighter than a phosphorous mine. He was alive, and she intended to keep him that way. This time she wouldn't fail, the way she'd failed Ana and Sam. This time she'd keep him safe.

She jerked away, drawing Bane's attention. "Life," she whispered. "I choose life." Wizard's life, because with Bane gone, he would stand a chance of escape.

Not a perfect plan, given that she was likely to die right along with the lowlife snake who had devastated her entire existence, but the only plan she had.

"A wise decision. One that pleases me greatly." Bane let the plasgun fall away, but he kept his punishing grip on her arm.

Raina swallowed. Her gaze shifted back to Wizard. He'd lied to her, tricked her, brought her here as bait. But in her worst moment he had not left her to stand alone. He was here. With her. Willing to die for her.

She loved him. *Frig.* Typical of her luck—she found

a guy to love, and she was going to go and die before she really had a chance to enjoy him.

God, what a pair. Two fools determined to die protecting each other.

She looked at Bane. "Your word." As if his word were worth anything, but she needed to make him think she believed him. "You will let him walk away."

Bane didn't even bother to glance at Wizard. "If he can walk, my dear."

He didn't mean it. She knew that, but she nodded.

"I accept." God, she sounded so calm.

The toxic pellet was tucked in tight to her cheek, hard against her back teeth.

Bane leaned a little closer, and she purposely flinched back. "Don't kiss me," she whispered, knowing that he would now, only because she asked him not to.

"Kiss you?" Bane repeated, frowning. Then he shrugged and pulled her roughly to him.

No more time. Raina closed her eyes and bit down hard on the pellet. A bitter taste flooded her mouth. Opening her lips as Bane crushed her in a brutal parody of a kiss, she let the poison flow into his mouth.

She knew the second he realized what she'd done. He stiffened, threw her to the ground with a guttural sound, and raised the plasgun. It wavered in his grasp. His eyes darted frantically about.

"Luc," Bane spoke into the lip-com. His voice was hoarse and faint, tight with panic. She doubted if anyone heard him. It wouldn't matter if they did. He'd be dead before help arrived.

The lousy thing was, so would she.

* * *

Wizard knew his chest was ripped open where Bane had shot him, the wound deep, the edges burned black by the plas-shot. On another man it would be fatal.

He pushed himself to a sitting position, gritting his teeth against the searing protest of his damaged muscle and skin.

The pain was inconsequential. Only the agony in his heart, the bitter ache of his desperation penetrated his thoughts. Frantically he tried to push the emotion aside, to regain his equilibrium and focus only on the analytical requirements of the tasks at hand.

He should alert Yuriko and the other rebel troops.

Raina.

He should secure the perimeter.

Raina.

He had to save Raina.

Struggling to his feet, he refused to look away from her fallen form. She lay on her side, back curved, arms and legs drawn protectively inward. She was so still.

He could not lose her. This was worse than Tatiana's death, worse than any loss he had ever sustained. Before Raina he had not understood. He had been able to maintain the compartments in his mind, had been able to lock away that which was not logical. He had mourned his sister, but he had survived her loss.

This loss, this mind-numbing sense of emptiness and heartache, this blinding terror . . . he did not know how to make it stop, did not know how to put it in its limited space.

Pressing one hand over the gaping wound in his chest, Wizard staggered toward Raina. His foot connected with something and he glanced down, taking in the twisted posture of Bane's body. He stepped away, but before he could move forward, something closed around his ankle.

"She dies with me," Bane whispered, his plasgun aimed at Wizard's heart. "That was her plan."

"Negative. Her plan was for you to die. Alone."

Bane gave a strangled gasp, his face a mask of twisted agony. He swung the plasgun toward Raina, cocked it.

"The pain," he whispered, his gaze shifting back to Wizard, too bright, too wild.

Pain. Bane had caused untold pain to untold thousands. Did he not deserve the same back tenfold?

Wizard knelt by the dying man's side, hating him, a dark and ugly coil of emotion that grabbed his viscera and twisted them mercilessly. He swallowed. Justice, not vengeance. Justice. "Do you remember what I am, Bane?" he asked softly. "What *you* made me?"

He knocked the plasgun aside, sending it spinning across the ice. Bane stared at him, his mouth working but no sound coming forth.

"Remember what I am." Looking directly into Bane's eyes, Wizard closed his hands around the man's skull. "I am your assassin," he said softly.

With a sharp twist, he ended Bane's life.

Straightening, he turned and staggered forward, pulling off his gloves as he went, unwilling to touch Raina with the cloth that had touched Bane.

He dropped to his knees at her side.

So this was love, he thought as he dragged her into his arms. The realization failed to surprise him. Somehow, it seemed inevitable that he would love Raina

Bowen. Brave, brash, beautiful Raina Bowen. The woman whose life was inexplicably twined with his, daughter of his savior, enemy of his enemy.

The woman who had taught him to *feel*.

The woman who had taught him to laugh, who had unearthed his humanity, who had taught him to love.

The woman who would leave him.

Raina lay on her side, feeling the numbness overtake her limbs. Cold. She was colder than she'd ever been in her life.

"Raina." Wizard's voice reached her through a long and hazy tunnel, and then she felt his touch on her back. He was alive. *Alive.*

"My dream," she whispered, forcing the words past a tongue that felt swollen to three times its normal size, desperate to say them before she lost this one shining chance. "I wanted to feel the kiss of the sun, to walk on a beach. With you."

He tried to kiss her lips, but she turned her face away.

"Poison. Diotoxin." She couldn't let him be tainted by the poison. She closed her eyes, felt his lips on her cheek and then a warm wetness. Tears. God, he was crying. For her.

"Stay with me, Raina."

As if she had a choice.

She tried to focus on his face, to see him one last time, but the poison had already dulled her senses. "I would have been happy with a life in the Waste . . . if I could be . . . with you."

Live to see peace. Live well. She was too weak to say it, but she wished it. Oh, how she wished it for him, the dream that she could be by his side dancing a ghostly waltz past the edge of her desperation.

"Raina, I love you." The words were wrenched from him, from the deepest part of his soul. "I cannot lose you. I cannot calculate the logic in your loss."

Love. You. She wanted to tell him, but she was too far away now. And to tell him. About. Tatiana.

A gray fog slunk through her body, draining her strength, her breath, her life. She felt Wizard's touch on her cheek, warm, so warm. He always made her warm.

On a slow exhalation, her world went black.

EIGHTEEN

She breathed. Wizard could see the minute movements of Raina's chest, see the barest cloud of moisture form before her lips and then quickly dissipate. If
she breathed, she lived, and if she lived, there was a
possibility that she would continue to do so.

So this was hope.

Diotoxin. A lethal poison. The probability of human survival was zero.

But still the hope swelled inside of him, despite
logic and probability. Raina *would* survive. She had his
blood. She had her strength.

She had his love.

Wrapping her in his embrace, he closed his mind to
the inexplicable agony as his torn body cried out in
protest. He forced himself to his feet, arms tight
around his precious burden, and began to walk toward
the horizon, toward the flight machine that Bane had
arrived in.

He had no qualms about using the possessions of a
dead man to leave the ruined camp and Bane's life-

less body behind, no qualms about leaving his task unfinished.

Trey and Sawyer and the others would come to round up Bane's hirelings. Yuriko would come. She would clean up the mess.

Yuriko liked things tidy.

Raina opened her eyes to a light so bright it burned. Her lids felt gritty and dry as they scraped shut. She moaned, turning her head aside.

She was hot, and every part of her felt stiff. The heat was amazing, but she could do without the pain.

Running her hands over her body, she felt for the catch-seam of her thermal wear. She felt so numb, so weak, her hands dragging sluggishly along cloth and then skin. Skin? With a squeak of surprise, she bolted upright, then fell back, battling a wave of nausea and weakness.

There was no catch-seam. Actually, there wasn't much of anything except a thin, sleeveless scrap of cloth that reached a little below her hips.

"Drink this." Wizard's voice, detached, calm, issuing a command. Some things never changed.

Hope flared inside her. "Either I'm . . . not dead . . . or . . . you're dead with . . . me."

Words she'd intended as a joke fell flat. Her voice was so hoarse she could barely speak, and the sentence came out as a nearly indecipherable croak.

"Drink."

She felt the edge of whatever she was lying on dip under his weight. One solid arm lifted her, and the rim of a cup came up to her lips. The first sip of the cold water was ambrosia sliding down her parched throat, and she angled up, trying to guzzle as much as she could.

"Slowly."

That was Wizard. The guy just couldn't get over his chattiness. He'd have to work on that.

She opened her eyes, letting her vision clear, and she took in every precious chiseled angle of his perfect face. Running her palm along his side, his jaw, his chest, she marveled that he was here, unharmed. Gloriously, beautifully alive.

Her touch lingered at his chest, on the already fading scar that bore witness to the wound that had almost stolen his life. Her arm shook, protesting against any activity, and she let it fall back to her side.

Frig. She felt as if she were swimming through tar, every movement a colossal effort. She quickly lost the battle and felt herself sucked into unconsciousness.

When she woke, Wizard was by her side. Tears pooled in her eyes, seeping out the corners and running down her cheeks.

"You're alive," she whispered.

"Acknowledged."

"And I'm alive."

He nodded, his gaze fixed on the wall behind her.

Uncertainty welled inside her. Why wouldn't he look at her?

Then he turned his head and met her gaze, and she *knew*, because there, glittering in the stormy depths of his gray eyes, was an infinite treasure of emotion that swirled like a storm-tossed sea.

She swallowed, mesmerized.

"It was . . . *unacceptable* for you to die." His eyes burned into hers. "The possibility of it was . . ." He gritted his teeth, balling his fists in the light sheet that was drawn up to her waist. "The possibility of your death was *painful*."

She nodded slowly. "Painful."

"If I lost you, Raina, I would die of grief." He stated it as a fact. No melodrama. Barely a hint of emotion in his tone, but in his eyes—*oh, God*—in his eyes, she read the truth of it. He would not have survived the loss of her.

"Then I guess I'd best live a good long while," she said softly.

He inclined his head. "Longevity is an advantage of genetic enhancement."

She frowned. That would give him a nice long life, but what did that mean for her? Pushing herself to a sitting position, she noticed that she already felt stronger. The lethargy and nausea that she had experienced earlier were gone.

"So all that . . ." she ventured. "About you giving me your blood, and about my genes changing to make me stronger . . . it was true?"

Leaning forward, Wizard lifted a plate from the table beside the bed. There was an array of fruits arranged there, sliced and peeled. She recognized apple and orange, but the others were unfamiliar to her.

"Eat this." Wizard fed her a slice of a sweet, juicy fruit that made her taste buds tingle with pleasure. "Mango," he said.

"Wizard," she prompted. "Your blood . . . my DNA . . ."

"Yes. Your genome sequence is structurally enhanced, modified for vitality and longevity, the chromosome shape distinctive in length. Though not as strong as myself or Yuriko, you surpass the expected human norm."

"Why didn't I ever notice this . . . enhancement before?"

Wizard cocked his head. "Didn't you?"

Sorting through memories, she realized that maybe she had. She'd taken on gun truckers, pirates, fended for herself from an unbelievably early age, and managed to survive unscathed. She'd assumed it was her skills, her brains, her attitude, but in retrospect, she could see that although all those things contributed to her survival, there had always been some intangible quality that had protected her. She'd noticed times where she'd been just a little faster than an opponent, just a little tougher.

"Maybe I did." She hesitated. "What of Bane?" The name nearly choked her.

He gave a curt nod. "Justice was served."

"So he didn't survive the poison? You're sure?"

He hesitated for a bare instant. "Affirmative."

She frowned, unsure of his hesitation, and then not caring. Bane was gone. Dead. He would never hurt anyone again. They were safe from him, all of them, Wizard, Beth, and Yuriko . . . everyone. "Why did I survive? Because of what you said? About my DNA?"

"Affirmative. In conjunction with the preadministered antidote."

"How did you know about that?"

"You spoke in your delirium."

Oh. Nice. What else had she said?

He plucked another fruit from the plate and popped it in her mouth. As the flavor exploded on her tongue, she murmured her appreciation. Wizard met her gaze, and the corners of his mouthed kicked up; then he took a morsel of fruit for himself.

Glancing around, Raina wondered just where in the frigging frozen Waste they were. There was no plasti-glass over the windows, and an unfamiliar sound washed over her senses. She blinked, feeling as if she had entered a surreal dimension. She wasn't dead. They were sitting here conversing as though they hadn't just rid the world of a sadistic tyrant. And they were eating fruit. Was she dreaming?

She looked at him, confused and a little afraid. How cruel if this moment was only a product of her imagination. "Where am I?"

"Where you asked to be." He leaned forward, press-ing his lips to hers in a hard kiss; then he scooped her up in his arms. Holding her tight against his chest he walked through the doorway. She gasped as the light hit her full force, and the warmth of the sun pene-trated her skin. She blinked and squinted, ducking her head against the stinging brightness.

Oh, this was not real. This could not be real.

Sand. To the right and the left, an endless stretch of white sand such as she had seen only in holopics, and before her, water lapping gently at the shore, a clear pristine blue. Ocean. Not the swirling, frigid darkness of the Northern Ocean. Blue and green, shimmering in the light, so beautiful she held her breath in awe.

Tightening her arms around Wizard's neck, she felt the movements of his body as he walked, carrying her toward the beckoning waves.

"I *am* dreaming." She buried her face in his shoul-der, then quickly looked up again. Everything was ex-actly the same.

"You said you wanted to walk in the sun. With me. So I brought you to the sun."

"How?" He had done this for her. Given her her dream. God, it was impossible. She would have settled for the coldest reaches of the Waste if he was with her.

"We flew. In Bane's plane."

Okay. That was unbelievable. "How did you know how to fly a plane?" And then she laughed, the sound catching in her throat. As if there were anything he couldn't figure out. Her amazing, magical Wizard.

He let her down, sliding her along the front of his body until her feet touched the warm sand, sinking in. He kept his arms around her, anchoring her, supporting her, and despite her physical lassitude, she felt strong. So strong.

Lowered his head, he kissed the laughter from her lips. His hands roamed her body, running over her back, her shoulders, tender, careful.

"I won't break," she whispered, smiling as she realized it was true. She felt amazingly good for a woman who had just finished a trip to hell and back. Trailing her hand along the hard plane of his abdomen, she paused at his waist, then dragged her fingers lower. "I feel good. Great. Perfect."

"Understood." He closed his fingers around her wrist, stopping her quest, and then glanced at the sand. "A gritty and uncomfortable pallet."

She tugged the scrap of cloth from her body, tossing it on the ground. "I don't care," she whispered, weaving her fingers with his and dragging him with her as she walked into the warm surf and sank down into the gentle waves.

Wizard shook his head and smiled, that perfect,

beautiful, masculine smile that melted her heart and heated her blood.

The kiss of the sun was warm on their naked skin, and the ocean lapped at their bodies. Opening her arms, Raina welcomed him, laughing as he floated her out until the water was just deep enough to buoy their tangled limbs, warm enough to caress their skin, adding to their pleasure as he kissed her, his mouth delicious, carnal, stroking the flame of her desire to life, and her flame of life to a roaring inferno.

He made love to her there in the water, slow, languid caresses that drove her mad with need until she gasped and moaned and, in the end, cried her release to the heavens.

As the sun sank below the horizon in a glorious celebration of pink and orange, Raina laughed as Wizard pulled her from the hammock that hung in front of their tiny hut and into his arms.

"Again?" she asked.

"Possibly." His eyes were dark and slumberous. Lowering his head, he kissed her, deep and wet. Her body tingled, then sizzled as he ran his hands over her, kneading, stroking, awakening the passion he had slaked only moments past. "After we contact Yuriko. We must tell her what you learned of Tatiana. We must begin the search."

Raina closed her eyes and smiled. She could still see the look of wonder and guarded hope that had shone in Wizard's eyes as she had explained that Tatiana might be alive. That Bane had suggested as much. There was the strong possibility that he had lied, but where there was the smallest hope that Tatiana survived, Wizard would search for her.

Facing the ocean, Raina leaned back against Wizard's strong chest. "Paradise," she whispered. "My every dream come true."

She felt Wizard tense. "You can stay if you wish," he said, his voice tight. "I must return to the Waste, but I will visit when I can. Tatiana may be alive—"

Stopping his words with a kiss, Raina cradled his face in her hands. "*You* are my paradise. *You* are my every dream come true. And while I appreciate your willingness to sacrifice your preferences for mine, if you go to the frigging frozen North, then I go, too."

His gray eyes burned into hers. "Until you, I never knew that I could dream. You are my first, my last, my only dream. Say it for me, Raina. I want—no, I *need* to hear the words."

She read the naked emotion in his face, and it called to her. "I love you, Wizard." She pressed a kiss to his hard mouth. "Love you. Love you."

He smiled and twined his fingers with hers. "Remember that when you are cursing the cold."

"Oh, I'll remember it. But it won't keep me warm."

Wizard yanked her tight against him, his kiss sizzling through her like wildfire. Together they tumbled onto the hammock that swayed and twisted beneath their weight, almost dumping them to the ground. "*I* will keep you warm, Raina Bowen."

Arching one brow, she closed her fingers around him, guiding him home. "And I'll keep *you* safe."

Raina sat in front of the holoplayer, her throat tight. Wizard's warmth, his strength, poured from him into her as he rested his hands lightly on her shoulders.

She tipped her head back, searching his face.

"I'm afraid," she whispered.

Leaning forward, he kissed her, his mouth hot, wet, his tongue twining with hers, sending a frisson of awareness rippling through her.

"You are the bravest woman I know."

"Yeah." She blew out a breath. "Yeah."

She swallowed, hit the play button.

An image shimmered and coalesced, a young girl, her blond hair caught in a ponytail.

"Hello, Raina," she said softly, her eyes shimmering. "I'm your sister. I'm Beth."

Turn the page for an exciting look at

DARK PRINCE

A riveting Gothic set in nineteenth-century
Cornwall

By Eve Kenin's alter ego,

EVE SILVER

Available now wherever books are sold.

Desperation made for a poor walking companion.

Jane Heatherington studied the horizon, dread gnawing at her with small, sharp bites. The sky was a leaden mass of churning gray cloud that hung low on the water, and the ocean pummeled the shore with a strength that heralded the furor of the coming storm. Breathing in the tangy salt scent of the sea, Jane clenched her fists. The edges of the delicate pink shell in her hand dug into the skin of her palm, grounding her as she struggled to hold her misery at bay.

Life was burdened by tragedy. Naive girl, to have believed that fate had dealt out all her cruel jests years ago. Jane shook her head. No, not fate. She could blame no one but the true perpetrator of this terrible thing that had come to pass. Her own father had consigned them both to uncertainty and despair.

How much money?

Five hundred pounds.

Yet fate *was* there too, lurking, laughing, playing

her horrible game. Was not Jane's presence here this morning some act of chance?

Ill chance, to be sure.

Less than an hour past, as the cold, gray dawn had crawled into the heavens, Jane had left her father's hostelry, needing a few moments to understand, to accept the terrible choices he had made, the dreadful consequence he had brought down upon them. She had walked along the beach, mindless of any destination, seeking only to calm her concerns and fears.

She shuddered now, studying the two men who stood in the churning surf. They waited as the waves carried forth a grim offering, a single dark speck that dipped and swayed with each turbulent surge, growing ever larger, taking on defined shape and macabre form.

Indeed, desperation made a poor walking companion, but death even more so.

Wrapping her arms about herself, Jane watched the dark outline float closer, closer, discernible now as human, facedown in the water with arms outstretched, long tendrils of tangled hair fanning out like a copper halo.

A woman, bobbing and sodden.

And dead.

Heart pounding in her breast, Jane took a single step forward as the men sought to drag their gruesome catch from the ocean's chill embrace. She was held in thrall by the terrible tableau unfolding before her, and she swallowed back the greasy sickness that welled inside her. 'Twas not morbid curiosity, but heart-wrenching empathy that froze her in place.

Most days she could look at the ocean as a thing of great beauty.

Most days.

But not today.

Today there were disquieting clouds and churning surf and the icy kiss of the mist that blew from the water's surface to touch land. Too, deep in her heart, there was the awful knowledge of her father's actions and the terrible feeling of foreboding, of change, unwelcome and unwanted.

'Twas all too similar to a day long past, a day best buried in a dusty corner of her mind. The sea. The storm. And there, just beyond a great outcropping of rock, the brooding shadow of Trevisham House, looming silent and frightful against the backdrop of gray water and grayer sky.

Separated from the sweeping curve of sandy beach by swirling waves, the massive house was a lonely, empty shell balanced atop a great granite crag that rose out of the sea like the horny back of a mythical beast, a fearsome pile of stone and mortar that offered no warmth. Trevisham was linked to the mainland by a narrow causeway that was passable at low tide or high. Unless there was a storm, and then it was not passable at all.

Chill fingers of unease crawled along Jane's spine, and she tore her gaze away, glancing to her right, to her left, feeling inexplicably wary. She was given to neither fanciful notion nor wild imaginings, yet today it appeared she was subject to both. Her heart tripped too fast, and her nerves felt raw as she scanned the beach, searching for the source of her unease. She could swear there was someone watching the beach. Watching *her*.

'Twas not the first time she had suspected such.

Twice yesterday she had spun quickly, peering into darkened corners and shadowed niches, finding nothing but her own unease. She sighed. Perhaps it had been a portent rather than a human threat, a chill warning of the news her father had been about to share.

"She's been in the water less than a week, I'm thinking," Jem Basset called grimly, drawing Jane's attention to where he stood thigh-deep in the water, the corpse bobbing just beyond his reach.

"Where's she from?" Robert Davey asked, wading a step farther into the waves. "A ship, do you think?"

"There's been only fine weather for more than three weeks. No ship's gone down here. If she's from a ship, then it was wrecked on the rocks to the north, I'm thinking."

The two men exchanged a telling look.

Jem grunted and reached as far as he could, but the waves carried the body just beyond his grasp. He glanced up, saw Jane, and shook his head. "Go on, now, Janie. No need for you to see this."

He was right, of course. There was no need for her to watch them drag this poor, unfortunate woman from her watery grave, but Jane could not will her feet to move. The talk of wrecks and rocks haunted her.

There had been whispers of late that the coast to the north was safe for no ship, that in the dark of the night wreckers set their false lights where no light should be. They were vile murderers bent on luring the unsuspecting to their doom, tricking a ship into thinking it was guided by a lighthouse's warning beacon, only to see it torn asunder on jagged rocks.

Torn asunder like the fabric of her life.

But at least she had *life*, Jane thought fiercely as she watched the corpse bob down, then up, long copper hair swaying in the current like snaking tendrils of dark blood.

Pulling her shawl tight about her shoulders, Jane blew out a slow breath, steadying her nerves, battling both her fears for her future and the ugly memories of her past. Dark thoughts. Terrible recollections of storm and sea and Trevisham House.

Jem lunged, and this time he caught the dead woman's arm, and then Robert came alongside him, and together they wrestled her from the frothing waves.

"You think there'll be others?" Robert asked, breathing heavily as they slogged toward the shore, the sand sucking at their booted feet, the woman's body dragged between them, her head hanging down, legs trailing in the water.

Shaking his head, Jem cast a quick glance toward Jane. "Not likely. Bodies usually sink into the deep dark. Strange that this one didn't."

"They sink only until they fill with bloat, and then they float up again like a cork, don't they?" Not waiting for a reply, Robert waved his free hand and continued. "Her skirt. See the way it's tangled about her ankles? It must have caught the air when she went into the water and held her afloat. That is why she did not sink."

Drawn despite herself, Jane took a step along the beach, and another, gripped by the image of this poor woman, her limbs growing heavier and heavier as she was tossed about on a cruel sea. Struggling, gasping, praying.

And finally, dying.

Such an image.

Such a *memory*. She could *feel* the tightness in *her* chest. The great, gasping breath that brought only a cold, burning rush of water to fill her nose and throat and lungs. With her heart pounding a harsh rhythm in her breast, Jane struggled against the strangling recollection, determined to hold it at bay.

Jem laid the drowned woman in the back of a rough wooden cart, mindful of her modesty, though such was long past any value to her. With a twist of pity, Jane saw that the woman was both bloated and shriveled at once, her face white-green, in frightful contrast to her copper hair, and her eyes . . .

With a cry, Jane stumbled back a step, pressing her palm to her lips. Horror seeped through her veins, a terrible dismay that chilled her to her core.

The woman's eyes were gone from her skull, leaving only empty black sockets.

Jane wrenched her gaze away, swallowing convulsively as she stared at the wet sand dusted with a smattering of white and pink shells.

Shells.

She had come to walk on the beach to soothe her soul, and to fetch a handful of shells to carry with her. Just a handful of shells for her mother. Those were her reasons for being on the beach. Now, instead of shells and ease of mind, she would carry the memory of the dead woman's bloated face and the empty holes that had held her eyes.

A new nightmare to haunt her rest, Jane thought. Imaginings of another woman's suffering, as though her own were not companion enough in the darkest hours of the night.

Suddenly she froze, and her head snapped up. The hair at her nape prickled and rose. Jane rubbed her hands briskly along the outsides of her arms as apprehension chilled her from within, swelling in tandem with the rolling waves.

Someone *was* watching them.

Lips slightly parted, the tip of her tongue pressed between her top and bottom teeth, Jane turned to face the great wall of sea-carved cliffs that rose alongside the long, slow curve of sand. Tipping her head up and back, she studied the stark precipice with measured interest. The sound of the waves hitting the shore surrounded her, punctuated by the cry of a lonely gull high overhead. From the corner of her eye she caught a hint of motion, a shadow, far, far to her left, up on the cliff.

There was a blur of movement, a dark ripple of cloth that might have been a man's cloak.

She spun so quickly her balance was almost lost. Reaching down, she pressed the flat of her palm to her left thigh, adding sheer will and the strength of her arm to the paltry force of the muscles that would straighten her knee and hold her upright. If she was lucky. If not, her leg would crumple as it was often wont to do, and she would sink to the sand in a graceless heap. After a moment she righted herself and turned her attention to the place she had glimpsed the shadowy stranger.

The cliff was barren. There was no one outlined against the ominous backdrop of gray sky. The man—if in truth she had seen one—was gone.

But the sinister unease that clutched at her remained.

WIN
A PUBLISHING CONTRACT!

Ever dream of publishing your own novel?

Here's your chance!

Dorchester Publishing is offering fans of
SHOMI a chance to win a guaranteed
publishing contract with distribution
throughout the US and Canada!

For complete submission guidelines and
contest rules & regulations, please visit:

www.shomifiction.com/contests.html

**ALL ENTRIES MUST BE RECEIVED BY
MARCH 31, 2008.**

The future of romance where anything is possible.

WIRED

LIZ MAVERICK

Seconds aren't like pennies. They can't be saved in a jar and spent later. Pluck a second out of time or slip an extra one in, the consequences will change your life forever.

L. Roxanne Zaborovsky discovers that fate is comprised of an infinite number of wires, filaments that can be manipulated, and she's not the one at the controls. From the roguishly charming Mason Merrick—a shadow from her increasingly tenebrous past—to the dangerously seductive Leonardo Kaysar, she's barely holding on. This isn't a game, and the pennies are rolling all over the floor. Roxy just has to figure out which are the ones worth picking up.

ISBN 10: 0-505-52724-3
ISBN 13: 978-0-505-52724-0 $6.99 US/$8.99 CAN

Blood Moon

✠ ✠ ✠

Dawn Thompson

Jon Hyde-White is changed. Soon he will cease to be an earl's second son and become a ravening monster. Already lust grows, begging him to drink blood—and the blood of his fiancée Cassandra Thorpe will be sweetest of all. Is that not why the blasphemous creature Sebastian bursts upon them from the London shadows? But Sebastian's evil task remains incomplete, and neither Jon nor Cassandra is beyond hope. One chance remains—in faraway Moldavia, in a secret brotherhood, in an ancient ritual and in the power of love.